Teach First,
Die Later

Brian Smith

Although this novel is based on my experience of
teaching in state education, it is important to note that it
is a work of fiction.

Front cover design by Brian Smith

ISBN:979-8-84-862278-2

DEDICATION

To all those teachers and teaching assistants who have dedicated their lives to helping and encouraging others in the face of the most difficult pressures. A special mention to the staff at All Saints who are some of the most talented, conscientious and humorous group of people I have had the privilege to work with.

ACKNOWLEDGMENTS

To my friends and family for their ongoing support, to Lyn for her immense contribution and superb eye for detail.

Brian Smith

PROLOGUE

In 2020 the national press reported on an unusual story. A middle-aged man, on the run from the Italian police, decided to hole up in The Six Arches caravan site in Preston, Lancashire. This man was no ordinary man, he was the head of a feared crime syndicate in Naples. Unbelievably, he still managed to conduct all his affairs and business deals whilst living in a caravan. Local residents and neighbours happily lent him a phone to call home. It didn't occur to anyone at the time that this was a bit odd, given he clearly had money. Gennaro Panzuto or Genny as he was affectionately known was thought to be in the shoe business but in reality was the boss of the Torretta quarter, a clan that forms part of the notorious Camorra mafia. Eventually, he was arrested and extradited back to Italy. Rumour has it, that some of the friends he made in Preston are still in contact with him today.

Brian Smith

1

FAST ASLEEP

Something was amiss. To the uneducated or the unobservant, it would not be apparent. A person would have to look carefully to realise that anything was wrong. After all, Mr Jones was still sitting upright facing his laptop, appearing to be immersed in his work. And the world would be none the wiser if it were not for Charlie Spicer, a renowned teacher spotter.

To those who are unacquainted with the term, a teacher spotter refers to one of those pupils, most feared in educational circles, who notice things, often embarrassing things about their teachers; the wearing of the same socks for three or more days; a small crumb of cake in a beard; the sprouting of an inch long hair on an eyebrow. Charlie had a way of pointing these things out – seemingly innocent at first. "I like your socks, sir. Nice patterns, good choice." And then the sting. "But weren't they the ones you had on yesterday, and the day before, and the day before that? A tad sniffy maybe?" According to his classmates, his chirpy assassination of a teacher, especially a cover teacher, was a thing of beauty.

Initially, Charlie didn't see anything of note with Mr Jones, apart from a few small ink stains on his tie, but like all good spotters, he was prepared to wait. His patience was rewarded when, after a lengthy stare, he spotted something…

"Mr Jones is in the land of nod." he declared quietly.

"What do you mean?" replied Becky, one of the girls sitting next to him.

"You have to look carefully. It's not easy to see, but he's fast asleep."

3

Becky peered over her teacher's laptop. "Oh my God, you're right." She waved her hand across his face – no reaction. "It's like a bad internet connection where the image has frozen."

Charlie laughed. Becky's little observations and descriptors often made him chuckle.

"Do you think I should wake him up?" he asked earnestly. "He looks so peaceful, like a babe in the wood."

"I'm not sure, I don't think so," replied Becky. She looked intently at her teacher's face. She had always been interested in portraits; her sketchbook was full of them. Mr Jones would have made a good addition. In this motionless state, his features fascinated her. It seemed as though gravity had tugged everything down to the floor. He'd always had slightly saggy cheek jowls, but right now they were positively droopy. The bags under his eyes had become enlarged, as though somebody had pumped air into them. Puffy, she thought, definitely puffy. His complexion was ruddy. Becky liked that word, she'd used it in an essay recently. She liked the way it went with puffy. Ruddy and puffy, they're like two peas in a pod. And then she had fun trying to put them together in a sentence. Almost immediately one bubbled to the surface like the froth of a freshly opened soda water. "Old man Jones's puddin' puffy cheeks showed off his bloody ruddy complexion." She laughed to herself. But then she looked closely at the tip of his nose. It was more than ruddy, it was a deeper red. She amused herself by trying to think of the exact hue. Tomato sauce she said to herself. No, no, it's raspberry, or is it crimson? She made her eyes wider so that she could fully take in the small patch of colour. Definitely crimson she thought. And then it occurred to her.

"I think he's got drinker's nose."

"What's that?" asked Charlie.

"It's when you drink too much, my granddad's got it. It's a special name, but I can't think of it right now."

"Maybe he's got a bottle of brandy in his draw," chuckled Charlie.

"Yeah, with some long straws so that he can just suck it up when he needs it."

They both laughed – before resuming their trance-like stare at the petrified figure. Charlie needed to say something quickly before they became completely bewitched.

"Sir," he whispered loudly but there was no response.

"What are you doing?" asked Becky perplexed at Charlie's actions. "We can have a right laugh."

"If the others spot him they're gonna do something terrible," said Charlie. "You know what they're like, especially Biggsy."

Becky looked round to where Biggsy sat. He too was fast asleep. His crumpled form lay slumped over the desk absolutely bored stiff by the video of Romeo and Juliet. As Becky looked on, she had to acknowledge that his mischievous and malevolent spirit was best subdued particularly in this situation. But he wasn't the only one who'd dropped off. Several other boys were in a similar position, rendered quite inert by the dark stuffy room and Shakespeare's tragic love story.

For a second Becky tried to guess who the boys were from the tufts of hair that sprouted up from behind their thin scrawny elbows. She quickly realized that she would rather be playing silly mind games than witnessing the havoc those boys could wreak, even if it would be funny.

Reluctantly, she turned to Charlie, "Yeah…maybe you're right."

Charlie didn't need a second invitation to rescue Mr Jones. He had rather a soft spot for the 'grumpy old geezer' and besides, Biggsy's coarse approach was far too crude for him.

"Sir," he whispered but this time a little louder. Still no response.

"Do you think he might be dead?" said Becky.

"No, no I can hear snoring," said Charlie, "and look his chest is moving up and down, he's breathing."

"Sir. Sir, Mr Jones," implored Charlie in the loudest whisper he could muster.

Becky laughed. "Poke him."

"What with?"

"A pen. I don't know. I dare you to do it on his big fat stomach. You know that you'll probably burst him."

"Shh," said Charlie trying to stifle his giggles again, "Biggsy's gonna hear."

But it was too late. Charlie's worst fears were soon realised. Biggsy's head suddenly popped up like an inquisitive meerkat sniffing an interesting scent. His small beady eyes pierced the gloom of the darkened classroom. A slow sadistic smile spread across his lips. He looked up to the heavens and quietly thanked God for this wonderful opportunity. He then went to work quickly mobilizing his troops with a series of nudges and winks. It took less than ten seconds for Taff, Knob 'ead, Boner and Lurch to be fully awake and ready. No words were spoken but they all knew through a kind of rogue telepathy what they had to do.

Biggsy was first. He rose silently out of his chair swiftly followed by his acolytes. Clearly in stealth mode, these shadowy figures were like ninja assassins as they gingerly walked over to where the sleeping beauty lay. They stopped no more than two feet away from their prey. Like gunslingers, they smoothly drew their iPhones out from shabby blazer pockets. Holding them carefully at arm's length, the black blazered carrion, headed up by the pointy-nosed Biggsy, began filming the unfortunate victim. A close-up of Jones's face lit up every screen as hungry young adolescents feasted on the carcass of the poor defenceless figure.

"Christ it's like feeding time at the zoo," said Charlie.

"I know," said Becky, "but he only has himself to blame, it happened three weeks back, same time – just after lunch. He's probably had a pint and a pie. That's what happens to my granddad, he just falls asleep."

"Yeah, but in the middle of the lesson?"

"Well watching Romeo and Juliet is pretty boring, it's not exactly interactive."

Suddenly Biggsy peeled away from the crowd. Becky stopped talking and watched him closely as he went over to his bag and pulled something out.

"Oh Lord," she gasped out loud. "He can't use that. No!" She'd only ever seen a sex toy on the internet. In the flesh, it seemed grotesque. Becky knew what her classmate was going to do with it, and it was going to be hideously funny.

Biggsy didn't disappoint. He took the giant phallus, stuffed it down his trousers, undid his zip, and let it pop out. He stood

6

there for a few seconds showing off his newly acquired member to anybody that would look. He then shuffled close to Mr Jones, gripped the ginormous stiffy, and delicately balanced it over his teacher's bottom lip being careful not to let it touch. The phones were ready. Without really thinking, Becky screamed.

"Sir!!!!!"

Mr Jones woke up with a start.

"What… what the?"

Dark shadowy figures scurried back to their seats like cock roaches running for cover. Biggsy gave Becky the eye, she'd woken him up too early. Fortunately, Mr Jones still wasn't quite with it.

"What…who, what the devil… Biggs, what were you doing? Why are you and Allen out of your seat?"

"We noticed you were asleep, Sir, we were just seeing if you were alright," replied an alert Biggsy.

"I was not asleep. My eyes were just resting."

"Can we just rest our eyes too, Sir?"

"Who said that?"

Becky put her hand up. She thought it was quite funny and didn't mind owning up to it, but Mr Jones didn't find it humorous at all.

"No, you can't," he said grumpily. "Now get on with…" But he couldn't quite remember what it was they were supposed to be getting on with.

"Romeo and Juliet, Sir," said Biggsy. "We were at the point where someone was gonna get poisoned…the really exciting bit."

There were a few titters from the class and gasps of amazement that Biggsy had some idea of the plot.

"Was it?"

"Yes, Sir," said Biggsy earnestly. He then went over to the machine, pressed rewind, and then play. He turned to Mr Jones.

"See?" There were further smirks from the class.

"Yes, yes I know," said a befuddled Mr Jones. He then frowned. That scream from Becky Taverner had given him quite a start. It had thrown him, and she'd been cheeky. He looked over to where she was sitting.

"I'll see you afterwards," he said sternly.

"What! I was helpin'…" but Jones cut her off.

"That scream, it was enough to wake the dead."

"Well, we thought you were, Sir," said Becky indignantly.

"That's enough."

"But…"

"I'm sorry, you're going to have to stay behind."

"You're not sorry you fat, old twat," yelled Becky, "and I'm not staying behind." And with that, she took her bag, stomped out of the room and slammed the door. A few seconds later she marched back in; gave Mr Jones a dirty look; walked over to where she'd been sitting; snatched the jacket that she'd forgotten and promptly stomped out again. This time she gave the door an extra slam. Mr Jones then turned to Charlie.

"You know, I think she's right with the fat part. That's fair enough and I will admit that I can be a bit of a twat but I'm not that old. I'm only in my fifties! I take umbrage at that. What do you think Charlie?"

"No comment," said Charlie diplomatically.

2

TARGETS

He wasn't entirely sure what went on in that lesson, but Mr Jones knew that the kids were taking the piss. That didn't particularly trouble him he'd learnt to use a glib comment as a defence against their dark arts. What alarmed him most, was that on reflection he didn't seem to care.

Harry Winston Jones to give him his full title had become pretty hacked off with the whole teaching business. A fifty-seven year old English and history teacher, he was aware that he was on the way to becoming one of those gnarly old "gits" who grumbled about everything all the time. He made pronouncements about the decline in standards, lamenting the loss of those good old days where the teacher's word was sacrosanct (if there ever had been such a time).

He was already one of those teachers who barked at every child who knocked on the staffroom door and gave a health warning to any teacher just starting their career. It wasn't beyond the realms of possibility for him to grab some unsuspecting "newbie" by the arm and tell them, "You must be absolutely crazy. Teaching! Couldn't you find anything else?" The trouble was that nobody knew whether or not he meant it, least of all the startled trainee he'd accosted. To others, particularly those who were in that mid-life crisis, he would delight in telling them that thankfully he had only three years to go before retirement. He would pat his man friends on the back and comfort himself by whispering in their ears. "Not long to go now. I can see the light at the end of the tunnel."

If you dared to peer into the corner of the staffroom you would see a monument to Harry's time at St Peter's, a scruffy old chair with a saggy old cushion. He sat there each break time supping his large mug of coffee, complaining about the same things time and again.

And much to his dismay, as Becky Taverner had pointed out, he'd become quite fat. It was after he turned forty that he noticed how easily he put on weight. His love of wine, real ale, and Frampton's large steak and kidney pies hadn't helped. It was a source of great frustration that he was continuously involved in a battle against the bulge. Still, he had managed to keep all his hair, but just lately even that was starting to recede.

But something was about to change. He wasn't looking for anything to happen, quite the opposite. He was slowly winding down like a battery running out of juice. Harry Jones was fading away and he was letting it happen. But that day of change, the accident – it hadn't arrived yet. There was still time for a good old moan in the staffroom about school inspectors and more specifically their "eduspeak."

"Apparently, it's not breadth they are focussing on now," said Harry, "it's depth." He wheeled round to the two who were paying attention, looked them in the eye, and paused for dramatic effect. He then continued.

"Listen to this, they're going to do a deep dive and drill hard. Ha, ha, have you ever heard of anything so ridiculous?"

"I take it you're not too keen on being drilled hard Harry," said Vicky the smart thirty-something head of the English department. She wasn't part of the audience, but she couldn't help butting in. Everybody laughed at her comment except Harry who was quite serious, which made it all the funnier.

"No, I am bloody well not," he replied gruffly, "and deep dive, what on earth? Deep dive, for heaven's sake. When they say that, I just can't get muff dive out of my head. Muff dive, deep dive…what a load of bollocks."

"I prefer that to being drilled hard," said Vicky.

"Well, you would," said Harry provocatively.

"I take it you disapprove of my relationships with other women?" said Vicky clearly trying to goad Harry further.

"Vicky, please don't get him started," came an impassioned plea from across the room.

"Yeah okay," said Vicky acknowledging the request. She then turned to Harry. "You're right it is a load of bollocks."

It wasn't so much his opinions that entertained people (they generally agreed with his moans about inspectors) it was his willingness to offer them in such a belligerent manner. He was about to sound off some more when the bell went for the end of lunch. Before he knew it everybody had started to shuffle out.

"It's just a warning bell, there's still a few min…" His voice trailed off as the staffroom suddenly became empty. "Slave to the shrill mistress," he said out loud. They were far too conscientious and diligent. No, he corrected himself, they just don't want to be seen slacking, and there's a difference. He could see them all now, dashing to get to their classrooms before the second bell, worried that if they weren't there exactly on time, they'd have a black mark.

He said as much to Carrie Philips in his line management meeting, but she wasn't impressed with his observations.

"It's working," she said, "all consistent, all pulling in the same direction."

"Okay," said Harry, "that's fine, but don't you think there's something a bit Stepford wives about the whole thing. All teachers at the start of each lesson hovering at the entrance to their classroom – "one foot in, one foot out," greeting children with a smile whilst reciting the Academy's mantra, 'We strive to learn.' Next, we'll be pledging our bloody allegiance to them arm across our chest all American style."

"No, I think it works," she repeated as she typed something on her laptop. Harry was used to her dismissive response to his sarcasm. He was going to wait for her to finish before speaking again but then he realised that it was *his* line management meeting in *his* time. She could do this in *her* time. It irritated him and it was taking too long, so he decided to say something and not just wait there.

"You know sometimes I don't smile," said Harry defiantly.

Carrie said nothing but simply carried on typing.

"When they come in, I deliberately don't smile." he repeated, "In fact, I've got a face like a smacked arse." Again, there was no reaction from Carrie who continued to type even more vigorously. But Harry wasn't going to relent. "And I make sure

11

that I am either in the classroom or on the corridor. I never ever have one foot in, one foot out. On the odd occasion, I step from side to side, do a kind of Irish jig in and out of the classroom, you know – a Michael Flatley thing." Still nothing from Carrie – except the relentless clicking of the keyboard. Harry couldn't help himself and needed to say more.

"Sometimes, God forbid, I am sitting at my desk, and I just shout, 'Come in you ugly gits.' The kids love it, 'Something a bit different,' they say. 'At least you're not a boring fart, not like the rest of the teachers'."

Carrie suddenly closed her laptop with real gusto and immediately presented Harry with some printouts. "Let's have a look at your year 11 data, shall we?" It wound up Harry that she could be so unfazed by his ramblings and unmoved by his attempts to goad her.

"Yes, let's," said Harry in mock cheerfulness.

Carrie coughed a little and peered at him over her thin-rimmed glasses. For a second Harry stared back but then found himself wilting. It wasn't just her narrow-eyed gaze, it was the pointy chin and resolute jaw that appeared so unyielding.

"If you look at 11R," she continued, "there are five students whose current grades are two levels below their predicted grade. Why is this?"

There's no doubt, he thought to himself, this woman is a she-wolf. This office, it's her territory and this climate is just right, cold and icy. The smart dress and sharp jacket, her efficiency, she is so… Harry stalled, he couldn't quite think of the words.

"Harry? Are you there Harry?" said Carrie quizzically.

But Harry had to finish his train of thought before he answered. There was an awful silence before it came to him. So perfectly perfunctory. Yes, that just about sums her up. He repeated the phrase in his head. Perfectly perfunctory. He was pleased with himself. Good alliteration.

"Are you okay Harry?"

"Yes, yes just thinking."

A faint smile appeared across Carrie's thin red lips. Was she enjoying this? And then he realized that it was quite a nervous expression. It caused Harry to study her face more closely. He had to admit she had aged well. Now in her mid-forties, her face showed few wrinkles. He didn't want to think it, he pushed hard against the idea, but he found her quite attractive. He might have warmed to her, but he just found it difficult to get past the fact that she appeared to be such an ardent supporter of the system.

"Harry?"

"What?"

"The grades are 2 levels below where they should be. Any idea why?"

"Oh yes, yes," spluttered Harry. "Absolutely no idea, maybe they hadn't drunk their carrot juice the day before a test; maybe their mother had just left their father for another woman; maybe they had trouble putting coins in the electric meter and had to do their homework by candlelight."

"There's no need to be facetious, Mr Jones."

"Well, they're people, for Christ's sake, not just numbers on a spreadsheet."

"I agree but you're missing the point."

"And what's that?" sneered Harry.

"We have to have a baseline, something we can measure our students against so that we can track progress and set targets accordingly."

"You make it all sound neat and simple. And if that were the case we'd all be happy and glad but it's not. Kids are unhappy, mental health's a growing problem and we're being put on trial for every child that doesn't make these stupid targets." He looked over at Carrie. "Tell me you're not a real believer in this." And for a moment he imagined her positively drooling over a printout of numbers and targets; properly salivating over the pretty patterned data; making great big blotches of ink-stained puddles of spit.

"No system is perfect Harry... but we have to do our best for the students and if they are not getting the grades they should be...." Carrie let the unfinished statement hang in the air and then added, "we're all accountable."

There was something hesitant in her voice that suddenly made Harry aware that she may be under similar pressures. He desperately wanted to imagine her as some monstrous educational harpy. It would have slotted nicely into his narrative, but he couldn't. Annoyingly, Vicky had also said some good things about her. It made him reluctant to sound off anymore so instead he murmured something back that contained a mild protest but had an element of resignation. He could see that for all his remonstrations there was a feeling of inevitability about everything. He shook his head and sighed at the thought of it all. And suddenly he was back in the staffroom feeling very much at odds with the world.

Harry paused for a second and looked around. There was nobody there. He felt quite lonely. There was something quite sad about an empty staffroom, like a seaside town out of season. He took a last gulp of his tea, sauntered over to the sink, tipped the dregs out, and watched as the contents slowly drained away. "A bit like life really," he muttered to himself. He then rinsed his cup and used his short thick fingers to wipe away the brownish stains that had collected around the rim. One last fierce rub made sure that no trace of a stain or mark was left. As he reached for a paper towel, he stopped and reeled backwards. A look of horror descended upon his startled features. "Un-bloody believable!" he bellowed out loud. "How could someone be that selfish? Vandalism, that's what it is…vandalism." He was in a fair old state when the door burst open and in rushed Tom Bailey the head of IT.

"Are you still here Harry?" chirped Tom as he rushed around frantically trying to locate his missing laptop. Harry didn't reply but simply carried on staring at the heinous sight. Tom sensed that something wasn't quite right.

"Harry? Harry, are you okay? You look a bit red, well redder than usual."

"This sort of thing bloody annoys me," cried Harry in disgust. "Does it annoy you?"

Tom looked around the staffroom and couldn't see anything. He shrugged his shoulders. "I'm not sure what you are referring to."

"There, right there!" said Harry pointing to a blue roll. "It was left on the chair. Can you believe it? It's obviously run out, but rather than taking the time to fit a new one in, they've left it there." Tom still looked bemused, so Harry walked up to the blue roll and pointed. "Right there, right there on the chair! Not even on a table or placed by the dispenser but tossed on the

14

seating. Look how the end has unravelled all over the seat. It's an affront to a civilised way of living. It's like those people who scoop the dog crap up in a poo bag and then leave it dangling on a branch or tied to a gate as though that's okay. Can you believe it? He or she got a new roll out, used it, but then couldn't be bothered fitting it in the dispenser. Well, why not, it's easier just to tear a piece off - leave the roll there for somebody else to fix - like somebody else will put the bag of dog shit in the bin. I'll bet you it's one of the younger members. Selfish bastards they are. No sense of staffroom etiquette."

Harry then strode over, picked the offending blue roll up, and attempted to rectify this blot on the landscape. But it wasn't quite as easy as it should have been. He huffed and puffed as the roll somehow refused to be fitted. In the end, Harry virtually bullied it into submission. The climax to this little piece of theatre was a slamming of the metal fastener shut. PPHAPP! "There!" he said sharply as he brushed his hands. "All done." As if to emphasise his point Harry angrily ripped off a piece of blue towelling. Shhhyaack! It was quite vicious and caused Tom to chuckle nervously. Harry looked at him despairingly. "You know I've brought this up at staff meetings. This isn't the first time that this has happened."

"Let it go, Harry," said Tom quietly.

"Let it go? What do you mean let it go?"

"Harry it's just a blue roll that's not been fitted in the dispenser. It's not exactly life or death."

"You let this kind of thing go and before you know it people are treating this place like a cesspit. We have to be vigilant." Tom smiled faintly. And for a second Harry could see how ridiculous his outburst sounded. "You're right," said Harry tersely, "no sense in getting wound up over something so trivial." But it was said with little conviction.

Harry then focussed his attention on using the blue towel to dry off his mug. He gave an extra rub around the rim. It calmed him down. No sense taking it out on Tom.

"You're right," repeated Harry. This time, it was said with a little more deference.

"No worries," said Tom who then picked up his laptop that he'd forgotten and dashed back out.

Harry looked carefully at his mug and became acutely aware that he had performed this rinsing and drying ritual for the last twenty-five years. There were some variations, he hadn't always put his cup in the same place in the locker and sometimes he took the half-drunken cup of tea into his lesson, but it was pretty much like this at the end of every break.

It didn't bother Harry that the bell had already gone for the start of the lesson. He was in no rush. Fitting the blue towel into the dispenser was important for staff morale and anyway, his classroom wasn't that far away. They can wait, thought Harry. As he left the staffroom, he was acutely aware that these days he was more often than not the first one in and the last one out.

There was a time, thought Harry, when we were all just a bit late to leave – passionately making that last point about something or other. We used to go into the lesson fired up. We were never *that* late and it never did the kids any harm. There used to be a bit of life then, the staff room was buzzing. What's happened, where's it all gone? It's just not the same and suddenly he found himself in that doleful place that seemed all too familiar. "Come on you old fart," he said out loud, "get a grip, at least look as though you mean it." He then forced a quick march along the corridor but immediately slowed down as he came across a very good display of year 9 cubist portraits that Carruthers, the new art teacher, had put up. It annoyed him.

3

A WORLD OF FANTASY

In truth, Harry was a bit jealous of Carruthers and his art displays. The problem was that they were near enough to his classroom to show up his relatively dull offering. Principal Michael Cavendish seemed to point this out at every opportunity. He did it in a jokey kind of way, the sort of way that annoyed Harry. "Come, come, Mr Jones, you can't let Carruthers get away with commandeering the imaginative. Just because he's art he's not got a monopoly on creativity you know."

Harry felt like telling him to piss off. One time he made what he thought was a valid point. "Well, if you insist on putting the same blue background and the same academy trust logo on every bit of display work, it kind of takes away a bit of creative motivation do you not think?" That last remark had a little sting to it but before Cavendish could answer, Harry jumped in. "Carruthers doesn't have that same problem, not with artwork, and besides he's covered up virtually all the hideous blue background anyway."

Cavendish simply ignored his point.

"Look, let's get you on a trip over to our partner school, they've got great displays."

"Oh, for God's sake," mumbled Harry under his breath.

"What was that?"

"Yeah great."

"Fab," said Cavendish, "see Debbie, she'll book you in."

"Indeedy, it's fab," said Harry sarcastically beneath his breath. There was then a strange pause as Cavendish looked at him waiting for some facial acquiescence. Harry just about forced a smile. Satisfied with this response, Cavendish then wheeled round and walked off briskly. Harry held his smile for a second or two longer before the smart grey suit disappeared down the corridor. Safe in the knowledge that the head couldn't see him, Harry gave Cavendish a wave goodbye. At the same time, he squeezed out "patronising twat," through a clenched-teeth smile.

"What was that, Harry?" said Janet Allen, one of the nice support staff, who happened to be passing by. Harry had known her for a long time. She was one of the old brigade and therefore to be trusted. He didn't mind telling her what was on his mind.

"Bloody Cavendish. Fab! Everything's bloody fab. If the world was coming to an end; an apocalypse had descended and we were all doomed, it would still be 'bloody fab'."

Janet laughed and then comforted Harry by patting him on the shoulder. "There, there," she said and then gave him a mint imperial before moving on to her lesson. It was an odd gesture, thought Harry, rather like giving a stressed pet a treat to calm it down. He popped it into his mouth and strangely enough, it worked.

Harry was about 5 minutes late when he saw his class lined up outside his room.

"Okay make your way inside...QUIETLY!"

The year ten class shuffled into the RE room compliantly. It was the first lesson after the lunch break, normally the kids took an age to settle down, this time, however, they were calm. It can be like that thought Harry, you're ready for a battle and then nothing, no rhyme or reason. Probably a full moon last night he mused. Anyway, he wasn't complaining.

Just get them in, sit them down and call the register. Do it quickly before it all changes.

"Right, listen for your name. Megan."

"Yes, sir."

"Ben."

"Yes, sir."

"Rylie. Rylie?"

No answer. Harry looked up from his laptop and saw that Rylie was fiddling with an elastic band. The boy was so engrossed with pulling and stretching it that he simply hadn't heard his name. Harry couldn't be bothered saying anything to him, he just sighed and marked him present. As he looked back down at his laptop, he heard a snap and a yelp. He didn't need to look back up to know what had happened.

The class laughed. Harry shook his head and was about to continue when in walked Principal Cavendish with a visitor. The brief surge in noise that accompanied the accident suddenly died down as all eyes fixed on the two smartly dressed figures. Harry stopped what he was doing.

"Please don't let me disturb you Mr Jones," said Cavendish. He turned to the rest of the class and smiled. "Please, do carry on."

That bloody smile. There was always something irritating about that smile. Despite this Harry duly continued his role call but felt slightly uncomfortable. It wasn't just the smile, it felt as though they were checking up on him.

"Harry, this is Brian Edwards," said Cavendish smiling again. "I think you two may know each other."

"Yes," said Harry hesitantly. He didn't recognize him at first. Edwards had lost quite a lot of hair and he looked slimmer than last time he saw him. "Yes, it was a long time ago," Harry murmured.

Harry then took the time to look at Edwards more closely. He noticed that what little hair he had was well groomed and nicely trimmed. And it wasn't just that he was slimmer, Edwards looked fitter, leaner and much healthier. It was as though he'd just come back from holiday. Harry also noted his manner. He appeared very confident. It pained him to admit it, but Edwards looked better than him. Even though they were the same age he looked a good few years younger. A frown appeared on Harry's brow. He turned to Edwards and commented on what was obvious.

"I see you've gone up in the world. What's your job now?" he asked knowing full well what it was.

"Inspector," said Edwards. He added no more. The reply was firm and concise.

Harry could tell that he wasn't here in a friendly capacity even before he spoke. It wasn't just the tone of his voice it was the curt handshake and formal greeting that gave it away. No real warmth. Was it deliberate he asked himself? Of course, it was.

He didn't need to think too hard. Edwards is just as much of a twat now as he was back then. He was always up his own arse.

But something distracted Harry from thoughts about the past. He couldn't put his finger on it, but as the two men stood side by side, it suddenly occurred to him that Cavendish was a younger version of Edwards. They both had that air of self-importance and the same immaculate sense of dress code. The suits they wore fitted perfectly and had that appearance of being fresh from the dry cleaners, the only difference was the colour. Edwards' was dark blue and Cavendish's was light grey. Obviously to signify a difference in rank thought Harry.

Although Cavendish did have a little more hair than Edwards it was groomed in the same fashion. And then it came to him. They used the same stylist! Harry was sure of it. Even their fingernails – so well trimmed, so neat, so much alike. They definitely had manicures and almost certainly had them at the same salon. They probably have a latte together there, thought Harry, where they shower each other with accolades and speak in hushed tones of ways to get ahead….

Fantasy 1…Harry and the Spa.
Edwards and Cavendish are lying back on sun loungers with loosely fitting but luxurious white bath robes draped around their semi-naked bodies. Two attractive women tend to their needs by offering plates of treats, but they are dismissed as troublesome interferences. The room is hot and sultry. Harry finds himself slowly wafting a giant palm tree branch. He looks around and sees some strange vapours floating by. On closer inspection, they are thin wispy strands of text that appear to be emanating from the frothy milk of their lattes. They dance and swirl around before gently coalescing to form sentences of spectral flattery that hover expectantly over the balding sweaty heads of Edwards and Cavendish. They sit back and anticipate the hit of these ethereal compliments. As the sentence "Brian you're so very commanding" floats by, Edwards leans forward and sucks it up. He takes it in like that first-morning drag of a cigarette; absolute relief followed by complete and utter joy. Cavendish feverishly gulps in "Michael, you're the best." With each deep swallow of the compliment, he experiences the high-octane rhapsody of an

addict getting a good fix. A knowing grin spreads across his lips. They nod at each other approvingly and then the rest of the sycophantic script comes flooding into their open mouths.

"Brian you are so wonderful, so sensitive and kind."

"Michael you have such authority."

"You are so masterful."

"Oooh, you inspect so well."

"You are truly great."

A sickly sweet smile lights up their faces as their eyelids gently close in sweet rapture. Both figures then recline further to fully experience the heady hit of self-adulation. And in one final moment of pure ecstasy, they cum together – but not before a few last words snake their way up Cavendish's left nostril…

"You're so fab, so very ab fab…"

"Are you OK, Mr Jones?" Harry looked vacant. "Mr Jones," repeated Cavendish.

"I'm sure he's fine," said Edwards nonchalantly. Suddenly Harry was back in the world of the living, annoyed that Edwards should be answering a question that was meant for him. Harry shot him a look.

"I'm here for support," smiled Edwards attempting to justify his intrusion.

"Is that what you call it?" said Harry mockingly.

The head brushed Harry's comments away and in a quiet aside whispered in his ear, "We'll talk later."

"Can't wait," said Harry quietly. He wasn't sure whether Cavendish heard that last comment but if he did, he didn't appear phased.

"Thank you, Mr Jones," he said and then turned to the class. "Thank you, 10…"

"10R," said Harry.

"Thank you, 10R."

Cavendish always made a point of saying thank you to the school children at any given opportunity. Harry found it nauseating. They hadn't done anything! Why the hell was he saying thank you? Then, just to satisfy his own sense of ironic humour, he decided to get in on the effusive gratitude. As they were leaving he called out.

"Thank you, Mr Cavendish and Mr Edwards." It was said with a hint of sycophancy but there was no reaction. Either they ignored it or didn't get it, thought Harry. After they had gone he turned round to the class and put on his best smile.

"Thank you, 10R."

The class looked mystified.

"What are you doin', Sir?"

"You never say thank you."

"No, I don't," said Harry wistfully. He had to be careful, some of the brighter students would pick up on his ironic mockery. He quickly dropped the false smile and tried to go back into professional teacher mode but the irritation of Cavendish's "niceness" wouldn't leave him. It was like something out of the Waltons. As he looked out at the sea of blank faces he couldn't stop himself from imagining....

Fantasy 2...Harry and the Waltons.

Somewhere in Jefferson County, the sun is setting on an old country house that sits just below Walton's mountain. The crickets are chirping peacefully and the small flame of an old oil lamp bathes an All American family in a soft orange glow. They are getting ready for bed but one member of the household is ready before anybody else – Cavendish. He is underneath the covers waiting eagerly for old granny Walton to tuck him in. He is wearing his wee Willie Winky night hat that she especially knitted for him to keep his "lovely balding head warm and cosy." But something isn't quite right. It is his glasses; they need to be removed before she arrives. Cavendish takes them off quickly, he doesn't want to disappoint her. She always tutts when she sees that he still has them on. He places them carefully on his bedside cabinet. Then he brings the covers back over himself and grips the top of the quilt tightly. His nose just about peeps out. He is all of a tremble as he waits expectantly, almost feverishly. And in she comes.

Cavendish's face is flushed red with excitement as the old lady stoops forward and plants a big sloppy kiss on his forehead. A small frisson of energy surges through his body as her ample bosom brushes his chest. She then gently tucks a loose part of

22

the quilt in. She makes sure it's tight and constricting, she knows that he likes it that way.

"Good night, Michael Cavendish," says old granny Walton warmly.

Cavendish positively glows. "Good night, grandma," he replies contentedly. And then the chorus starts.

"Good night, John Boy."

"Good night, Michael."

"Good night, Mary Ellen."

"Thank you, Michael."

"Yes, thank you, Michael Cavendish."

And then old granny Walton puts a glass of milk and a cookie by his bedside. Cavendish speaks, his gratitude is effusive.

"Good night, granny…oh you're just so fab."

John Boy then pukes up over this cloying scene, not just a small wretch but huge projectiles of vomit, "hhgghee, hheeeegghh…ooogheg!!" It's everywhere, wrecking bed linen and splattering crisp white walls. And then Mary Ellen pukes up. It is a foul-smelling green-brown bile and then her head spins round violently spraying everything in its path. The glass of milk on the bedside table starts to bubble and froth. Cavendish is frightened and hides under the covers. Suddenly music plays. "You spin me right round baby right round." The whole scene is now a bizarre mixture of a 1980's rave and The Exorcist. Harry finds himself rather enjoying it when he is suddenly interrupted by the sound of reality.

"Are you ok, Sir?" came a voice from the front row.

"You wouldn't get it," said Harry snapping out of his daydream.

"I think I might."

Harry knew who that voice was straight away, Emily Bradshaw, a scrawny-looking ferret-like teenager with long mousy hair. She was also a highly intelligent extremely lazy and very malevolent spirit, something akin to a poltergeist. Harry had to be careful.

"I do not wish to engage you in this conversation thank you."

But Emily was not to be fobbed off that easily. "Are they going to be observing you?"

Thank you, Emily," repeated Harry firmly but Emily continued undeterred.

"You were a bit narky if you don't mind me saying so sir and I could understand why – all those smiley thank yous from Cavendish, it seemed a bit false."

Harry said nothing but simply stared at the diminutive figure.

"And you, you were taking the piss weren't you, Sir? Before Harry could say anything, Emily turned to the girl next to her "What do you think?"

And in the blink of an eye, she was conducting a full-scale debate on the matter. This is Emily thought Harry – taking great delight in manipulating the class in any direction she pleased. He understood why teachers could literally be seen dancing a jig of delight if she was absent on the day of their lesson.

"That's enough!" shouted Harry. Most of the class wheeled round. Emily then took it upon herself to tell the others who were not listening to turn round, be quiet and listen to the teacher. She then looked at Harry and smiled sweetly. He couldn't resist a comeback.

"Not much difference to Mr Cavendish then Emily."

"What?"

"Your false smile."

"That's a bit rude, Sir."

"Yes, I suppose it is," laughed Harry.

"Teachers aren't supposed to be rude," replied Emily smugly.

"Well, I am, I can be and if need be, I will be."

That last comment seemed to quieten Emily down – maybe a little too easily. She did stare at him for a minute or two, but he ignored her. Much to Harry's relief, she eventually got on with her work. The rest of the lesson then went without incident apart from one minor thing at the end that unnerved him. She strode up to his desk and politely thanked him.

"What for?" said Harry "I didn't do anything."

"It's just for being you, Sir." And with that, she giggled, linked arms with Matilda Beavis, and pranced out. Harry remained sitting at his desk. She had been up to something he could feel it in his water. Nevertheless, he was just glad that the lesson was over. He would be the first to admit that he wasn't feeling it especially because it was a cover and an RE one at that.

There were, however, some positives. The class didn't give him any trouble and Emily Bradshaw was surprisingly quiet. He was even able to text his friend without being detected. And joy of joys the fishing trip was still on! Despite these little fillips he still begrudged doing the cover. It wasn't just the fact that he had to do it that annoyed him most, it was doing it for Clare Guppy. She was off with stress again; she was always off. Most people knew that she was skiving. Apparently, she was once spotted on a cruise when she was supposed to be off sick. She never denied it and even said that her doctor had prescribed it. Now that really was taking the piss. I would never do that, thought Harry, no matter how hard it got.

Every time he thought about her, Harry got irritated and very hot under the collar. He could feel it now as he envisaged her breezing into the staffroom having had six weeks rest. She'd be all chirpy, full of the joys of spring with that awful cockney swagger of hers… "Ello lav, 'ello my lav, orwight. 'Ows ya farver?"

"She's got a nerve," mumbled Harry, "a bloody nerve."

Fantasy 3…. Harry and the crying teacher.
Harry is with Cavendish in his office. Guppy is there in a smart white jacket, a sprinkling of glitter resting on her shoulder pads. It is obvious that she'd partied the night before, maybe the last evening of the cruise.

"Please sit down, Clare," says Cavendish sympathetically. As she does so he hands her a letter slowly, sadistically, gleefully.

"I'm very, very sorry," he says in that horribly smiley way of his, "but I am going to have to sack you, yes sack you!"

Plink, plink! A few large tears splash down onto a glass-topped desk from the big brown eyes of Guppy. The mascara begins to run down two puffy white cheeks and her aging face begins to droop.

Cavendish laughs. "The letter tells you (Cavendish laughs some more) that effectively (laughs again) your contract here at

St Peter's is terminated. Yes terminated." (laughs even more)
Harry is impressed and gives him a jolly good round of
applause…
   "Well done, Cavendish, good one."
   Cavendish turns and bows to Harry in acknowledgement of a
fine performance and then the curtain comes down.

"Strange," said Harry out loud, "quite a bizarre daydream even
by my standards." He looked around at the empty classroom and
began gathering his stuff together. Suddenly a head popped in
the doorway.
   "How did that go?"
   "Oh, you know, I just love covering for Guppy whilst she
goes on her latest cruise."
   "Harry!" That's no way to speak about a fellow colleague"
said Vicky who laughed as she said it. "Anyway, what time do
you fancy going?"
   "Going?" said Harry.
   "We are car sharing, remember?"
   "Yes of course we are. As soon as possible then," said Harry.
   "I'm thinking 4.30 ish."
   "Yes, yes that's fine," said Harry with a sigh.
   The sigh was because he knew full well that four thirtyish
meant five o'clockish. It irritated him that Vicky dithered so
much. She always had something to do, that in his opinion,
didn't really need doing. It wasn't as though he wasn't grateful
for the lift, he was. It was Vicky that suggested the car share in
the first place. She was fed up with Harry moaning about
driving. "C'mon you fat bastard, share a car with your lesbo
mate. I'll drive, we're on the same route." Harry just couldn't
refuse an offer like that. And to be fair he enjoyed the chat in the
car after school. It's just that he'd like a quicker getaway some
of the time.
   But there was something about Vicky. Her short black hair
and pixie-like features combined with a confident swagger and
mischievous smile were appealing combinations. When she first
got the job at St Peter's she kept her sexuality hidden but now
that she was established, she pretty much flaunted it in front of
the principal's face, a fact that Harry loved. He was sure that he

26

could see the few strands of Evangelical hairs on the top of his head bristle with righteous indignation.

Harry stared at an unmarked set of History books. He was just about to pick one up when a smiling Tom Bailey poked his head round the door.

"Could I have a word?"

"Yeah sure," replied Harry.

Tom started to run his hand through his untidy grey hair, always a sign that something wasn't quite right.

"What's wrong?" said Harry.

"Well, I know I'm smiling," said Tom, "but it might not be funny, particularly if Cavendish gets wind of it."

"Wind of what?"

"This." Tom then pulled out a phone from his jacket pocket. "Have a look. I confiscated it earlier today."

Harry put on his glasses and peered at the small bright screen. Tom pressed play and a recording started up. Harry squinted his eyes and looked closely. In the foreground, he could make out a couple of silhouetted children's heads. Beyond those were a pile of books and several items that lay strewn across a desk. Just behind the desk through a small gap in the books, an ageing rather portly figure could be seen using what looked like a mobile phone. The figure sat immersed in what he was doing paying no attention to the class. It was evident that it was Harry.

"It goes on for a few minutes," said Tom, "but it's what appears next…"

Harry peered intently at the screen and immediately saw a caption pop up. "SCANDAL AT SAINT PETERS SCHOOL. TEACHER FOUND PLACING ONLINE BETS IN LESSON." And just after the caption, Harry's image appeared close up courtesy of a zoom feature. He could be seen having a furtive glance around as if to check that nobody was looking. It was quite clear that he was texting.

"Well...I don't know..." mumbled Harry.

"That's not all," interrupted Tom, "there's more."

Harry re-focussed his eyes on the phone, his brow now quite furrowed. He watched as a competent piece of editing saw the text and the image fade away, only to be replaced by a new one of himself. His face now filled the screen completely. He could see that his eyes were closed and by the sound of things he was snoring. It was loud. And then another image appeared over his, of a pig's snout snorting and grunting.

"That's not me making the snoring," protested Harry.

Tom couldn't help laughing.

"It's the little bit of dribble coming out of the side of your mouth. It's so sweet."

"It's not funny," said Harry getting quite annoyed.

"It's still not finished," said Tom laughing.

Another caption came up. "MR JONES THE DOSY BASTARD." And for a moment all was quiet.

"Well, they've spelt dozy wrongly," said Harry and they missed the apostrophe off Saint Peter's.

"Yes, that's right," agreed Tom, "but I don't think that the powers that be, will be too concerned with that. Harry, it's gone round year 10 like wildfire. I have seen them having sneaky looks on their phone chuckling away. The kids think it's a hoot."

"That's ridiculous…I... I…" Harry was clearly flustered but then tried to compose himself. "Well, in the first instance I was organising a fishing trip. I know I shouldn't. But who the bloody hell recorded me?"

"I took this phone off Matilda Beavis," said Tom, "but she wasn't the culprit. I'm pretty sure it was her friend…"

"Emily bloody Bradshaw," said Harry completing the sentence.

"Yep, you got it," affirmed Tom.

Harry shook his head. "But I never fell asleep in *that* lesson, I…" Harry stopped in mid-sentence to try to figure it out. And then it dawned on him.

"Biggsy! He must have sent her the image from the previous lesson, the crafty bugger."

"Did you actually fall asleep?" said Tom grinning.

"Yes, yes," said Harry irritated. "But she must have put it all together in my lesson." Harry sighed aware of the trouble that may ensue. He shook his head once again.

"Emily bloody Bradshaw," he repeated. "I thought she was bloody quiet."

4

SOMEWHERE IN NAPLES

The little girl pulled at the trouser legs of the crumpled figure resting in the chair. "Uncle Massimo, what happened next? Uncle Massimo?" But the figure didn't answer, so the little girl went to tug at his trouser leg again.

"Diana, don't disturb him," came a commanding voice from across the hallway. The little girl paused as a high-fashioned, well-dressed lady strode elegantly through the main room. She then calmly put her hand on the little girl's shoulder. "Can't you see, he's fast asleep?"

"But he was in the middle of reading me a story," replied the little girl insistently.

"I'm sure he'll finish reading it to you," said Maria, "just let him finish his nap, he's very tired."

The grandmother's voice was soothing but firm. Reluctantly Diana gave in. Nevertheless, she wasn't going to let her uncle off that lightly, so she pulled her phone out and took a picture of him. She found it funny and grinned. With his eyes closed and the stern features somewhat diminished he looked very peaceful, almost heavenly. A long way from the gruff persona he often liked to present to her. As Diana reviewed the picture on her phone, her grandmother looked at her and frowned.

"It's evidence," exclaimed Diana, "that he never kept his side of the bargain. He said that he would read me a story."

Maria smiled; her darling little Diana was definitely a De Rosa. Although she was only seven she was already displaying some of the traits needed to be a part of The Family. Would she be as important as her great uncle, who knows? Although Maria had reservations about any of her kin being involved, she knew that, in this part of Italy, her granddaughter would be better off being very much on the inside, as part of the System, than on the outside.

Maria watched Diana stomp off and then glanced over at her brother. She too noticed how peaceful he looked, a far cry from the frowns that had grown on his features over the past few months. They had always been there, but they were now a little more indented. In a funny kind of way, they added to his character and made his ageing complexion an "interesting road map of experience" as he himself put it.

Maria noticed that in the short time she had been observing him, Massimo had sunk further into the soft armchair so that his slightly fatty chin rested firmly on his chest. His balding head, now tipped forward, reflected the soft yellow glow of an art deco lamp. She thought that it was a shame that the males on her side of the family lost their hair so early and deduced that the moustache was a way of compensating for this. She looked at the small bristles of black and grey neatly groomed strands that hovered over his top lip and smiled. Maria often taunted him about it but her brother would never shave it off. He first grew it in his early twenties. After a successful business enterprise, he swore that it brought him good luck, and from that point on he vowed never to get rid of it. He trimmed it every three days. The neatness of it made him look very official and gave birth to his nickname of l'investigatore after the Belgium detective Hercule Poirot. There were worse names he could have had.

"Is he okay?" said a voice handing out a chilled Martini. Maria took the glass without looking at the tall black haired, well-tanned figure that was her son and little Diana's father.

"Oh yes, absolutely," replied Maria with more gusto than was needed.

"Hmm," said Paolo unconvinced. He was just about to say something more when suddenly a loud sound of something percussive pierced the soft chit-chat of the family gathering. Diana had found an old dinner gong from the kitchen and had sounded it right at the side of her great uncle's ear. Massimo got up with a start.

"Piccolo diavolo!!" You little devil.

But before he could get his hands on her, she was off. And then everybody laughed, not just a little, but a lot. Maria looked slightly concerned but couldn't quite stifle her giggles either.

"Can't you control that granddaughter of yours? Diana!" Massimo shouted again. "Diana!!" There was real annoyance in his voice. At first, she hid behind her grandmother's legs but then after a second or two slowly stepped out from the protective shield. Gingerly she walked towards a very grumpy old man. By the time she had got there, head bowed Massimo's anger had virtually disappeared. He found it very difficult to be at all annoyed with his favourite grandniece. He tried to frown but couldn't. Instead, he let out a long gentle sigh.

"Look you mustn't...."

"But you said that you would read me a story," interrupted Diana with a hint of guilt in her voice.

"I know but..." and then Massimo smiled and looked at Maria. "You know if it was anybody else." He shook his head. "Okay, get me a drink from the kitchen and we'll finish off." And with that Diana skipped away and came back with an especially cold beer in a frosted glass.

"Thank you," said Massimo, "gratefully received."

After he'd finished reading the story, Massimo walked over to Maria. They both shook their heads in acknowledgement of Diana's charm and the hold that this little monkey had over them. As they looked on, enthralled at her antics, Massimo turned to his sister.

"You know you must not give me that much pasta," he said accusingly. "It is yours I take it?" Maria nodded proudly.

"Yes, it is mine. I would not let anybody else do it. My chef did the rest of the cooking and put the menu together, but the pasta is mine. I insisted."

Massimo patted his growing waistline that appeared to be trying to free itself from his shirt.

"You know I can tell it is yours, I cannot resist it. I eat too much of it and then I fall asleep. But then you know that this will happen. You are a wicked sister."

Maria smiled. "You need the rest. Speaking of which...you look tired. Is everything ok?"

"Yes, yes everything's fine," replied Massimo quickly but Maria seemed unconvinced. She frowned and looked at him closely.

"Hmmm."

"What?" said Massimo innocently.

"You need a break."

"Well as a matter of fact I am thinking of going away."

"Where?"

"Not sure yet."

"Things must be bad if you are thinking of having a break," joked Maria.

"No, no," said Massimo gently. He smiled as if to reassure her. "It's just the job, you know what it's like – but you're right I need a break."

Maria accepted the vagueness of Massimo's answers. She knew not to ask too many questions about business, but she couldn't resist one last need for reassurance.

"You are okay though?"

Massimo nodded and smiled. "Of course."

If her brother went away, he would of course miss Diana. Massimo had become quite attached to her but hopefully, he wouldn't be gone too long. Without somebody as pivotal as Massimo, things could go south fairly quickly. He was only a cog in the machine, but his work was underrated by many, not so much by Alfonso, but by other members of the clan. It was partly because her brother shunned the limelight and eschewed any glamour associated with the family. He was more than happy being in the background; balancing the books and crunching the numbers. And once that was done, burying himself in his books, listening to his classical music, and drooling over his beloved Caravaggio.

It never seemed odd that her brother developed such an obsession with this great artist. Maria's theory was that after his mother died, he needed to look up to someone. Their father spent little time with him back in England. Massimo said that he only remembered seeing him three times whilst he was there. Losing his mother was hard enough but then coming over to Italy proved almost unbearable. He was a very lonely boy. In one sense it seemed perfectly logical that he should latch on to such an outlandish figure from history. She never forgot the day he "found" Caravaggio here, in the church in Naples; he was ecstatic…

"What are you thinking," asked Massimo interrupting Maria's train of thought.

"Will he be going with you?"

"Who?"

"You know, your beloved Caravaggio?"

"Ah yes, my beloved Caravaggio. Yes, I should have known," said Massimo smiling. "Well, that would be highly irregular not to mention quite horrific. He has been dead some four hundred years and being with a bag of bones would not be my preferred choice."

"No, of course not," responded Maria quickly, "but I can arrange for a framed piece of his artwork to be packaged up and sent to your apartment, ready for travelling with you – as a sort of companion to help your well-being. You can even take it to bed with you if you like."

"No, thank you," replied Massimo curtly.

They both smiled but Maria couldn't quite dismiss the thought that something was looming. It cast a small grey cloud over an otherwise bright sunny afternoon.

5

THE CAR JOURNEY HOME

"So, what's this I hear about you placing bets online during a religious education lesson?" enquired Vicky laughing as she said it.

"Bloody hell, let me get in the car first," said Harry, who seemed irritated at his friend's glee. "You're gonna have to wait," he added, "until I'm good and ready, and besides you're not the only one in the car. He looked across at Romy, the young German trainee, camped on the back seat of Vicky's nippy little Volkswagen.

"Maybe Romy doesn't want to hear," said Vicky impatiently. But Romy wasn't listening. She was too busy doing something or other on her iPhone.

"Are you okay there Romy?" said Harry but rather than answer she simply gave him the thumbs up. Harry took it as a sign that she couldn't be bothered to speak. He sighed at what he perceived as a lack of manners. He then sighed again as he contemplated the ever-increasing problem of fitting his expanding frame into the smallish front seat. As he bent down he felt his back stiffen and his knee joint crack. This was nothing new but the involuntary puff of air that gushed out with the effort was. And to add insult to injury his leather trouser belt then dug into his midriff. "Ouch."

"Are you ok Harry?" cried Romy from the back of the car. She was much more alert now that she'd put her phone away.

"Never better my dear," replied Harry.

"Good I am glad to hear it," said Romy earnestly.

Harry shook his head. Romy never quite got his sarcasm and she always seemed to take what he said at face value. He found it endearing and at times annoying. Right now, it was annoying as he tried hard to buckle up his seatbelt and make himself reasonably comfortable, but it wouldn't quite click. Usually, after a few goes it worked, but this time it didn't. He tried several more times but to no avail. He then started to bash it just as Romy asked another question in that forthright tone of hers.

"Some students told me that they saw you making some bets on your phone and they have video evidence, is this true? Were you betting on your phone?"

Harry could feel a few beads of sweat trickle down his forehead. He was getting bloody annoyed. No matter how hard he tried, the seat belt still wouldn't click. He looked red-faced at Vicky who was trying desperately not to laugh for fear of upsetting her colleague.

"No, I was not!" said Harry firmly. He looked in the mirror and could see a frown appear on Romy's face that upset the delicate equilibrium of those smooth young features. He'd been upsetting quite a few people recently. He wasn't unduly concerned, but he didn't want to upset sweet Romy. No definitely not, thought Harry, even though she needed toughening up.

"Well, c'mon Harry, tell us what happened," prompted Vicky.

"I will if I can get this bloody seatbelt of yours in!"

"Harry, you have to be gentle, she's got feelings." Vicky then removed Harry's hand from the strap and eased the buckle in. Click! First time. "Like most men you just try to ram it in bish bosh. That's far too crude, you have to ease it in gently. Let that be a lesson."

"Thank you," said Harry ironically. "Where were we?"

"You were about to tell us what happened."

"Oh, yes. Nothing, absolutely nothing. I was just texting a friend."

"In class?"

"Yes," said Harry feebly.

"Christ Harry! You need to be careful; Cavendish is gunning for you. What were you texting anyway?"

"It was about a fishing trip."

"A fishing trip!" exclaimed Vicky. "Is that all? Bloody hell, it took long enough. Apparently, you were being filmed for about five minutes."

"Look!" bellowed Harry as he spread out his thick podgy hands. "They're not exactly a concert pianist's fingers. It takes me one minute to put one word in. And besides, you're in a different world to me, you lot type quicker than you speak."

"Text, Harry, text. We don't type on a phone," said Vicky correcting him and smirking at the same time.

"Whatever," replied Harry.

"Aren't we missing the point?" interrupted Romy.

"What's that?" said Harry.

"Nobody's supposed to film or video anybody without their permission, and the school policy states that mobile phones should not be used in the classroom." The authoritative tone in Romy's voice startled Harry into silence.

"We know that," interjected Vicky," but Harry was using his."

"But she still videoed you," said Romy.

"Cavendish will be more concerned about my use of the mobile phone, I'd bet my mortgage on it," said Harry regaining his voice.

"You can always say it was your sick mother who'd rang," said Romy trying to be supportive.

"Maybe," said Harry surprised at Romy's suggestion that he tell a lie. "Maybe."

Harry then spent the next few minutes of the journey trying to work out how he'd left an opening for anybody to see him, let alone film him. A part of him admired the ingenuity and sheer audacity of Emily Bradshaw. She quite literally spotted the gap and went for it.

Harry thought that there was a possibility she may get excluded for a day but that would have little effect. In her mind, it was worth taking such a hit. Exclusions never bothered her in the slightest. It had happened so many times before. She often boasted about what she did on that "day off." More than likely, she'll be in the isolation room thought Harry, where she could wreak more havoc, and I'll be in the head's office again. He sighed and looked out of the window.

"Don't worry," said Romy trying to comfort him, "maybe Mr Cavendish will not see it."

Harry said nothing but simply carried on staring. They were coming up to the lights that always turned red as they approached. And, sure enough, they did. He looked on ahead and could just see the Spar where they sometimes made a pit stop. Further ahead would be the sign for St Johns primary school followed by a string of 30 and 40 mph signs that often caught out some unwitting driver. He'd had enough, he needed a moan.

"How many times have we driven along this same route? I mean it's not a terrible journey but it's half an hour there half an hour back. That's an hour of my life doing the same thing. It's not exactly edifying, getting in the car; going through the gates; passing spotty teenagers giving you the finger through the Preston traffic; past the Spar; on to the bypass; blah, blah, blah." There were a few minutes of silence and then he started again. "I suppose it's not too bad when you get out of the centre, the traffic's easier, there are a few more trees but it's all the same. All the bloody same."

"Well, I've got something to cheer you up," said Vicky sensing that Harry was about to descend into one of those glum moods.

"What's that?" said Harry impassively.

"Tom Bailey's going to do an assembly tomorrow."

Suddenly Harry perked up. "Does Cavendish not know? Hasn't anybody warned him?"

"No," said Vicky excitedly, "nobody knows. The last time he did one was a few years ago. All the management are new and Cavendish has only been here a year or two."

Harry was now livelier than on any part of the journey. He rubbed his hands together in anticipation.

"Interesting," he said slowly, "but I thought cheery O'Leary was going to do it."

"No," said Vicky, he had to cancel last minute. Tom stepped up and said he'd do it, and here's the funny part, the head was really grateful."

"Bloody hell," spluttered Harry. "I think that may change."

"Why is that?" piped Romy from the back seat.

"You haven't seen one of Tom's assemblies, have you?" interjected Vicky.

"No, but please tell me," said an intrigued Romy.

"Christ, where do I start?" muttered Harry.

"The Mrs Doubtfire one," said Vicky gleefully.

"Yes," said Harry smiling, and then they both started giggling.

Eventually, Harry got it together to explain to Romy that it was when Tom first started at St Peter's.

"I think he wanted to impress," said Harry "but he came to school dressed as Mrs Doubtfire to present an assembly. The first time I saw him in the staffroom I thought it was the cleaner sitting down having a cuppa. I actually thought that this person's got a real nerve. He/she just sat there not saying a word drinking our tea from our mugs."

"I think it was the method school of acting," said Vicky.

"Yes, that's right," said Harry. "He was completely immersed in character, never said a word. Just stared at the floor. 'Tom, is that you?' I said. He just nodded and said something about an assembly."

"What was it like, the assembly?" said Romy enthusiastically.

"Bizarre," said Harry. "He'd even gone to the length of photographing himself at home tucking the kids in bed, doing the ironing, kissing his wife goodnight all dressed up as Mrs Doubtfire. And then he showed them to the kids using the big giant projector."

"No!" said Romy in a low and hushed tone clearly shocked. "What did the kids do when they saw the pictures?"

"Well, here's the thing," said Harry, "the kids, they never seemed to bat an eyelid. At that time everybody's half asleep anyway. There were a few chuckles but on the whole, all was perfectly fine, apart from when he did the Lord's Prayer at the end." Harry turned round to look directly at Romy. "He never came out of character, he continued to pray in that same hopeless Scottish accent." And then Harry attempted to imitate Tom imitating a Scottish accent. "Oour farther whoo art in heeven hallo wood be thay nayem." Romy and Vicky fell about laughing. It took a minute or two to die down before Harry chirped up. "I think there was a message in there somewhere, maybe something biblical, but it was lost on me."

Harry then went on to describe his other notable assemblies including the captain Pugwash one which featured Master Bates and Seaman Staines.

"How did he get away with them?" said a shocked Romy.

"I have no idea," replied Harry, "because they were funny for all the wrong reasons, politically so incorrect. I think eventually some of the parents complained and he was banned from doing them." Harry turned to Vicky. "About seven years ago?"

"Something like that. Oh, and there was that one where he got a water pistol out and fired it from his hip." Vicky turned to Romy and explained. "From a certain angle, it looked as though he was peeing on the kids."

"No," said Romy again in that shocked way of hers. "Why didn't the staff try to stop him?"

"You're joking," said Harry, "and spoil all the fun?" He and Vicky laughed again. They were still giggling away as they pulled up outside of number 2 Appledown Lane – Harry's house. He stepped out of the car and groaned again with the effort.

"It's not that bad is it Harry?" said Vicky.

"Get a bigger bloody car, it's like being in a dinky."

"That's no way to talk about my baby," said Vicky patting the steering wheel. "Anyway, see you tomorrow."

"Sure," said Harry. He then smiled at Romy, nodded at Vicky, and shut the car door. He stayed and watched as his two colleagues drove off. He always did that. It was so impolite to walk off straight away without seeing people go. Lots of people do, thought Harry, it's just so rude. As the car became a spot in the distance, Harry realised that for all his moaning he still liked that little drive home. It was like a transition phase before the re-entry into his personal life, which in the next couple of minutes would hopefully include a cold beer. The day had been a scorcher and Harry was a bit hot under the collar. The phone recording debacle had pissed him off, he needed something to take the edge off.

A couple of steps and I'll be there he thought to himself. He could feel his tongue starting to stick to the roof of his mouth. He opened the small white gate that marked the entrance to the house and strode purposefully up the path towards the largish Edwardian Semi. Normally Harry would be a little slower so that he could take in the well-tended mature shrubs and flower beds that lay on either side of the path. He would usually take the time to acknowledge the work of his green fingers and say out loud that it looked pleasing without being too pretty. But not this time. He needed something cool and refreshing right now. He marched on but then stopped and stared hard at a very red front door.

He'd forgotten that he had just painted it. That colour was quite dominating. He still wasn't sure. It wasn't his first choice. He originally wanted something dark and less ostentatious, navy blue or maybe even black. He always thought that there was something sturdy and strong about a black front door but his wife, Mary, wouldn't even entertain the idea.

"For goodness sake," she said, "why on earth would anyone want black on a front door? It's, so...unwelcoming."

Harry did protest, but any attempt at a counter-argument was quickly extinguished.

"No, no, a nice warm red. Yes, warm and inviting," said Mary firmly. "Definitely not anything dark. That would be wrong!

Harry would have said something more but it was said with such finality that he found himself just giving in. "Okay," was all he could muster. He very nearly said, "Okay, dear." but just stopped himself in time. Mary never liked being called dear. Later on that day she googled "red doors." Harry knew that she would do that, it was just like her to back up a point of view with evidence and sure enough, he was right.

"See," she said, "welcoming. That's what it says right there. It's symbolic. A red door, it's a welcome."

Harry put on his glasses and sure enough, his wife was right but then he looked further down the Wikipedia description and spotted something that amused him,

"It also means that you are mortgage free in Scotland."

Mary looked exasperated. Harry knew that look.

"Okay, okay," said Harry recognising the need to be less flippant, "but nothing too bright. I don't want a really bright red,"

"Well, that sounds okay," agreed Mary. "So why don't we have a look at some colour charts." It took both of them an age to settle on a colour. Eventually, they plumped for Farron and Ball's rectory red.

Back in the present Harry suddenly became aware that he had been staring at the door for some time. I suppose it doesn't dominate too much, he thought. I can live with it. He then pulled out his set of keys that were always in his right-hand jacket pocket, found the brass-coloured Yale, and slowly turned the lock. There was a satisfying feeling as the mechanism revolved easily and smoothly. The WD40 he had sprayed on yesterday had done the trick. And then he remembered that he was very thirsty and needed that cold beer. No, not yet, he thought to himself, I'll just say a quick hello to Mary first. It would be remiss of me not to greet her and ask about her day.

6

ALL ABOUT MARY

Everybody always told Harry how fortunate he was that he'd married Mary. His stock reply to any such comment was that she was extremely lucky to have him. That always brought about a few laughs amongst his male friends and indeed from some of the women but in those instances it was usually proceeded by a dismissive look at his figure and then a comment like, "Yeah right."

Harry would often protest that, "Women have fought over this body."

"Yeah... fought to get away," would be the swift reply.

And then Harry would feign being emotionally wounded.

"Well...I'm...staggered...you could even think such...a thing...no...no really I am."

And if Mary was there, she'd bash Harry in the ribs and tell him to be quiet. She used to like Harry's humour. She liked the way he could poke fun of himself as well as others. Back then he never took himself too seriously. It was a quality she found extremely attractive and was one of the main reasons she married him. But he was more thoughtful then and she quite liked his forthright views on politics and religion even if she disagreed. There was also a brightness to Harry in those early days but just lately she recognised that some of his spark had gone.

Mary felt as though she too was fading away, although she had looked after herself far more than her husband. She had kept in trim with a well-maintained diet, regular swimming, and a weekly yoga class. Her dress sense was quite eclectic with some clothes bought from stores but others, unashamedly, purchased from the local charity shops. Whatever she wore, worked. She knew that she was still attractive, but it was on the inside where she felt somewhat diminished. She called it her 'dull ebb.'

To offset this, she had recently started helping with the food bank at their local church, just down the road. She began volunteering there six months ago, just after she was made redundant from her job at the council. Mary didn't mind being laid off; she was getting tired of the job anyway. There was no real sadness at leaving, even though she'd worked there for a number of years. Harry was annoyed about it though and vented.

"So, this is how things are done these days," he said. "When they think you've outlived your usefulness, bang, gone. Never mind about your experience, never mind about all that you have contributed. Bastards, that's what they are."

Mary tried to tell Harry that she was knocking on a bit and that she wasn't as enthusiastic about her job as she used to be.

"Well maybe so," he said, "but age should be no barrier to your being able to do the job, you should have been able to choose."

"I did, I took redundancy."

Harry got quite cross by that remark, "You know what I mean, you were pushed." He then got up in a huff and went to the kitchen to get a beer. "And anyway 56 is not that old," he shouted from across the hallway.

"That's not the point," said Mary quietly to herself so that Harry couldn't hear. "I am growing tired of everything. It's been the same for too long. I need something new… maybe somebody knew." Just as she had finished muttering to herself Harry walked in with a small glass of sherry. "For you, my darling," he declared.

Mary smiled at the kindness shown by her husband that day as she tried to dismiss thoughts of 'someone new' out of her mind. She listened with one ear as Harry chuntered on about the injustice of the political and educational system. Her distracted mind agreed with most of what her husband had said but she had heard it all before.

And in that moment, she was grateful for her new friend, Tanya, who had fresh words and a different perspective on life. She was a few years younger than Mary, and it showed. She had so much more energy. They met at the yoga class and they just seemed to hit it off. It was Tanya who suggested helping out at the local food bank where she was the project manager. It wasn't long before Mary got involved; two hours a week soon developed into two full days a week.

One afternoon just after they'd finished work, Mary invited Tanya back for a quick coffee. She was careful not to be too pushy and made it clear that she would not be offended if her friend declined. To her surprise and delight, Tanya accepted the invitation. As they strolled down the lane Mary turned to Tanya.

"You know I quite enjoyed it today even though lifting all those boxes made it quite physical."

"Yes," said Tanya, "you will soon have muscles like these." And with that, she rolled up her sleeves and flexed some impressive biceps. It came completely out of the blue and was said with such gay abandon that it made Mary suddenly laugh out loud.

"I don't know why I did that," said Tanya giggling childishly. "It's such a sunny afternoon I think I've caught some of its spirit."

"That's fine by me," said Mary. And as the two of them walked merrily onward, Tanya turned to Mary.

"Are you sure Harry won't mind?" Mary looked puzzled. "About the use of your fridge and freezer, are you sure he won't mind?"

"No," said Mary quite confidently.

"But all that food bank stuff, in your fridge."

"It's not your fault the church one has broken. No, Harry won't mind and besides, you know I am always glad to help," said Mary reassuringly. Even if Tanya wasn't her boss, Mary would still have been happy to support her. There was something about her new friend that inspired loyalty.

"Home!" said Mary suddenly as the two stopped at a pretty white gate. "After you." There was a lightness to her voice. She watched as Tanya sauntered up the path in front of her. She couldn't help but notice how well the primrose yellow blouse fitted her friend. It brought out the best in her slender back.

"That blouse, it looks so pretty. It really suits you."

"Thank you," said Tanya, cheerily. "A little treat from Oxfam."

"Really!"

"Are you jealous?" said Tanya turning round and grinning.

"No, it's just that I like buying from charity shops but if I could get something that fitted me that well…" She then paused, "yes, I am jealous."

They both laughed. Tanya then hopped up two steps to the front entrance. As she did so the bottom of her right cotton trouser leg rode up slightly to reveal a small butterfly tattoo on the base of her ankle. Mary was just about to comment on it when Tanya stopped.

"You've changed the colour of your front door, much warmer, more welcoming."

"That's what I said," exclaimed Mary. "Harry wanted black!"

"Oh no," said Tanya, "who'd want a black door?"

"That's what I said," repeated Mary. And then the two women burst out laughing at the absurdity of their conversation.

"Right," said Mary once they'd stepped inside, "let's have a cup of tea." It was after she said it that she wished she'd suggested something different. A cup of tea seemed so mundane, so very, very English.

"You haven't got anything stronger?" asked Tanya. "I know it's cheeky but I just fancy something a little spicier."

And in a flash, those little grey clouds that had gathered over Mary's head suddenly vanished to be replaced with two large gin and tonics complete with ice and lemon.

"Great minds think alike," said Mary as she handed one over to a grateful Tanya. "Do you need a cushion? These garden chairs can be quite hard."

"No, no," said Tanya "I'm fine." She then looked around and bathed in the glow of the gorgeous sunlit afternoon.

"Mary, I must say what a beautiful garden you have," said Tanya eagerly.

"Thank you," said Mary, "although if it was left to Harry, it would be absolutely awf…No, no," she corrected herself, "I'm not going to be horrible. He did do a lot of the planting. Let's just say it wouldn't work as well if he had a more creative role."

45

"You *can* be awful," said Tanya. "I always used to slate my husband even though I loved him." Mary smiled. They'd touched on Tanya's husband's death before but right now it wasn't a cue to talk about him, it was more an invitation for Mary to be a little wicked. Tanya was giving Mary permission to moan about Harry and not to hold back. She jumped at the chance.

"Yes, yes," said Mary, "he's got absolutely no sense of colour...red tulips and white roses together!! I ask you. And his idea of a black door, for heaven's sake. But the worst thing is that he thinks he's right. The kitchen, you've seen the kitchen. That beautiful sunflower yellow, he wanted sailor's blue. Honestly! We argued for ages about it. He should just stick to his fishing, stamp collecting and his beloved Caravaggio! Honestly! He's got this obsession with him and bloody late Renaissance art; you'd think he'd have some idea about colour, you know, what goes together and all that, but honestly, he does for colour what Domestos does to a germ: kills it stone dead."

And with that, they burst out laughing again. Maybe it was the gin and tonic, but it was as though some imaginary shackles had come off. Whatever the reason Mary found herself talking freely about all sorts of things. And she continued to have a moan, which was most unlike her. For Tanya, that's what made it so funny, this quiet, private, well-spoken middle-aged woman suddenly letting rip. She started to laugh again. Great big hyena laughs. Mary joined in with equal gusto. They both laughed so much that they became breathless. "Please," said Mary, "I can't. Don't, don't I think I might wet myself." After a few minutes, they eventually calmed down. Mary suddenly noticed how vivid the colours in the garden seemed, how alive the earth was. In that moment everything seemed so wonderful, so idyllic.But every bubble has to burst.

"Halloo," Harry shouted as he marched into the hallway.

"In the garden, Harry," shouted Mary trying not to laugh.

Harry was thrown by the fact that he could hear two voices. He poked his head round the back door.

"Hi, Harry," said Mary giggling, "Me and my friend Tanya, we've just done a shift at the food bank."

"Oh," said Harry in a rather non-descript manner. Mary then gave her husband a look. Harry then smiled and greeted Tanya with a little more warmth. The fact that someone unexpected was there when he came home from school threw him. He liked that time, when he first came in, to sit down and relax. No matter he said to himself, I'll just get a beer and sit in the spare room after I've done with the pleasantries.

"I'm just going to get a beer," said Harry. "Anybody want anything?" Both women shook their heads and carried on giggling. Harry frowned. He could see that they already had a large something, but he thought it was still polite to ask. He slipped away quickly. He just couldn't wait for that beer. He'd had a crap day really, what with the phone debacles; falling asleep in the lesson; doing the cover for Guppy and an impending doom-laden meeting with Cavendish and Edwards yet to come. He was suddenly aware again of his tongue sticking to the roof of his mouth. "I can't wait," he muttered out loud as he opened the fridge door.

"Oh, Harry!" shouted Mary.

But before she could say anything more Harry saw a terrible truth. Gone were his cans of beer. Not one was visible. Instead, the fridge was packed top to bottom with milk and various other dairy products.

"I hope you don't mind," continued Mary, "but I've had to take your beer out of the fridge. It's just that we had nowhere else to store the food bank stuff. We needed a fridge, the church one is broken so I kindly offered ours for a day. I hope you don't mind."

"Where is the beer?" said Harry tersely.

"Oh, the beer, yes. I think I left it on...."

"The side," said Harry disdainfully as he completed Mary's sentence. He hadn't noticed it at first, but now he could see several cans of Budweiser resting on the worktop drenched in warm sunlight. He walked over; felt them; his worst fears confirmed. "Not just warm," he muttered angrily, "boiling bloody hot!"

"They're hot!" he shouted.

Mary caught the annoyance in his voice and tried to placate him.

"We've still got some ice in the freezer. Just pop some in your beer."

"Ice in my beer?" said Harry exasperated. "You don't put ice in beer. Couldn't you have left just one in the fridge?"

"Why don't you have a gin and tonic then?"

"I don't want a gin and tonic. I want a cold beer. Correction, I wanted a cold beer, because I know I can't have one, now!"

"Oh, Harry, it's not the end of the world, just chill out and have a gin and tonic. Come and sit down with us."

Harry stopped for a second to consider his wife's suggestion. There was a possibility that he could have taken her up on it, but such was his sense of indignation that he couldn't let it go. It was only a couple of weeks ago that he tripped over several large boxes of cereal left in the garage and before that, several tins of beans had slightly warped the lightweight pantry shelf he had erected. All this in the name of food bank storage. No, this was getting out of hand.

"No, thank you," said Harry as he turned around and stormed back into the house.

"Miserable old fart," said Mary. She laughed a little, but the spell had been broken.

Tanya smiled. "Look, I've had a great time but I really must be going."

Mary was disappointed. She was going to protest but stopped herself. Instead, she smiled back.

"We must do it again sometime soon."

"Yes, we will," said Tanya, "definitely." And with that, she knocked back the rest of the gin and tonic and stood up. She smiled again. "Strong stuff."

"Yes, it is," replied Mary knowingly.

As the two of them walked back through the house Tanya cheerily said goodbye to Harry who barely raised a grunt back. The two women then reached the bottom of the path and embraced warmly. Tanya opened the gate, stepped through with a little bit of a wobble, and then closed it carefully behind her, making overly sure that the bolt was back on.

"Strong stuff," she repeated.

"Are you okay?"

"Yes fine," said Tanya laughing, "don't worry I've got a lift."

"I never thought…Harry could have given you a lift."

"No, honestly I'll be fine." With that, she walked a few paces then turned round and waved one last goodbye. Mary waved back and smiled as she watched her friend disappear down the lane.

As soon as Tanya was out of sight, Mary's smile disappeared. She walked back inside and slammed the door. She then marched into the living room to find her husband sprawled over the couch, feet up, idly watching some sport with a ball in. To make matters worse he was sipping a glass of beer with bits of half-melted ice bobbing around in the froth.

"I hope you fucking choke on it!" said Mary furiously.

Harry could tell that Mary was going to be annoyed even before she came in, but he didn't quite realise that she would be that angry. His wife hardly ever used the F word and when she did it never sounded quite right. A part of him wanted to laugh, not because he found it funny but because it sounded so shocking. He only managed a one-word response.

"What?"

"What? What? You know what!" scowled Mary. "Don't give me all this innocent business. You were rude. What did I do that was so wrong? I left your precious beers out of the fridge and for that, you showed your backside and embarrassed me in front of my friend. It was for the food bank, Harry - you know the people who can't afford any food, let alone beers. Correction, a cold beer. It was a mistake. I was going to put them in the garage, but God forbid, I left them out." And then Mary got upset and tears started to well up. "I was having such a nice time." (sob) "AND YOU SPOILT IT!" And with that Mary stormed out and slammed the door.

Harry felt numb. He continued to watch the television but wasn't really paying attention. He barely blinked as a slow-motion clip of a Nadal topspin forehand winner was replayed. After a second or two, he looked over at his glass of beer resting neatly on a coaster on the coffee table. He could see the drips of condensation running down the side caused by the cooling effects of the ice cubes. It looked appetising. He took a sip – no real loss of taste. And the beer in the freezer, that would be ready in about half an hour. And then he realized that he could have been more magnanimous, even kinder. He just felt so wounded at the time. Thoughtlessly leaving the beers out in the hot sun, after his day at work, what was she playing at? It only confirmed what had been on his mind recently: that his wife did not care for him. But that did not excuse his being rude to Tanya. And on reflection, Harry realised that Mary was also right about the food bank stuff.

Mary did eventually come back after an hour or so, as Harry knew she would. They patched things up. He was quite remorseful and when he said sorry, he meant it. She graciously accepted his apology and when he told her about the day he'd had, Mary understood her husband's reaction and she in turn apologised. They hugged each other and then Harry cleared away the glasses in the garden and tidied up.

7

TOM'S ASSEMBLY

The following morning Harry woke up well before the alarm sounded. He pressed the off switch so that it wouldn't wake Mary. He eased himself out of bed, put his dressing gown on and set about making his wife the nicest cup of tea and the tastiest piece of toast he could muster. He decided to use the best china teapot and a posh little ramekin for the marmalade. A small red rose freshly picked from the garden placed in a tiny glass vase finished it all off nicely. Harry carried the breakfast tray up the stairs with a sense of pride and presented it to his wife who was finding it difficult to come round.

"On the side," mumbled Mary. She then turned over and said something about a few too many gin and tonics.

Harry gave a disappointed sigh. There was no acknowledgement of his efforts, no gratitude. He stood still for a few seconds and then gently placed the tray on the side as his wife had asked. He left the bedroom with a real sense of deflation. "Not a great start to the day," he muttered.

After his muted breakfast, it wasn't with any great sense of excitement that he stood on the corner waiting for his lift to school. It didn't help that he wasn't a morning person. He didn't fancy too much chat on this journey. Thankfully none of the others spoke much. Vicky had had some kind of night out and was a bit worse for wear and Romy was, as ever, engrossed in her phone. Like a group of zombies, they all processed out of the car; up the steps to the school; stepped into the staffroom; had a cuppa and then went for a pee. Harry muttered something about it being like the lemmings shuffling mindlessly to their doom. The morning briefing went in a blur and before he knew it Harry was standing in the Hall waiting for the students to arrive for morning assembly.

His job was to usher the youngsters in and direct them where to sit. As he waited for the masses to arrive, he looked around at the ageing panels of the large side walls and took in the scent of the freshly polished wooden floor.

Despite his growing antipathy towards much of school life, there was something deeply comforting about that smell. And when he thought about it, he had a similar feeling towards the structure of the old hall, which in many respects was a remnant of a bygone age. After the various extensions and modernisations to the building, this seemed to be one of the few parts of the school that had real authenticity.

It used to be Harry's self-appointed job to lead teams of deviant year 11 boys to clean up the "old quarter" as it was known. He used to get them to scrub the aging magnolia-coloured walls and restore the beauty of the decorative wooden panelling. He also gave them a mission to rid the interior of any graffiti however small and insignificant it was. And for those who had done particularly well, their job was to polish up the brass fittings on the altar. They used to love that; they used to love being there. "And so did I," muttered Harry out loud. He'd never really acknowledged that to himself but in this reflective moment, he allowed himself to feel some pride in his work.

He used to like the banter with some of the older more streetwise boys. There was one group of lads, he could still hear them now. "Come on Jonesy show us how it's done." He would have shown them how it's done but he hadn't a clue what they were on about.

It was always Archie, Archie Shufflebottom, the poor lad with a surname like that. They all called him Shuff for short. He'd always be the one who couldn't resist saying something. Harry remembered one time when they were all polishing the brass and it was Shuff, who else, who asked a question.

"Do you believe in all this stuff, Sir?"

"What stuff?"

Shuff pointed at the Altar. "You know, this religious stuff."

"Well, we are a church school. I think…"

But before Harry could complete his answer, one of the lads clambered on the altar for a dare and did a kind of jive dance. It was a black lad they called Token. He made all his limbs move in different directions but miraculously he had timing and rhythm. In the middle of his routine he stopped, put his hands together in prayer, and looked up to the ceiling. Then he came out with a kind of Gregorian chant.

"I can play dominoes better than you can." He then crossed himself.

At first, Harry was shell-shocked and did nothing except let his jaw drop wide open. Then Token started dancing again.

"Get down from there!!" bellowed Harry who then made an instinctive move to grab the boy. In doing so he tripped and pushed Token, who duly slipped and fell on his arse. There was shock followed by uproar as cleaning fluid had inadvertently spilled over Token's crotch. The poor lad looked as though he had wet himself. Harry tried his best not to laugh but he couldn't help himself. Suddenly they were all in hysterics. It was a full 5 minutes before any of them recovered. After that, Token did his dance at least once a month. Harry told him off every time, but it was never with any great force.

"Why do they call you Token?" Harry once asked.

"Because I'm the token black lad on the football team. Anyway, look around."

Harry didn't need to. It wasn't just the football team; he was the only black lad in their class.

"I'm not sure about that name, it doesn't feel quite right," said Harry thoughtfully. When he tried to explain why, the boy just shrugged his shoulders.

"I don't mind," he said. "I've been called worse."

"Well, I am calling you by your proper name. Peter."

"If you want." Suddenly a chant roared out from Shuff.

"Pissy Peter, Pissy Peter, Pissy Peter." Token's response was quick,

"It's better than Short arse Shannon." (Shannon was Shuff's thirteen-year-old girlfriend!)

Suddenly the two boys would start to wrestle, but never quite seriously. It would often take a minute or two to calm down but eventually when they did it was good. They loved scrubbing cleaning and polishing and they were very proud of their work.

Away from the constraints of the classroom, these "bad 'uns" were different. They used to like chatting with Harry. He had a way with them, and back then he took an interest. He even persuaded Token to attend some extra English classes after school. He was failing in almost every area, but Harry recognized something in him: a spark.

A few years after he left, Pete, as he came to be known, took the time to thank Harry in a letter to the school. Harry remembered showing it to Mary. He was quite proud of it. "Look at this!" he exclaimed, "he says he's fine now, married with two children. Well, would you believe it? He's now a journalist. And he's said that I was instrumental in his success. Good on him, good lad." Harry remembered that inner feeling of pride. He made a difference, but that seemed such a long time ago.

A melee of students noisily entered the hall bringing Harry's mind back to the present. A voice then hissed down his left ear hole causing him to instantly recoil. "The kids are definitely fatter these days." Harry couldn't see who it was but that didn't matter. He recognised the rhythmic, if slightly sardonic, tone of Hughesy, the Welsh fire-breathing dragon of a PE teacher. He gave a dig which made Harry wince. "Look at them," he jeered, "what a load of fat bastards."

Harry rubbed his side and then watched as a bunch of year 7 students waddled past him. Hughesy wasn't kidding. They were a bag of jellied fruits. He swore he could see huge bulges of "trifle belly" poke out from underneath ill-fitting shirts and large neck folds of jam-roly-poly billow out from tight school ties. Suddenly he could hear the imaginary voices of teachers and the sound of smacking lips…

"Raspberry or strawberry thighs anyone? I think young Dickens's legs are looking quite scrumptious"
"I quite fancy some of Smith's Satsuma shoulder."
"Is that a bit of lemon posset elbow?"
"Yes, indeed it is"
"Mmmm, lovely."

"Mind if I have a sample?"

"Be my guest."

Would you mind holding young Simpkins down? He does tend to kick up a fuss over a bit of elbow. One would think it's a whole arm I'm eating."

"Yes of course."

"At least it would keep them in check."

"What's that?" said Harry startled by Hughes's interjection on his daydream.

"A good thwack around the ears…and I'd have them on a run each morning." Harry wasn't quite with it and didn't respond enough so Hughesy gave him a very hard tap on his left shoulder. It forced Harry to turn round and face him.

"I'm right, aren't I?"

"Yes, I suppose so," said Harry meekly. He didn't necessarily agree but the unrelenting tone and "friendly" man pats made it difficult not to. Harry always felt pressurised into siding with him. It was Vicky leading a large group of year 9 into the hall that offered the possibility of some respite. He walked over to her. He didn't know what he was going to say but he had to get away from the chummy bullying. But to his dismay, Hughesy followed him straight towards Vicky. The next sentence came as no surprise.

"Hey, Vicky, look, they are getting fatter. What a load of fat bastards, hey?" He gave Harry a dig in exactly the same place as before. "Aren't they?"

Harry rubbed his side whilst Hughesy annoyingly laughed at his own comment. There was no real response from Vicky, so Hughesy looked at Harry for more manly affirmation. There was a brief pause before Harry simply said, "Yes," in a very monosyllabic and unenthusiastic way.

Vicky looked at Harry's bulging waistline as if to say you can talk but she didn't stop to say anything. She was too busy marshalling her troops. Some rowdy boys were deliberately pushing the chairs to make that horrible scraping sound. Harry watched as his colleague walked over and ticked them off. The boys got the message and calmed down. Vicky was like that. She had a way with some of the more difficult ones. They tended not to mess her about.

There was no doubt in Harry's mind that the youngsters were becoming more badly behaved. He could see it in the way they came in. They were a right shower. It was so clichéd, but he couldn't stop himself thinking…youngsters these days, no respect. As he watched the last of a year 10 class sit down he glanced to the front of the stage and there, sitting on a chair all alone, at the front was a little old lady with, what looked like, a bundle of knitting on her lap. That figure, thought Harry, there's something vaguely familiar. And then it dawned on him.

"Tom?"

Harry looked across at Vicky. He watched her expression change as she too suddenly realized who the old lady was. She looked around at Harry and if it were possible pulled a face that contained agony and ecstasy at the same time. Then she mouthed, "Shit," at Harry who nodded gleefully and then smacked his hands together as though he was about to be served a 16-ounce filet steak with all the trimmings.

As the hall went quiet for Cavendish to make his entrance the only real sense of anticipation came from Harry and Vicky. For the others, it was nothing more than a dull numbness, a grim resignation that they would be consigned to experience yet another turgid assembly. Little did they know that it was about to become exciting for all the wrong reasons.

It was when Cavendish haughtily floated in with Edwards in tow that Harry's grin became even wider. He couldn't wait for them both to experience the unique embarrassment of one of Tom's special assemblies. Harry watched on intently.

Cavendish did his usual thing of eyeing up the students as he walked up and so never quite noticed the figure sitting at the front until he was virtually on top of her. If he was thrown by her presence, it never showed as he turned round to Edwards and smiled. He seemed to remember booking in one of the old church ladies to do some appeal on behalf of Age for Concern. He was sure it was next week but if it was today, so be it.

Harry listened intently as the Head made the introductions to the old lady.

"This is Brian Edwards lead inspector for North West Schools,"

Edwards nodded with reverential deference to his title but stayed seated. Cavendish smiled at his friend and let a moment or two pass, for his title to sink in. And then in rather brusque fashion stepped forward. "And I'm Cavendish, Michael Cavendish, Principal of Saint Peter's." He then extended his hand for the old lady to shake

Tom never grasped Cavendish's hand but instead lowered his head (which was already bowed in respectful submission) and curtseyed. Without looking up he then held out the back of his hand, in ladylike fashion, for one of them to kiss. Cavendish hesitated and squinted. And then it suddenly dawned on Vicky and Harry that Cavendish didn't have his glasses on. He really did think it was a sweet little old lady sitting there. They started to giggle as Cavendish found himself caught up in a mini dilemma. Should he kiss the old lady's outstretched hand or not? In the end, he clasped her hand with both of his and smiled. It looked quite tender. (More giggles from Vicky)

"You are doing the Age for Concern appeal aren't you? Mrs...."

"Doubtf..."

But before Tom could complete his sentence Biggsy's meerkat head and neck shot up. He knew full well who the old lady was.

"Get 'em off!" he roared. The rest of the assembly gasped and then laughed.

"My office now!" bellowed Hughesy who took on his more familiar guise, that of the enforcer.

Harry revelled in the look of alarm that spread over Cavendish's face. He still hadn't got who the old lady was. Meanwhile, everybody watched as Biggsy shuffled his way out deliberately clattering into chairs and grinning from ear to ear.

"I do apologise," said Cavendish turning his attention back on Tom/Mrs Doubtfire, "I assure you that the boy will see you later to apologise." He then paused and frowned. "You are doing the Age for Concern appeal?" he asked.

"Noo laddie, nooo," said Tom in the most ridiculous Scottish old lady accent. And with that, he jumped up, snatched the microphone and did a little Scottish jig before greeting the masses.

"Morning children. How are yooo?"

And then he got it, Cavendish recognized who it was, but it was too late, Tom was in full flow. He had no option but to go with it. If anybody questioned him afterwards, he could just say that he had been playing along all the time. So, a well-rehearsed fake smile appeared across his face which quickly crumpled as Tom hoisted up his frock and flashed his sloggy, droopy draws. Several bulges were seen around his nether regions. These were his visual aids which he duly pulled out much to the gasp of the audience. The blood drained from Cavendish's face.

Harry and Vicky were in hysterics not so much at Tom's actions but Cavendish's reactions. It was the uncomfortable body language followed by the twitching that gave the game away. And that smile was now a nervous thin-lipped half grimace that he unwittingly flashed at Edwards – who responded by putting his head in his hands. That sealed it. This was a red-letter day.

As Tom continued to flash his knickers and pull all sorts of things out, Cavendish got up. He'd had enough. It had gone too far. It was too unpredictable; he wasn't in control. The students were laughing for all the wrong reasons. Something needed to be done quickly. He stood up, stepped over to where Tom was and patted him on the back. He made it look friendly, but it wasn't. It was a bit of a thump. "Thank you, Mr…"

But Cavendish couldn't be heard over the riotous laughter. He snatched the microphone out of Tom's hands and addressed the audience.

"THANK YOU, THANK YOU," he bellowed forcefully. But the students weren't listening, they were too busy having a riot. "THAT'S ENOUGH!!" he shouted. It was fierce enough to make some sections stop but the older ones carried on. "THANK YOU!!!!" he bellowed again. He was almost there but some assistance was needed. "Mr Hughes, could you just go over to those year 11, thank you."

In the end, all went quiet as Cavendish took back control. His smile then returned. He again thanked Tom for his assembly and asked Mr Hughes to dismiss the students. As he did so he and Edwards marched purposefully down the steps; along the hall and out through the double doors. Tom looked quite pleased with himself.

Harry turned to Vicky. "I'd completely forgotten that Tom was going to do an assembly."

"I know, so did I," chuckled Vicky. "I'd love to be a fly on the wall in Cavendish's office. I bet Edwards was none too pleased."

"Hopefully," said Harry.

"Do you think there's going to be some comeback?" enquired Vicky. "It was a bit risqué to say the least."

"I don't know," said Harry now feeling rather concerned." I do hope not."

Vicky shook her head. "What gets into Tom? When he gets on stage, he becomes a different person."

"I don't know," confessed Harry. "Maybe I should have stopped him, but he is so entertaining, if not baffling. What was the point of his assembly anyway?"

"I think it was something to do with God's presents being in the most unlikely places," replied Vicky.

"You mean God's presence," said Harry, and then it dawned on him. "Oh, I get it…God's presence/presents being in the most unlikely of places…like in his knickers, that's actually quite clever."

"I don't think Cavendish will see it that way," said Vicky mournfully. "I hope they don't do something to him."

Harry thought about that last comment, and he suddenly realised that with this academy it may not just be a case of taking him off assembly rota; they may give him a proper warning. Suddenly he felt a bit guilty and a little sorry for his friend.

"Let's hope he's alright," sighed Harry, "he means well."

8

A CARAVAN HOLIDAY

Massimo chose to leave Maria's family gathering a little early. He eschewed the short taxi ride home preferring instead to walk. Only by foot could he fully appreciate the changing views of the trees that lined his route. As he strolled across the smooth grey paving stones he caught sight of the old Chilean Palm. Had it grown an inch or two? The leaves seemed to be greener. Further on he could see the large Cassia. It was now in full bloom, its yellow fingers spilling out from crispy branches. It was a good time of year to be viewing trees. Naples had over a hundred different species and several of them were in his neighbourhood.

With all that tree spotting it was a while before he arrived at a large oak door…the entrance to his two-story apartment. Once inside he stepped through into the main living room; ambled over to the cocktail cabinet and poured himself a small cognac. As he did so he viewed the art-adorned wall with a mixture of pleasure and satisfaction. He smiled at the energetic lines of a Giacometti sketch and stared longingly at a small Lowry painting of a Northern Mill town. It was a slightly incongruous piece, but it was a prized part of his collection. His first real art purchase; it gave more than a passing nod to his Lancastrian roots. At that point, he decided to access his playlist for some musical accompaniment. "Chopin," he said out loud.

With a soothing piano solo playing in the background, he then opened the large patio doors and stepped outside onto the grand terrace to soak up some of the late evening sunshine. He poured himself a rather expensive glass of Remy Martell and slumped down on the old wicker chair. He took a sip and reflected on the evening with his family. As always, a smile came to his lips when he thought of Diana. He was also touched

by Maria's protective attitude towards him. It was nothing new.
Ever since he'd come to live with the family, as a young boy,
she'd always looked out for him. Suddenly the phone rang. It
was Rudi. "Ah Rudi my old friend," said Massimo oozing
charm. "How are you? To what do I owe this honour?

"I think you've gone crazy," said a very surprised voice on
the other end.

"I'm not sure what you mean."

"That last move, it's suicide."

"Really?" said Massimo frowning. "Let me take a look."

Massimo walked over to the coffee table and studied the
pieces on the chess board. After a minute he concluded that Rudi
was right. He knew that he had been terribly distracted recently
but what on earth was he thinking?

"It's the 'Lada Manoeuvre'," explained Massimo.

"I've never heard of that one," said a puzzled Rudi

"Ah yes," said Massimo, "it's based on those old Russian
cars. You know that if you use it then you risk crashing or
breaking down."

Rudi laughed. "It's not like you. Usually, you are so precise.
This seemed so reckless." Massimo agreed. For a second he
contemplated the crime that he had just committed. Had it
affected his play?

"I think you will have to concede," said Rudi

"Yes," sighed Massimo, "I think you are right."

"You sound as though you need that holiday."

Massimo agreed.

"Maybe you've got some femme fatal shovelled away
upstairs," laughed Rudi. "Maybe she's there with you now and
that's why you made such a big mistake with that rook."

"No, no I can assure you…"

"I am just teasing you, my old friend. You like your solitude.
I know that." There was a pause before Rudi continued. "I hate
to say this, but I think it will be checkmate soon."

Massimo looked at the board again and sighed. "I fear that
you are right. Yes, I concede. Well done my old friend."

"I think I have caught you on an off day," said Rudi
magnanimously. Look I really must go. We'll chat again soon.

You make sure you have that holiday wherever it is and good luck. Ciao"

Massimo bid his friend goodbye but purposely didn't tell him that he'd already booked that holiday – in a caravan, of all places, in the north of England. It was Rudi that gave him the idea. At first, he suggested he stay in his apartment in Paris. He'd have a maid to clean and cook for him and then jokingly he suggested that Massimo's lifestyle was far too luxurious and much too comfortable. All that fine wine and art appreciation had made him too soft. He needed to toughen up, maybe to "rough it in a caravan!" They both laughed at the time but as soon as Rudi said it, he knew that that was exactly what he wanted to do.

Massimo took another sip of his brandy and allowed those happy childhood memories of growing up in those rolling Lancashire hills to surface again. He closed his eyes and before he knew it, he was there, in that rickety old caravan drinking hot chocolate looking out over the Ribble Valley. He could still hear the pitter-patter of raindrops spitting down on the hard metal roof. It never mattered if the weather was terrible outside, he could do his puzzles and write his stories. It never mattered that his father was never around, he had his mother and he loved her dearly.

Thoughts of those times quickly faded as the present came back into focus. He popped his brandy down on the mosaic coffee table and walked over to the set of drawers in the living room. Once there, he pulled out the bottom drawer. He looked at what he had stolen. He never intended to steal it, but an opportunity presented itself, so he took it. He had no choice in the matter. If he didn't do it, then something awful was going to happen. For him it wasn't just a matter of life and death, it was something far more important.

9

FAMILIAR GROUND

It was going to be an arduous journey. Massimo knew that, but he was as ready as he could be. At first, he was fine, but it wasn't long before he found his travel experience far from relaxing. He could never escape that feeling of being watched. Every stranger that walked toward him invoked an element of fear. Even taking a piss seemed fraught with danger.

But in the end, despite looking over his shoulder most of the time, Massimo arrived at his destination in one piece. He afforded himself an inward smile. L'investigatore had done it. And his timing could not have been better. He had arrived in the evening, just as it was getting dark, so luckily, he wouldn't be noticed. It didn't matter that he couldn't see much. He knew to some extent what it looked like anyway. Yes, there would be major growth, maybe new trees and the layout would most likely be different, but the land: the soft undulations of hills and fields would be the same. The smell of the air *was* the same. He then closed his eyes and welcomed that secure feeling that crept over him. It was a good five minutes before he opened them again. He slowly got out of the car and walked up the driveway.

The front door to the reception was locked so he tapped on the glass pane of the window. It was just the right kind of tap, not too loud to be offensive but loud enough to be heard. A small figure came dashing out, apologising for any delay.

"Sorry, sorry. You are staying?" Massimo nodded. "Right, well if you wouldn't mind filling out these forms. Don't forget the car registration number at the bottom, for some reason lots of people miss it out." The old guy pointed a bony finger at the small space at the bottom of the form where the registration number should go. Massimo turned around and looked out of the doorway to see if he could see the number plate. He squinted.

"Rented, is it?" said the old guy. "Don't worry I'll go 'n look, you stay 'ere and fill out the rest."

Massimo smiled and nodded. He didn't really want to engage in conversation. The old guy sensed it and never pursued anything. He did, however, ask how far he'd come. It was more polite conversation than anything else. Massimo simply answered, "Quite far." The old guy handed the keys over.

"Just as requested yours is a lovely plot with its own bit o' land and a view over't Ribble Valley. Lucky we 'ad that cancellation." Massimo nodded in agreement.

The old guy then gave Massimo directions like he'd done it a million times before. "First left, up the drive, take the right fork past the large pine tree, shower block on the right, straight up to the top, plot 32." Massimo nodded, took the keys, and started back to the car. "Oh, and be careful," he added, "we're very clean and tidy here but your neighbour's dog can be a bit messy, if you know what I mean? We do our best, and 'e does, but I'm just tellin' you cos it's a bit dark and you never know."

That's what I love about the English, thought Massimo, so very helpful. On autopilot, he shut the car door and started the engine again. There was a feeling of anticipation as he drove off slowly down the gravel path.

Soon, he reached a good-sized caravan that lay perched on top of a small plateau of hard standing in a well-looked-after field. Massimo didn't hang around. He walked straight inside to have a quick look around and to ensure that everything was okay. Carefully he unzipped his suitcase. He looked closely at what he had stolen. It was still intact. Satisfied, he packed it away again and slid it under the bed.

In no time at all, he was fast asleep.

10

FIRE, FIRE!

"Cavendish, he's not going to be in a good mood, is he?" said Harry sipping his coffee.

"Tom's Mrs Doubtfire show stopper hasn't helped," replied Vicky trying to contain her laughter. "I think old Cavendish might be just a tad wound up, especially with Edwards being there."

"Poor Tom, we shouldn't laugh," said Harry dolefully. He looked up at Vicky. "Please don't make me laugh."

"It was Cavendish's face – priceless," spluttered Vicky. She puffed out her cheeks; made her eyes appear large and stuck her front teeth out. "Like a rabbit caught in headlights." Harry couldn't hold it in any longer and fell about laughing. As he paused for breath, he looked round the staff room and could see a few other colleagues were having a good old chuckle, probably at the same thing.

"You know Tom's assembly has done wonders for staff morale," said Vicky. "Look at them, I've not seen them looking quite so happy for some time."

"Well, we must be doing something wrong then," said Harry.

"What do you mean?"

"Wasn't it the chief inspector, Wilshaw, who said that if staff morale is low, the management must be doing something right? Following on from that, if staff are happy, then management are doing something wrong. What a load of crap it all is." And suddenly Harry went into a more sombre mood.

"What's wrong?" said a concerned Vicky.

"I've got my meeting with Cavendish today. I think Edwards will be there too."

"Oh shit," said Vicky. "Harry, why didn't you tell me you've got your meeting with Cavendish today? I would have stopped Tom doing his assembly or at least had a word with him."

"Well, it doesn't matter. I'm for it anyway," said Harry with a certain amount of resignation.

"What do you mean?"

"They are after me, I can smell it. I'm getting on; I'm at the top of my pay scale; I'm costing the academy money and I'm a bit of a relic."

Vicky smiled faintly. She had some sympathy for her friend's distress. She'd heard some terrible stories about academies making life incredibly difficult for people like Harry and they'd found ways to get rid of them or made life so unbearable that they had to leave. Younger teachers had more energy but most importantly they were far cheaper. Harry also found it hard to keep up with all the changes. There was real pressure on him, but he didn't always help himself.

"You'll be okay," said Vicky, trying to reassure her friend, "you've got a thick skin, just don't let them intimidate you."

Harry smiled. He knew that his colleague had his back.

"Yeah," said Harry, "you're right." With that, he took a last swig of his coffee; wiped his mug vigorously with some blue towelling and thrust it back in the locker. He then marched down to Cavendish's office in bullish mood, ready for the fight. Then the fire alarm went off.

Harry groaned; it wasn't just that his dreaded meeting would be delayed he was going to have to don the high-vis jacket complete with walkie-talkie. He was one of the fire stewards recently appointed by Cavendish to justify their upper pay scale. He hated wearing it. Others loved it but he didn't. What's more, people could see that, with his expanding waistline, he looked uncomfortable, which made it all the funnier. Sometimes shouts of 'Oi, fat controller!" were launched in his direction from the groups of thuggish year 11 lads.

But Cavendish was in his element. Very, very visible in his own specially made high-vis jacket. Out in front, he was organising, calling the shots, issuing commands to students and teachers alike, all with the assistance of a large booming megaphone.

"Clearly a penis extension for a man with a small dick," said Vicky who then commented on his other favourite accessory – the walkie-talkie, suggesting that he was holding it so close to his mouth he was practically giving it cunnilingus. Suddenly Harry was on the set of a trashy eighties porno movie called 'Megaphone Massage and The Walkie-Talkie Wanker.' Cavendish was the director showing the young wannabes how it should be done. Harry shuddered at the thought and quickly pushed the unfolding apparition away in disgust.

It was Cavendish's love affair with the officious nature of the fire marshal role that got on Harry's nerves. He suddenly remembered a fire drill that just about summed him up. A student was seen slipping out of the front gate. Harry simply couldn't turn down the opportunity. He reached for his walkie-talkie. "A pigeon has flown the coup. Over. I repeat a pigeon has flown the coup. Over." Everybody that was listening knew full well what it meant but Cavendish told him it was frivolous and unprofessional and that he should take more care when a student was absconding lessons and was in his words, 'making an unsanctioned exit from the school premises.' I definitely need to be on my best behaviour on this fire drill thought Harry. Definitely.

As the fire alarm continued to reverberate through the school, Harry realised that it could be the real thing, so he quickly donned his high-vis jacket. "Best not be too frivolous," he muttered as he took his position near the East fire escape. He watched as the students funnelled past in an orderly fashion. Harry was loathed to admit it, but it was well orchestrated and well handled by Cavendish and everything ran pretty smoothly. It wasn't anything too serious, a science experiment had gone wrong. The ensuing smoke had set off the fire alarm. Harry continued to be reluctantly impressed as the rest of the students filed out submissively, apart from the usual suspects in year 11 and Biggsy, of course, who saw the whole thing as a joke. But Hughesy was on them, and they were quickly dealt with.

Harry looked on as Cavendish appeared to look at Edwards for validation. It was a moment between the two. Edwards gave a slight nod. He approved and Cavendish was positively beaming. The brownie points he had lost through the assembly had been won back. Buoyed by this, the Principal then walked over to Harry. He seemed intent on sounding decisive. Ah, thought Harry, Edwards is looking.

"It will have to be Monday."

Harry looked at Cavendish quizzically.

"Our meeting. I'll get Rachel to book it."

"Sure," said Harry.

"Fab," said Cavendish and then wheeled away to compile the fire report. Within the hour it was duly emailed to all staff.

FIRE DRILL REPORT 11 .15

1) Well done to all for a very well-ordered evacuation.

2) Time taken for all marshals to be in position- 2 mins 35 seconds. This is better than last time but could be improved further.

3) Location of walkie-talkies was an issue...several had not been previously returned. In future, please ensure that all walkie-talkies are returned after being on duty as soon as possible.

4) Time to evacuate the building – 4 minutes 10 seconds. Again, there is still room for improvement. Year 10 was sluggish. A reminder that target time is 3 minutes 55 seconds

5) Although students were quiet, they should be silent. Could heads of year please make sure that staff are in their positions early and that they are vigilant in ensuring that students are silent.

6) Registers- several inaccuracies led to some confusion. Mr Brown and Mrs Bennett need to see Vice-principal Perkins at one o'clock in his office.

7) Lastly, it would be helpful if staff did not take their mugs of tea or coffee out with them. We are professionals- a fire alarm is a serious procedure, and we could be seen to be giving the wrong impression.

Harry found the report tiresome. And that last bit about mugs of coffee, there was no need for it. It seemed as though every last bit of teacher privilege was being eroded. In the end, he was quite glad when the lunch bell sounded. But then he realized that he'd forgotten his packed lunch. He was going to have to use the canteen. "Damn," he said out loud. Ever since the new catering firm had taken over, the food had deteriorated. It wasn't so much the quality, although that wasn't great, it was the size of the portions. One rasher of bacon on a small white roll and only two of Asda's cheap range bargain chipolatas served with a meagre portion of chips. "Not even proper-sized sausages," muttered Harry.

But he wasn't the only one, everybody who used the canteen felt pretty much the same way, but he was the one who said something. He made a complaint. In hindsight, this was a mistake. The dinner ladies never liked him after that. Every time he came to the hatch they gave him a look or deliberately served somebody else first so Harry boycotted the canteen. But on this day he was far too hungry to stand on principle. He was going to have to queue up, be last in line, and generally suck it up.

As he grabbed his tray, he noticed that it was Nellie that was serving. There was no love lost between them. She was quite a diminutive figure with black hair tied back in a net and thin lips full of determination. She gave him the eye, but Harry ignored it. Instead, he tried a more charming approach.

"Good afternoon Nellie," he said cheerily.

She grumbled something in reply and frowned. Not a great start. Undeterred he soldiered on and tried to lighten the mood.

"Oh my, look at this wonderful array of culinary delights from tasty toasties to terrific tacos. Fantastico."

"What do you want?" said Nellie in deadpan fashion.

"Well, I'll have… let me see now…"

Nellie gave an impatient sigh.

"Right," said Harry trying to appear unflustered, "I will have chips and a terrific taco, oh and a couple of fried eggs…I am particularly hungry."

"You can't have that."

"I beg your pardon?"

"I can't till that in."

"What do you mean?"

"We have a set menu - you can have chips and taco; eggs, sausage and chips; or just eggs and chips, but you can't have chips, eggs and taco."

"That's ridiculous."

"I don't set the menus and I don't pre-set the tills."

"But if I'm paying surely, I can have what I want."

"Till says no."

"Right," said Harry forcefully, "I'll have two meals on two separate plates, taco and chips, and egg and chips. I'll pay for them both as separate items."

"Are they both for you?"

"I'm not telling you,"

"Well, I need to know."

"Why?"

"We have a policy that…"

"One's for a friend actually," interrupted Harry, "Mr Hughes, the P E teacher."

Nellie grinned triumphantly "The policy states that you can't buy a meal for a friend as well as your own."

"Don't be ridiculous. I'm a teacher for heaven's sake. A rule like that applies to the kids so they don't bully others to get their dinners for them."

"Well, you can't have one rule for one."

Just then Assistant-principal Carrie Philips walked up.

"Is everything alright?"

Harry looked at her tray, it had two dinners on! This was his chance!

"You've got two dinners on your tray Mrs Philips, that's quite an appetite you have."

"No, no they aren't both for me," laughed Carrie, "one is Mr Cavendish's, we are in a meeting. On that note do you mind if I pay first?"

"No, no be my guest," said Harry cheerily.

As soon as Nellie had finished at the till he turned to her and grinned. "I rest my case. Now could you please carry out my order? Thank you."

She glared at Harry and then with great reluctance slapped the taco on the plate followed by a scoop of chips but as she came to the last chip, she pulled the scoop back so that one small fry remained unserved. Harry stared as Nellie then dumped it back into the main tray of chips. He couldn't believe it.

"What… what on earth? That last chip why didn't you serve it? Why did you feel the need to withhold it? One chip that's all it was. Why put the one chip back?"

Nellie ignored him and simply carried on serving the second plate.

"I'm sorry said Harry I didn't quite hear you. It was a simple enough question and I think I am entitled to an answer as to why you withheld that last chip."

Still no answer.

"Well in that case can I have it…that last chip?"

Nellie pursed her lips together but said nothing.

"If there is no good reason then surely it will cost you nothing," stated Harry firmly. "Just give me back that last chip."

He stared at Nellie; she stared back. And then the students started shouting.

"C'mon Mr Jones we're all starving back here."

"Yeah, Sir, 'urry up."

Harry stuck an arm out and commanded the hordes to be quiet. Such was his tone that they instantly obeyed. He eyed Nellie some more and then decided enough was enough.

"Okay, okay," said Harry, "you win, but whatever grudge you have or whatever bad mood you are in, my advice to you would be, as they say in the musical Frozen, to 'Let it go, let it go, let it go." Harry sang the last few words. Nellie bristled with indignation; the singing had got to her. She looked at Harry's smug little face, but Nellie Noakes, queen of the hatch, wasn't finished. In a last desperate act of retaliation, she let out a melodramatic cry of anguish just as Assistant-principal Phillips looked her way. It worked; Carrie came rushing over. Nellie then feigned growing weak and breathless. She dropped her scoop in melodramatic fashion and went all wobbly. Soon, other staff were there patting her head and holding her hand.

"Are you okay Nellie?"

"What's the matter?"

Nellie then pointed an accusing finger at Harry and managed to sob some real tears.

"Is it Mr Jones?" asked Violet her long-time friend and colleague. Nellie nodded meekly.

"Has he been horrible to you again?"

"Oh, come on," interrupted Harry, "surely you are not falling for this?"

And suddenly he could feel the venom in the air as those tending to 'the victim' shot him a look of utter hatred. Just as Harry was about to say something Carrie jumped in

"I think it best that you go," she said, "we'll sort this out later."

"But…"

"Now please!"

As Harry sloped off, he thought he could detect a little grin on those thin determined lips. He hated losing these kinds of battles and to compound matters he hadn't even got all of his meal. He was missing an egg… and one chip.

Harry spent the remainder of his lunchtime mulling over what had happened. He was sure that he didn't do that much wrong, probably a bit flippant but of course Carrie wouldn't see it that way. After their recent exchanges, she would very quickly conclude that he had, as always, been rude and upset a poor defenceless dinner lady. Would he be given a warning to add to his other warnings? Maybe, but at the very least he would have to go on some course on how to better communicate with other members of staff. "Wonderful," he muttered out loud, "another nail in the old coffin." He couldn't wait for the bell to go for the end of the day.

Unbelievably, time passed quickly. The afternoon lessons came and went and before he knew it, he was back home, cold beer in hand flicking through the first few pages of a book on Caravaggio by celebrated author and historian Andrew Graham Dixon.

"Did you have your meeting with Cavendish?" Mary shouted from the garden.

"No, it's going to be Monday instead."

Mary strode into the living room. She placed the secateurs down carefully on the side cabinet, ensuring that she didn't stain or damage the veneer. After taking off her gloves, she patted away some dust that had gathered on the knees of her jeans. She looked at Harry.

"Are you alright?"

"I'll survive."

But Mary could see that her husband was anxious. "Look, why don't you go down to the caravan? I would come with you, but I've got something on. The weather is going to be nice, and you can take your fishing rod. It might do you good, take your mind off things." She glanced at the book that Harry was reading. "Maybe even take something interesting to read. Yes, why not 'Get Away From It All With Caravaggio'." She said that last part like it was the title of a television programme.

Harry chuckled at his wife's gentle humour, but the idea quite appealed to him. Mary came up to the back of the sofa and, reaching over, kissed his head from behind. He liked that. He looked up and smiled at her. She smiled back. There was a moment's tenderness and then Mary put her gardening gloves on and taking the secateurs off the cabinet, walked purposely out into the garden. Harry thought for a minute before shouting.

"Maybe you're right, dear. I think I will go. It will do me good."

"Don't call me dear!"

11

THE ACCIDENT

Harry parked the car next to the caravan, but it didn't feel quite right –maybe a little crooked. He opened the car door and checked his positioning. He knew it, it wasn't straight. The front end was a fraction out. To most people, it probably wouldn't have mattered, but to Harry, it was like a big black mark on his driving prowess. There was no second thought, he had to re-park the car. He shut the door and looked in his mirror, nothing behind. But just before he reversed, he tilted the mirror slightly and as he did so he caught sight of his reflection. He looked closely into his own eyes as they stared right back at him. They were neither piercing nor vacant, they were just there. At that moment he thought of his wife, Mary. He loved the times that she would look at herself in her small compact. "Just making myself look presentable," she would say. She tilted it in a similar way to the way that Harry now tilted his car mirror. And suddenly he missed her and felt guilty for how he had acted a few days ago. He blamed the stress of school for his insensitivity to his wife and of course, there was Cavendish. Thinking about him right now made him angry. Then it happened. BANG! A loud crack instantly sent a jolt into Harry's seat which sent a shudder through his spine. He'd hit something. His mind hadn't been in the present. It was now!

"Shit," he said out loud. "What have I done?" He needed something or somebody to blame. What was the last thing on his mind? "Fucking Cavendish!" He shook his head and tried to calm himself down. No sense in getting wound up, it was his fault and he just had to accept it. He turned the ignition off and for a moment sat completely still. Glancing up in his mirror there was a large black Audi camped at the back of him. It reversed a couple of yards and then stuttered to a full stop. There was a brief silence before something metallic dropped to the floor. Chink!

"Shit!" Harry cussed, "Shit, shit, shit!"

He steered back into the bay, composed himself, and then stepped out of his car. His first thought was the other car. He could see that the front right headlight was smashed. It wasn't terrible but it was enough. And then he looked at his car. There was a large dent in the bumper and car boot. He could probably get it fixed but it would still cost a few hundred. It wasn't just the cost, it was the ball ache of having to take it round to the garage, pick it back up and be without a car.

He waited for what seemed like an eternity before there appeared to be some movement from inside the other vehicle. A door opened and out stepped a fairly stocky, balding figure. Probably in his early sixties thought Harry. His movements were slow and deliberate. It made Harry more nervous. The man said nothing but just inspected the damage. As he did so he stroked a rather well-trimmed moustache.

"Look I am sorry, it was my fault," said Harry stepping out of his car, "I don't know what to say."

The man continued to walk around his car looking closely at the vehicle from different angles. He remained silent.

"Yes, definitely my fault," repeated Harry agitated by the stranger's lack of communication.

The man simply frowned and then grunted. Harry in turn folded his arms and waited.

"I will fix it," said the stranger in a sudden and forthright manner.

Harry was baffled. If it was him, he would not have been so magnanimous. He would have been very cross.

"But it was my fault."

"No problem," said the stranger once more but this time there was less gusto and more quiet assurance.

Harry shook his head and frowned. He was quite taken aback by the generous response of a possible adversary.

"I will fix it," repeated the stranger. "Yes, I will fix it."

But before Harry could ask what "fix it" meant, the stranger took out a wad of money…

"Your car, five, six, seven hundred?"

"But it was my fault. When you said fix it, I thought you meant your car," said Harry astonished.

"It is okay," said Massimo smiling, "I was not looking; it was my fault."

Harry knew it was his fault. He was the one who wasn't looking. The stranger smiled some more, walked over to Harry, and practically thrust the money into his hand. It seemed difficult to refuse.

"I'm not sure I can," he stuttered.

"No problem," said the man. He took hold of Harry's hand and closed it around the money. He smiled again and then sauntered over to his own car as though the business was concluded. Suddenly he wheeled round. "The boot, can you open the boot?" Harry was in a daze but still walked over to his Astra. The boot was normally a bit stiff. It might take a few tugs thought Harry but before he could do anything else the stranger was there giving him a hand. Suddenly the boot sprung open. A pair of stripy underpants had spilled out and lay spreadeagled across his luggage. Harry quickly stuffed them back in the bag. As he went to zip it back up, the stranger gripped his arm. It shocked Harry, but for some reason he didn't protest, nor did he draw his arm away. Instead, he looked on like some passive bystander. The stranger then slowly released his grip and pulled the zipper further back to reveal a book that had been poking out. He looked at it with reverence and stroked the cover affectionately.

"Michelangelo Merisi de Caravaggio," whispered Massimo lovingly.

Harry felt his adrenalin subside a little. It was the voice. The tones were warm, rhythmical and flowing. Although his English was good, only an Italian could have reeled off Caravaggio's name in such a way and only an admirer could have said it so lovingly.

Harry was mesmerised. "Yes, Caravaggio," was all he could muster in reply.

"Do you like him?" asked the stranger smiling.

"Yes, I am a bit of a fan."

"Un uomo appassionato."

"I'm sorry," said Harry somewhat perplexed.

"A passionate man...Caravaggio."

"Yes, I suppose so. That is if you include murder as one of his passions," said Harry dryly.

Massimo scoffed and waved his arms. "If you are referring to the brawl in Rome, it is most clearly a crime of passion. I cannot believe that anybody who paints with such theatre and brilliance would ever have murder as a part of a sentence in their story. The word seems so cold and brutal for one who is capable of such beauty." Massimo paused and stroked his moustache and then continued with gusto about the 'understandable misdemeanours' that Senor Caravaggio had committed. Before any of them knew it, they were in a deep conversation, arguing and then agreeing with each other about events and issues surrounding one of history's most notorious artists. All this occurred against the backdrop of the open car boot complete with stripy underwear strewn over a neat blue bag.

"I cannot agree with you completely," said Harry after Massimo had spent some time justifying the great artist's personal life. "I know he broke with tradition, but he wasn't just a rebel he was a troublemaker. I believe he caused many of the incidents. The police in Rome still holds records."

"Yes, that is true," said Massimo surprised at Harry's knowledge, "but it does not tell the whole story. An inventory in a book tells us very little, there is no context."

"But the fights he was involved in?"

"Yes, yes, but you have to understand Rome in that time was no different from the violent back streets we have now in Naples, full of menace. The only difference is that guns have replaced swords and knives. Killings are not uncommon now nor were they uncommon then. For all we know Caravaggio was provoked or attacked, perhaps, with a weapon." Massimo frowned and shook his head. "To be involved in one or two of these kinds of incidents was a part of life, a life that we know little about. You and I were not around at that time. We cannot judge."

"Oh no, I am not judging him," said Harry, "he is too much of a genius for any judgement I can make, but I hold opinions and that's all they are. We have no letters, no diaries and he never kept any kind of journal. I am a history teacher who should be able to back a view of any kind with evidence, but the only evidence is from the accounts of others. Nevertheless, I have always encouraged my students to have opinions even if the evidence is flimsy. I, therefore, feel obliged to do likewise… Caravaggio was a villain!" Massimo looked shocked. But Harry wasn't finished. He looked down at the book and read out the title. "Caravaggio: A life Sacred And Profane." He paused and looked back at Massimo. "But I will admit that the sacred far outweighs the profane."

Massimo smiled at Harry's theatrical delivery. "Perhaps we could drink to that."

"Why not," said Harry cheerfully. He had taken an instant liking to this Poirot-like figure. And for a moment the two of them stood there not quite knowing what to say next. Harry thought for a second. Was that an invitation; maybe for a glass of wine or two? But he brushed the idea off as nonsense.

"Look, are you sure about this?" said Harry suddenly remembering he had a wad of twenty-pound notes in his hand.

"Positive," stated Massimo, firmly. Harry knew that the stranger was not going to change his mind. But there was one thing he could do.

"I know a good mechanic, let me give you his phone number." Massimo looked perplexed. "For the damage to your headlight," explained Harry.

Massimo thought for a second. "Yes, that would be helpful."

"Damn, the phone needs charging," said Harry slightly irritated. "I'll get it to you later. Where are you staying?"

For a second Massimo seemed hesitant. It was clear that he didn't want anybody intruding, but after a brief pause, he pointed up the hill to an isolated caravan behind a few large poplars.

"Right then," said Harry, "see you in about 15 minutes."

Massimo smiled faintly and stepped back inside his car. Oblivious to the damage, he drove off up the small path. Harry went inside; put his phone on charge; lay down on the bed for a brief rest; and fell fast asleep.

12

SUPPER AT EMMAUS

Harry felt the compulsion to turn round and look at the painting.
Something seemed strange. The peasant-like figures that filled
the canvas seemed to flicker ever so slightly. They-were such
small movements. Then he noticed a finger unfurl, an eyelid
slowly close, a piece of raggedy clothing ruffle in a small breeze.
He rubbed his eyes and cleaned his reading glasses. As soon as
he put them back on, the Christ figure at the centre of the
painting coughed. The eyes that were originally cast downwards
then looked directly at him. Harry moved to the side and the
gaze followed him. Then the right-hand figure, the one with the
shell pinned to his brown leathery shirt, slowly turned his head
and smiled at Harry. Before he knew it, whoosh! He was sucked
in.

The next thing he knew he was sitting in a chair at the table
with the figures in the painting. The chicken, fruit, and loaves of
bread were now real and suddenly he was hungry. He reached
out to grab an apple.

"Don't you fucking move!" came the cry.

Harry wheeled round and there right in front of him was the
artist looking very angry.

"You buffoon! Do that again and I will cut your fucking
hand off!" The artist made a swish with his brush over his wrist
to emphasize the statement.

Harry froze. It wasn't just the threat. The bald head and
bespectacled features of the artist were familiar.

"Cavendashio, sir, Mr Artist," came a voice from the set.

"What is it now?"

"Can we have a drink; we've been here in this same position
for two hours?"

"No, you can't," said Cavendashio abruptly. He looked at Harry. "And what are you staring at?"

But all that Harry could think about was the name Cavendashio. How on earth did he let such a nightmarish name make its way into his dream? He tried desperately to wake himself up. But couldn't.

"Get back into your position!" roared Cavendashio.

It took a second for Harry to realise that the roar was addressed to him. The trouble was that he didn't know what the position was. He tried resting his arms gently on the side of the chair hoping that it would be okay. He looked up to the others hoping for some kind of affirmation. Instead, he got a few surreptitious rolls of the eyes, a couple of grimaces, and one furtive gesture from Saint Peter. They clearly didn't want Cavendashio to know that they were helping.

Harry had had enough. He went to get up. Immediately there were several vigorous shakes of the head, so he sat back down and started to fret. He could feel the heat of Cavendashio's wrath rising by the second. He looked down in a kind of submissive gesture and in doing so noticed his sleeves. They were dark green. He never wore green. He quickly scanned the bottom half of his attire. The trousers, only they weren't quite trousers, they were britches, they were orange. Orange! Something familiar was beginning to stir. He frantically felt the corner of his elbow, there was a worn patch. And then he got it! He wasn't just there as an onlooker or bystander. He was one of the painted characters in "Supper at Emmaus." And in that instant, he knew exactly what pose he should take. He crouched forward palms of hands pressing on the arms of the chair expectantly, face and chin thrust forward. He looked up to see smiles of affirmation from his companions. It was just in time as Cavendashio, who had strode forward menacingly, stopped and put away his sword.

"You are a very lucky peasant," he said begrudgingly.

"Yes," said Harry in simpering fashion.

Cavendashio went back to his easel and picked up where he had left off. Feeling a tad more comfortable, Harry took in the scene more fully. His eyes had now gotten used to the strange but dramatic lighting caused by the positioning of various candles. He could now make out the background. It was pretty bare apart from one or two unfinished canvases propped against the wall; two rickety old chairs; and a couple of vases. But they were not the only props. Two wooden struts supported Peter's outstretched arms.

"NO, NO, NO!" cried Cavendashio interrupting Harry's flow. "Still not fucking right. You're not dramatic enough. You, Christ, tell a fucking story! And make it good. Maybe somebody found a great treasure. No, boring. Maybe a fight, somebody's testicles were cut off!" Cavendashio eyed Harry. "But nothing funny. I don't want you illiterate bastards laughing. It's really not funny. I don't want anybody thinking this is some kind of costume fucking comedy. That's going to piss me right off." As he started to reapply the paint, he continued to mutter. "No, definitely not fucking funny."

Seemingly out of nowhere, Harry spotted a young girl playing in the corner of the room. Through the grubby dirt marks and grimy clothes, there was something familiar about her mischievous presence. He watched as she walked over and started to pull stupid faces in the hope that she would make somebody laugh. A boy with a large neck suddenly appeared and pulled out a mobile phone from underneath his loin cloth. He held it aloft so that everybody could see what was on the screen. One by one they all began to titter and chuckle. Cavendashio's face started to contort, and his lips curl up. Harry knew what the image on the phone was. He didn't need to look; he could hear the snoring.

"Jones! They are your fucking children can't you keep them in order," yelled Cavendashio.

"My children?" spluttered Harry.

"Jesus, man. Yes, your fucking children."

Harry muttered some kind of forlorn response that was barely audible. It annoyed Cavendashio even more. And then the Christ figure guffawed out loud. Seeing the image on the phone, of Harry fast asleep and snoring loudly, was just too much for him and a wet patch of pee formed around the middle of his loincloth.

"That does it," cursed Cavendashio. He sprung to his feet, took his sword out of its sheath, and with one fell swoop chopped Harry's hand off! Harry woke up with a start and couldn't feel his arm. It took a nervous second or two before he realized that he'd been lying on it, and that it was numb. A few shakes and rubs gradually brought some of the feeling back. "Thank the Lord," he said out loud as he continued to close and open his left hand. He then breathed a huge sigh of relief as his arm finally felt as though it belonged to him.

Meanwhile, just up the lane sitting alone in a modern well furbished static caravan, Massimo was desperately hoping that he hadn't been taken literally. He had wanted to keep a low profile but was it possible that he had inadvertently invited this rotund Englishman round to toast the great artist? Perhaps his Englishness will prevent him from doing so, they are far too reserved, thought Massimo. He'll just give me the phone number of the mechanic say a polite goodbye and then go. No, he won't expect to come in for a drink… and that's a good thing. He paused and sipped his wine, the Piedirosso seemed most agreeable and suddenly his outlook changed. Contrary to what he had been telling himself he realised that he wouldn't mind some company, a little light relief from the internal inquisition he was giving himself each night.

He waited a few minutes for Harry to arrive, but the few minutes turned into a half-hour and then one hour. He poured himself another glass of wine and played some Vivaldi on his iPhone. He lay down on his bed; closed his eyes; and started to drift off. Probably just as well, he told himself, I don't know who this Harry Jones is. He could be a spy for all I know. It was a ridiculous notion that caused Massimo to smile inwardly. Not quite asleep, his thoughts went back to his home in Naples where he recalled a lunch with the Family somewhere in the Spagnoli Quartieri, a few months earlier.

13

DINNER WITH ALFONSO

.

The large, suited, middle-aged figure of Alfonso dabbed the corner of his mouth with the napkin and ordered some more wine. As soon the waiter had left, he turned to the small gathering...

"Well, they can go and drown themselves in the Volturno if they think that we are just going to hand it over."

"We may not have a choice," said Vito. He, too, was a large, but slightly older, suited figure. "The law..."

"Fuck the law," interrupted Alfonso, "since when have we been too concerned about the law? Anyway, possession is nine-tenths of the law, and we are in possession."

"It isn't just the law," said Vito, "it is the church, they are powerful. Even for us, it is not good to be in conflict with the church even, though we have support there."

Alfonso grunted. He was about to say something more when the waiter came over to pour the wine. He waited and smiled politely.

"Thank you," said Alfonso, who made a point of being calm in front of the staff. The waiter nodded and then left quietly.

"I understand how you feel," said Carlo, a smaller figure with a bald head and wide girth. "I feel the same way. The painting has been in the family for ages and the evidence that it originally belonged to the church is flimsy, and besides, that lying, thieving institution is rich. No, no, there is some way to go in this matter. It is monstrous to think that we should simply hand the painting over."

"We could just destroy it," said Alfonso with more than a hint of malice. "Then the arguments would be over. Nobody would have it."

"Hmm I don't think that would be a good idea," said Massimo quietly.

"So, the l'investigatore has spoken," said Alfonso ironically. The others laughed, almost affectionately.

"And pray, tell me, Massimo, why is that?"

"You would not just be destroying art; it is our heritage and a thing of beauty. It would be like destroying the soul." The others listened as Massimo went on to make a heartfelt speech about the preservation of such things at all costs. "And that is why," he concluded, "I think we should consider handing over the Caravaggio…if we lose the fight."

Alfonso laughed again but it was a much more raucous laugh and then his demeanour became quite serious. "You stick to the financial advice and let us make the decisions." Alfonso slapped his friend on the back as if to say thank you for your contribution, but we'll take it from here. He turned to the rest and concluded by declaring that as long as he lived the church would never ever own "their Caravaggio." The rest of the meal was taken up with some business and finance matters that Massimo needed to advise them on and the lamenting of Napoli's demise as a top-class footballing province. Massimo joined in the football talk as much as he could, but he could never get himself to be as passionate about 22 men kicking a round object between two sticks as he was about art and Caravaggio. His mind was distracted anyway. He couldn't stop thinking about the threats to destroy the old painting. He tried to convince himself not to take it seriously, but the thought that Alfonso could do it, or something quite vindictive would not escape him.

"l'investigatore you look a little distracted," said Alfonso. "Is everything okay?"

"Yes, yes," uttered Massimo. "I think I just need some air. Do you mind if I go? I think that the business is concluded. The meal, it is finished, yes?"

"Yes, of course," Alfonso went to stand up, but Massimo put his hand on his shoulder and assured him that it was not necessary. He then turned to the assembled.

"Gentlemen, thank you for an excellent meal and some fine company." He then flashed them that warm, well-cultivated smile of his. The others reciprocated. Bidding them farewell; he left.

As he stepped outside, Massimo took in a breath of the fresh spring air. He felt better. Without thinking, he turned right. For a second he was puzzled as to why he took this direction. It wasn't the way home, but within a few paces, he knew where his feet were taking him – to the old quarter, more specifically to the Pio Monte della Misericordia. There, he would get his regular fix of aesthetic contemplation and consider the sacred. He was in no rush. It wouldn't be right to be frantic or impatient. He walked slowly down the back streets avoiding the busy main street of Via Toledo, past an array of trattorias. Normally the smells of pizza fritta or baba would whet his appetite but, he was full and did not stop to take in the sights and smells that permeated the colourful back streets.

It wasn't long before he reached the steps of the old church. After quietly crossing himself, he proceeded. As the elderly attendant waved and grinned at this frequent visitor, Massimo smiled and nodded his head in acknowledgement. He closed his eyes briefly as he strode forward through the front entrance. It was as though he were passing through some kind of threshold or portal to another world; a world full of the sacred. Once inside, he put on his spectacles that were specially made to view artwork in dim places. When he came to a piece of art that he found particularly moving he would stop and clean the lenses. He would then peer closer and see something that he hadn't noticed before – a detail, a blend of colours, a series of brush strokes. There was great reverence in Massimo's unwitting theatre. It would always end with a blissful sigh and a knowing smile as though something hidden had suddenly been revealed. But all this was a prelude to the central attraction, an hors d'oeuvre before the main meal.

Straight ahead, a large highly impressive panel dominated the hexagonal chamber. But somehow it wasn't right to go straight to it. It would show a lack of respect for other artists. It would be crude to gulp down the starters just so that you could get to the fillet mignon. Even the smaller morsels, the minor pieces had to be savoured, so Massimo deliberately averted his gaze from what lay ahead until he was directly in front of it. And then he stopped. He lifted his head and looked in awe at the large panel that towered above him, Caravaggio's 'Sette Opera di Misericordia', 'The Seven Acts of Mercy'. He closed his eyes and recalled the ghosts of his past, the visions of Caravaggio he had as a young boy, and once again he could feel the presence of the great master cursing through his veins.

He opened his eyes and was astounded as much now as he was the first time he saw it. The sheer genius, the audacity of the man, the drama. "Bellissmo, bellissimo," he said out loud. He was in full flow when a voice whispered in his ear.

"I knew I'd find you here."

Massimo smiled and turned round immediately. He recognized the warm husky tones of his sister.

"It's quite something," said Maria looking up at the dramatic composition that confronted her. "Although I must confess, I'd rather be on the high street looking at the art of a different kind. Massimo sighed at the intended crassness of his sister's comment. He smiled and kissed her on the cheek.

"You look well," said Massimo appreciatively. "Are you here…"

"Just by chance," said Maria completing Massimo's sentence. "I've not been here for an age, but I knew that there would be a good chance that I would find you here prostrate before your idol. There's too much in it for me," she said waving her hands across the panel, "far too many figures; too dramatic for my liking; too much theatre. I like the clean lines of modernism, give me the simple art of the Toledo Metro any day."

"Well of course the 'Seven Acts of Mercy' were originally conceived as several separate panels, so it would not have been so complicated," replied Massimo in a lecture-like mode. "Each panel would have had its identity and yet all be connected. Whether it was an inspired act to combine them in this way or simply an economic necessity, I am not so sure, but one only has to…" Massimo stopped mid-sentence. Maria was laughing.

"It doesn't take much to get a reaction."

"What?"

"One slight criticism, one unguarded comment about your precious Caravaggio and you are off. I pray for your sake that the sinkholes that are starting to invade this city don't swallow up this place whole and take your precious painting with it. I think if you saw it happening, I swear that you would jump in with it." Massimo didn't disagree. There was a lull in the conversation before Maria continued in a more serious vein.

"I hear there's been a disagreement about a certain painting."

Massimo frowned and shook his head. "It is ridiculous."

"I haven't seen the painting myself," said Maria. "It is definitely a Caravaggio?"

"Of course," replied Massimo.

"Has it been officially authenticated?"

"No, not officially but we have done the tests. It is undoubtedly of that period and has used the right kind of paints. There is also evidence of some provenance. Some private letters written three centuries ago have recently come to light. The painting is mentioned, and a history of sorts is given but this is not absolute proof.

"Really?"

"There is no record of Caravaggio ever having done preliminary studies before. He tends to work directly onto his compositions and finishes them like Mozart writing out a perfect manuscript with no mistakes, no rough copies.

"I see," said Maria, "but you still believe it to be a Caravaggio."

"Yes. I have spent my whole life studying his art. I do not need an expert to validate it."

"But the church is laying claim to it."

"Yes."

"Is it a legitimate claim? Do they have any rights to it?"

"Yes, they do, it is part of their original commission."

"I bet Alfonso's not too happy."

"No, he's not," sighed Massimo.

That last statement seemed to hang in the air as the scene in the church began to fade and the deep hues and tones of 'Seven Acts of Mercy' began to dissolve.

Massimo was now back in the present, inside the strangely comforting confines of his pod. "No, Alfonso won't be happy," he said out loud, "or at least he won't be if he finds out what I've stolen." As he said this Massimo looked up at the painting propped up on the table. He took another sip of wine and contemplated the dramatic beauty of its composition. But what on earth had he done? It was so impulsive for him, and now that he was here in his beloved caravan what next?

Suddenly there was a knock at the door. It provided a grateful distraction and stopped him from facing up to some difficult questions. He quietly put the canvas back in its case and sat back down. After a second or two, there was another more insistent tap.

14

PARTY TIME

"Hello, Massimo, it's me Harry, Harry Jones. I've got that phone number. Sorry I am a bit later than planned."

Massimo sighed and rubbed his eyes. He took another sip of his wine and opened the door. "Oh, and I've got this," said Harry as he held out a rather nice bottle of Chianti Classico. It took Massimo a little by surprise. It was a year and vintage he knew well.

"You shouldn't have," he exclaimed sheepishly.

"I already had it with me, well to be honest it was my wife, Mary. When I told her about the accident she insisted I give you the bottle that she packed for me."

"This wife of yours sounds like a good woman." Massimo smiled graciously and accepted the bottle lovingly.

"Well, I hope that's alright," added Harry. "Thanks again for being so forgiving but the money. I can't..."

"Please," said Massimo firmly. Harry sighed. He knew that he wasn't going to get anywhere. He smiled in acknowledgement and turned round to go back to his caravan but then stopped. He wheeled back round to face Massimo who was just about to shut the door.

"You know the so-called duel on the tennis court, it was a fight. The two men were pimps, they were arguing about the use of prostitutes. I think the idea that it was some kind of noble duel is exaggerating things a little."

"Argh, yes," said Massimo "I've heard that account too, but I would discount it. There is no real evidence to support that version and it would not alter my view on Caravaggio even if that were the case. Ownership of women was also a means of protection for those women. I'm not saying that Caravaggio wasn't some kind of pimp but…" Massimo stopped and looked more closely at Harry. "Why don't you stay here? Yes, stay a while and help me finish off this bottle. We can discuss the life and times of Michael Angelo Caravaggio and the great masterpieces together in a much more civilised way."

Harry instantly warmed to the idea and nodded his approval. Massimo pulled out a table and two chairs from behind the caravan and placed them in a spot bathed in the late afternoon sunshine. Massimo then poured a good glug of wine into Harry's glass and topped up his glass with the last remaining drops.

"Saluti," said Harry appreciatively.

Massimo smiled and raised his glass. "To the genius of Caravaggio."

Harry then responded by raising his glass further. "To the genius of Caravaggio."

After an immensely pleasurable gulp, they both plonked their glasses down and together let out a pleasurable "argh."

"Per'e palummo," stated Massimo. Harry looked quizzical so his friend explained. "It is Neapolitan dialect; it means red feet. It is the colour of the pigeon's feet and is the same colour as the grape used for the piedirosso." They both then savoured the taste some more by holding the next mouthful in the roof of their mouths. Harry felt quite invigorated and made an inquiry.

"There is one subject I must ask you about," he paused and looked at his glass of red wine glistening in the sun. "Caravaggio's Nativity with Saint Francis and Saint Lawrence."

"Ah yes," said Massimo half expecting the subject to be raised. "The great mystery that seems to be on the lips of every art lover every 10 years. What has become of it? Where has this great work of art disappeared to? Yes indeed. 1969 I think it was. That was when the thieves cut it away from the stucco in the oratory at Palermo." A wistful look came over Massimo's eyes. "Such butchery." He paused as if in silent prayer and then continued. "It has never been seen since, despite all kinds of investigations and confessions. And is it still alive now so to speak? I ask this question because of course the thieves made a great mistake. You know what that was don't you, Harry?"

"I think so. Did they roll it up?"

"Yes, they rolled it up in the carpet to protect it from rain. We know this because there were reports of a stolen carpet along with the painting. And rolling any painting up from that period..."

"Would cause the paint to crack and in some cases disintegrate," said Harry finishing off the sentence.

"Such idiots," said Massimo shaking his head.

"It was on the news recently," added Harry. "The priest, who was connected to the case all those years ago, he was talking about it."

"Ah yes, the priest, a good man Benedetto Rocco." Massimo again looked quite mournful. By the look on his face, Harry thought that he may even have known him. There was a small silence. "I beg your pardon," said Massimo snapping out of his mini slumber, "please, do carry on."

"Well," said Harry, "as you know the priest, God rest his soul, has been dead some years but they've just released an interview he did about twenty years ago with a filmmaker, some Italian name I can't quite remember, but the priest said that the Mafia sent him a letter saying that they, the Mafia, had stolen it and that they wanted a ransom. To support their claims, they included a small piece of the painting that had been sliced off!"

Massimo simply said, "Yes," in a dull kind of way and shook his head. There was a pause as he took a rather large gulp of his wine. "Can you believe it, Harry? Who would do such a thing?"

"Well, the Mafia did obviously."

"Yes, yes," said Massimo, swatting away Harry's interjection, "of course, but who could give such an order, not only to hack it away from its home but then slice a part of it off in such a fashion? Would you ever let that happen, Harry? If you knew that something so precious, so beautiful was going to be harmed or even destroyed, would you do something to stop it?"

"Yes, of course," said Harry defiantly.

"Thank you," said Massimo. "Thank you."

Harry didn't quite know what Massimo was alluding to or why he wanted his validation, but he had a good idea that his friend knew quite a bit about the darker side of life. When Harry thought about it, the whole car business and giving that cash away so readily seemed odd, as though he didn't want to go through any official channels, but Harry wasn't complaining. There was something quite intriguing about this charming Poirot-like figure that, for whatever reason, chose to holiday in a caravan on the outskirts of Preston. Whatever the circumstances, this presented a golden opportunity that wasn't going to be missed. He decided to probe away at events surrounding the theft of Caravaggio's masterpiece, hoping for some titbits of new information.

"That bit of painting sent in the post, a bit like cutting a part of an ear off or the tip of a finger. It's got Mafioso's signature all over it," stated Harry.

"Quite," said Massimo thoughtfully. "But you know we shouldn't be surprised. Mafioso's link with great art, particularly that of Caravaggio, has always been prevalent. It is nothing new. Many bosses of the Cosa Nostra and more recently Camorra have, how shall we say, 'acquired' great masterpieces. Sadly, for many, it is not for the passion of art, it is more a badge of honour, something to be shown off at dinner parties or to rival bosses."

This time Harry shook his head in disgust. Massimo nodded his appreciation at the empathetic gesture and then continued. "They have become so unguarded about their acquisitions. Only four years ago the authorities confiscated two Van Gogh's from a Camorra boss's house. It was a photo of him, with part of the painting in the background that alerted the authorities. Can you believe it, Harry?" Massimo let the question sink in. "A tour of these people's houses would be like a tour of the Uffizi." Massimo laughed. "But they are not always great art lovers like you and I, Harry."

"Have you been to any of these houses? Have you seen any of these great missing masterpieces?" asked Harry inquisitively.

"Of course not," said Massimo. It was a quick repost, but Harry could detect a little twinkle in his friend's eye. "Even if I did, I would not tell you," laughed Massimo.

"Perhaps it is a good thing you don't," added Harry but then he couldn't resist one last question on the matter. "So where do you think the painting is now?"

Massimo smiled and then answered. "In all seriousness, I do not know. It is common knowledge that Gaetano Badalamenti, the Sicilian boss, was responsible for its initial theft. A pentito named Mannoia Mannorino affirmed this in his confession to the police. But after Badalamenti was arrested, some thirty years ago, and prosecuted by none other than Rudi Giuliani, there was a search around all his properties, but there was no sign of it. There was talk of a Swiss art dealer being involved. Many people think that he has it somewhere, but what state it is in, I am not sure. That is what I know."

Harry sort of believed him. Massimo then took a bottle of Harry's Chianti, opened it, and changed the subject. "So, Harry you are a teacher. I think a very privileged position, to influence so many young minds, to do good in the world."

"Yes, I suppose so," said Harry meekly.

"You sound very unsure, Harry. It must be quite difficult, all those teenagers with all their problems and having to control them."

"Yes, it is difficult with young people…" Harry hesitated. "But there are positives. They can and often do surprise you." Then he remembered his present circumstances. He shook his head. "I'm not sure. The more I know the less I understand."

Massimo smiled. "I think that that is a very honest and perceptive statement."

"But it's not always their fault," interjected Harry. The system doesn't help."

"But systems are not always designed to help," laughed Massimo. "They are often designed to protect power or increase the powers of others." Harry didn't disagree. But then Massimo laughed again which annoyed Harry.

"I'm sorry, Harry," apologised Massimo immediately, "I am not suggesting that you are in any way naïve. Far from it, I think that you have a healthy cynicism if I can put it that way, but it is easy to see in our system. Nobody pretends that it is anything else. Quite simply the Clans control everything. It is an uncomfortable truth that people are forced to live with. Everybody knows it and everybody knows that all adjustments to 'The System' that have been made in the last 30 years have been designed to maintain power of Camorra and increase its foothold in society. I repeat, there is no pretending it is something else. Of course, it may benefit others but that is not its primary objective."

Harry took another sip of his wine and pondered Massimo's words. "You mention adjustments to the system, what adjustments are these?"

Massimo thought for a second. "More integration and diversification." He said it in a way that made it sound like whatever it was, was his idea. "Take shoes," he continued, "leather shoes. In the old days, these goods, along with others, would be stopped at the port. A simple levy on those goods and control over distribution would provide 'The Family' with a very sustainable income. You go anywhere in Italy and good quality leather shoes are always in demand. But if 'The Family' then found its own high-quality shoemakers to mimic the top brands and integrate these with said top brands and if the sales chains and the admin and the electric companies, that provide the power to run these shops, were all in one way or another tied to 'The Family, even appointed by the family, you can see how much more money they will make and how much greater their influence will be." Massimo laughed. "The Clan has made a lot of money on leather shoes…"

"Because they have altered the system to suit themselves," said Harry completing the sentence.

"Precisely," replied Massimo, "precisely."

I don't think we are quite at that stage yet and besides, we don't "take out people" if they get in the way."

"Quite," said Massimo dismissively, "but you must ask yourself, who has instigated such whole-scale changes in the system, and why have they been implemented so quickly? Everybody will use words such as 'reform' and 'improving standards' but there will be some at the top who will have instigated the changes so that they can make the most profit. It is most likely that their companies will, for example, have obtained many lucrative contracts for providing schools with equipment and access to their information technology. It would not surprise me if there were a bending of the rules somewhere along the line, improper lobbying of MP's, cash for questions, maybe a bribe or two. It happens all the time in Italy.

Harry didn't want to agree too readily. For all his distrust of the educational system, he still wanted to defend something, even a small part. But before he could provide a counterargument a rather ugly vision popped into his head. It featured a group of fat adult pigs dressed in public schoolboy uniforms all guffawing away around a giant trough of dirty lucre. They were stuffing themselves full of fifty-pound notes, so much so that they were vomiting and yet still they continued the feeding frenzy, their big fat stomachs growing larger by the second, pushing the small round buttons on their blazers to breaking point. And there, in the background was quite a porky little piglet that had round glasses on the end of its nose. Even though the features looked pale and emaciated there was no mistaking the look of Inspector Brian Edwards. He was trying desperately hard to muscle in. Every time he did, one of the fat pigs shunted over so that all he got was a face full of pig's arse.

"They're not all like that," said Harry quietly. Again, he surprised himself with his response.

"No, no of course not said Massimo sympathetically. "There will be many in power that are honourable. I paint a dark picture because of my own experience...it is the world I inhabit. He patted Harry's shoulder. "I did not intend to put a slight on your years of honourable service." There was a brief silence before Harry spoke.

"So, what is your job Massimo, what do you actually do?"

"Ha, what do I do?" said Massimo laughing out loud. "That is a good question, Harry. I advise 'The Family' financially, Harry. Yes, that is what I do. I suppose I also look at ways to make money flow more easily and for our financial operations to comply with the law."

"Right," said Harry. He kind of understood Massimo's role. "But going back to systems. Mafioso, Camorra whatever you call it, they've done some nasty things. I mean what's the word they use when they take out people? 'Whacked', that's it, 'Whacked'. I mean Naples is quite notorious and what I want to ask..." Harry hesitated.

"How can I work for them when they commit such acts?" said Massimo. "Is that what you want to ask?"

"Yes."

"Do not think that I do not ask myself the same question, Harry, and I cannot give you a definitive answer. But let me put this to you. One of the things that you expect your government to do is to protect you. And when there is a threat to the people of your country, whilst it may be regrettable, they will order killings and assassinations. I am sure that if they could have, for example, assassinated Saddam Hussein prior to the major conflict in Iraq, many in your own country would have found that acceptable, he was, after all, a threat. Do you see what I am saying, Harry?"

"Yes, I think so. But I didn't vote for this government and I opposed the Iraq war. And I am free to say that."

"And that makes you feel better? We all have to live with things we prefer not to think about, even if we oppose them. And the lies that are perpetrated, I never did believe in the weapons of mass destruction. It was always a lie to make killing morally justifiable. The Clan doesn't attempt that kind of propaganda, it simply takes out those who are a threat so that it can hold on to its power, keep its sovereignty and protect its own, but we don't wrap it in a morally justifiable blanket."

"Hmm, I'm not sure I quite go along with that."

"I admit it is an oversimplification Harry, but the Clan has done a lot for me, and I am pragmatic. I could agonise over the morality of which I am part, but I try not to do that, and I see very little of the more unsavoury aspects of Camorra activity. But enough of this talk. It does not always sit happily with me. If you don't mind Harry, we shall talk about something else. Despite our different backgrounds, I think we may have a good deal in common."

"Of course," said Harry who felt quite humbled by Massimo's openness.

It turned out that they did have quite a lot in common with many of the same interests and passions. They talked about all sorts of things and had some heated debates about politics, religion, and education. The more wine they drank the more passionately they argued, but always with a degree of mutual respect. Eventually, Harry got very drunk and had to be walked home. It proved to be difficult for two reasons. Firstly, Harry's legs had gone and secondly, Massimo wasn't much better. He just about managed to guide Harry up some small steps and into the caravan. On the final step, Massimo gave Harry one last affectionate slap on the back and propelled him forward until he collapsed face down onto the bed into dream time again – in downtown Chicago of all places...

There is a meeting of sorts. Each one of the assembled figures is wearing a sharp double-breasted suit complete with a kipper tie, spats, and a black fedora. So is Harry. By the sound of the accents and the look of their attire, he guesses that they are in 1920's Chicago. It is prohibition time and he is in the middle of the mob. He has a vague feeling that he mustn't be recognized so he pulls his hat down to cover a large part of his face. Careful to keep his features in shadow, he lifts his head up slightly and recognizes a familiar figure. It is Cavendish looking just a tad sharper than everybody else. Eyes are turned toward him in expectation. He is the boss; the big cheese. He stands on a crate and makes himself look big. A hush descends. The crowd waits. And then he starts to speak...

"He's godda new friend. Yeah, Harry Jones has godda new friend. They call him l'investigatore. He tinks dat he's gonna give him protecssiun. But I got dis covered." The audience cheers loudly. Cavendish then opens a violin case and pulls out a wad of typed paper. "See dis, it's an inspectas report and it says dat Harry Jones has not met his targets." Some of the audience jeer whilst others boo and hiss. Cavendish nods his head in agreement and then extends an arm to quell the noise. After a few seconds, he continues. "Yeah and you know sumtin else, he's not used an acronym, no DIRT time, nuttin."

Suddenly one of the audience shouts out. "What's DIRT time again boss?"

There is a loud gasp from the others as Cavendish suddenly wheels round.

"Who said dat? Was it you Mozzarella?" A rather hapless-looking gangster hangs his head in shame.

"Sorry boss."

"We've gon over dis so many times in ya trainin days." Cavendish then turns to his audience. "Tell 'im, tell 'im what DIRT time is."

All together the audience shouts out, "*Dedicated Improvement and Reflection time.*"

Cavendish acknowledges their unified response with another nod of his head. He's lapping it up. He then turns to Mozzarella "Don't you forget now, ya hear?" It is said quite lovingly. Mozzarella responds by nodding his head gratefully. Cavendish then continues his speech. "Not in any part of his lesson did dis Harry Jones ever demonstrate his PEE, which is..."

The crowd can't wait. "*Point, Evidence, Explanation.*"

"He never even had a CRAP."

Again, mantra-like the audience responds "*Celebrating Recording Assessment Procedures.*"

"If only he'd used da Bennet girl, dat utuber," continues Cavendish. "Da one dat sings dem acronyms."

"Yeah, she's a blast."

Suddenly Mozzarella pipes up, "Whaddaya gonna do wid 'im boss? What are you gonna do wid dis Harry Jones?"

"Cavendish's eyes light up maliciously. "Why I'm gonna let im have it… I'm gonna sling a poor performance management review right ad 'im, right between dee eyes."

"He ain't gonna recover boss!" urges Mozarella trying to gain some lost brownie points.

"No, he ain't," chuckles Cavendish sadistically. The audience shows their appreciation with loud cheers and riotous claps.

"Hey boss, what about l'investigatore?" Suddenly the noise subsides. Cavendish becomes stony-faced.

"What, dat liddle pumped up Poirot? Why he's gonna get what's comin.'"

"What's dat gonna be boss? Tell us."

"Why he's gonna get drilled hard. Dats after I've taken him for a deep dive…in da river."

The audience laughs wickedly and shouts, "Yeah!"

And in the background, away from all the excitement, a girl stands on her own. She is holding something, maybe a case of some kind. It's a curious vision. It's so apart from the rest of the events. Harry can't quite make her out. She's not quite in focus, half seen, almost recognizable but not quite and then she's gone.

15

MORNING BRIEFING

The shrill sound of an alarm clock woke up Harry with a start. He was confused. It wasn't his usual bed, and he wasn't in his bedroom. It took him a minute or two to realize that he had had rather a lot to drink, he was in the caravan, and it was Monday morning. Worst of all, school beckoned. There was no time to dwell on the fuzziness of his head or the heaviness of his eyelids, but it was still a slow ascent from supine to upright. "The three Ss," said Harry to himself. "Shower, shit, shave in any order – that usually helps." Sure enough, it did. Then teaching clothes on and he was ready to go. He didn't want to be late. He had a meeting with Edwards and Cavendish early in the day and needed to be prepared. There was also a good chance that both would come into one of his lessons for 'support'.

During the drive to school, Harry reflected on the evening with Massimo. There was an overwhelming sense of enjoyment even though he couldn't remember much. Events were patchy but the nearer he got to Saint Peter's the more his thoughts shifted. It was like going from light to dark. He couldn't stop thinking about the day ahead. It would all start with the Monday morning briefing in the hall. He knew what he would be faced with as soon as he walked in. Emblazoned across the big pull-down screen, it would be impossible not to notice. And it didn't disappoint. As soon as he stepped inside the hall, there it was, the academy logo complete with 'We strive to learn' beaming into the blurry eyes of every teacher that walked through the double doors. It was the last thing Harry wanted to see.

As people were shuffling to their seats Harry could see Cavendish chomping at the bit, dying to start his presentation.

Harry's bottom had barely touched his seat before Cavendish enthusiastically kicked things off.

"I'd like to start," he said, "by taking a moment to look at our mission statement 'We strive to learn.' Take a moment to reflect on what that means for our students; for our community and for ourselves." A minute's silence duly ensued as all the gathered bowed their heads in a prayer-like fashion. "Turn to the person next to you," added Cavendish, "tell them that we strive to learn." Harry was amazed that so many followed his instructions and mumbled the mantra to each other. He was, however, pleased when he heard some of the older teachers quietly protest. Harry and one or two others just laughed which seemed to irritate Cavendish. Not a great move he thought to himself as he looked over to see Tom Bailey quietly humming 'The Star-Spangled Banner'.

"Just one or two items for this morning's briefing," said Cavendish brusquely.

Harry looked at his watch. "Five minutes," he said out loud. He turned to whoever was next to him, "Five minutes before we get on to anything remotely important. What was all that first bit about? What a load of bollocks!"

Cavendish looked up and frowned. If he did hear Harry's comments, it didn't put him off. With a click of his remote, the mission statement transitioned beautifully into the agenda. Good use of the fade feature thought Harry. First up was the duty rota.

"People on duty," piped Cavendish. "Could they make sure that they circulate in their designated area? Please, do not remain in one place talking to other members of staff. Engage with the students. Research has shown that this informal time of talking with students fosters good relations and helps learning."

"Really?" whispered Harry. "We can't have a word with our friends and colleagues, and we have to talk to children? What on earth is happening here?" The person next to him smiled but Harry could tell he wasn't interested.

"Second item," continued Cavendish," is pupil progress. Vice Principal Prentiss will take you through this one."

A very neat, well-trimmed bearded suit stepped up; switched laptops; and clicked up a bar chart, all in the blink of an eye. There was a small but audible collective groan. Harry called this

100

slot the 'data dirge.' It didn't disappoint. So absorbed in his data mission, Prentiss didn't even say 'Good Morning'. No time for pleasantries. Straight in…

"As explained in the technical information table, where pupil progress is statistically, significantly different to the national average, the bar is highlighted in green or red. Grey bars indicate a difference (positive or negative) but that difference is not statistically significant. Groups with fewer than five pupils in the cohort will not be displayed in the chart. This is to avoid misinterpretation of results due to small samples.

Harry tapped the person in front of him. "Do you understand any of this? Better still do you want to understand any of this?" But there was no reply. It was as though Prentiss had cast some spell over the entire gathering. They all appeared strangely becalmed as the drone continued.

"A further 'progress gap' bar chart can be found on page six fig 4 of the handouts in your pigeonholes. This chart can also be used to answer the questions: One, within our FSM6." Several hands went up. "Ah! Yes," smiled Prentiss.

"Good God, people are actually listening," said Harry out loud.

"You are wondering what FSM6 is," continued the drone smugly. "These are pupils eligible for free school meals in the last six years." He then stopped for a second as Harry let out quite a yawn.

"Sorry," said Harry. And he was, it wasn't deliberate.

Prentiss seemed unruffled as though he was used to it. He carried on regardless. "As I was saying, FSM6 pupils and not-FSM pupil groups, do we have any other pupil characteristics that are underperforming? How wide are the gaps in progress between some groups of pupils? What are the strengths and weaknesses of our departments?" Prentiss pointed with pride at his bar chart, "This gives a detailed overview of how FSM6 pupils performed in relation to non-FSM6 pupils."

Harry could feel his eyelids getting heavy.

"The black dotted line," stated Prentiss, "represents national average progress for pupils with a similar prior attainment. Therefore, any group above or below the dotted line made greater or lower expected progress when compared with other pupils with the starting point nationally."

Harry felt like Mowgli being hypnotised by the snake in *The Jungle Book*. He even started to hear the soporific song 'Trust in me' running around his brain dulling all his senses. And still Prentiss continued.

"If you wish to look at how pupil context affects progress of FSM6 and non-FSM6 groups in your school, please refer to FFT's CVA progress analysis. Figure 4: horizontal bar chart depicting the progress made by different sub-groups of FSM pupils compared to their peers. The final graph in the FFT dashboard…Blah, blah blah."

Harry's eyes could not stay open any longer. The drone had caused them to close and still it carried on…

"The final graph is a scatterplot on page seven on your handouts." Prentiss then clicked his remote. "This scatter graph can be used to answer the questions: Do we have any under-performing groups of pupils, or are there wide gaps in attainment between some groups of pupils? N.B. Value-added is the default methodology used in FFT's dashboards."

The drone didn't notice Harry slumped in his chair. He was in full flow and never even came up for air.

"Therefore, when analysing progress data under this method, you are comparing the progress of your pupil groups against pupils with a similar starting point only. For example, when grouped by pupil characteristics, this school's male pupils happen to make more progress compared to pupils with a similar starting point. You will need to refer to FFT's CVA progress dashboard for data to support contextualised analysis…"

Suddenly Prentiss stopped. Everything went quiet. Nothing could be heard apart from the slow rhythm of someone snoring. At first, people were too stunned to speak until one of Harry's snores roared like a lion and then everybody burst out laughing. Prentiss was not amused. Vicky leaned over and poked Harry hard. He woke with a start.

"What, what, where..?"

"Harry we are in briefing," said Vicky laughing.

"Are we? So we are. Is it over yet?"

"No, Mr Jones, it isn't," smiled Cavendish tersely.

"Be careful, Harry," said Vicky.

"Christ, I didn't think he could hear."

Prentiss looked at Cavendish. It's okay, I think I've finished." He looked up at the rest of the assembled teachers. "Just make sure you read the last couple of pages of the handouts."

"Thank you, Mr Prentiss," said Cavendish. There were still a few titters, so he waited for a second or two before continuing. "And finally, a few pupil matters."

"Finally, finally," mocked Harry underneath his breath. "Has anybody got a copy of Prentiss's handout? I know how I'm going to get to sleep tonight."

The bell went for the start of lessons, but Cavendish ignored it and simply carried on undeterred. "Could staff please ensure that Sophie Reynolds is seated at the back of the class. We've had a long chat with her. I know that she can be disruptive and rude, but she feels anxious when sitting near the front. So please let's try to accommodate her wishes." Harry, irritated by that last phrase, sighed, rolled his eyes, and muttered something under his breath but there was still more. "Freddie Shields in year 8 wishes to be called Samantha. This has been approved by parents. Please do not call him Sam for short.

Next, Scott Luckhurst. This is a boy who joined us only a few months ago. He has had a particularly difficult time. There are a number of things going on with this young man. It would be helpful if you could restrain from raising your voice with him as this can often be a trigger for his more challenging behaviour.

And lastly, Emily Bradshaw. Please keep everything that is yours or valuable out of her reach. If there is something that is out on your desk, make sure it is secured. A search of her locker last night revealed a treasure trove of stolen objects from staff car keys to remote controls. If you have recently had items that have mysteriously gone missing, go down to the office. They have a collection of all the items that were found in the locker."

Harry shook his head. He wanted to say something to somebody, but people were never going to take him seriously, not after his little sleeping episode, so instead, he marched off up the stairs to the staffroom to get a cuppa before his meeting with

Cavendish and Edwards. After his little nap, he felt refreshed and surprisingly ready for the 'baldy brigade'.

The Meeting
Harry knocked on the Principal's door, mug of tea in hand, determined not to look too stressed.

"Come in," shouted Cavendish. "Ah, Mr Jones you know Mr Edwards. Please take a seat. How are you?"

"Fine, absolutely fine," said Harry sounding as unequivocal as possible.

"That's good. Yes, good. Now then there are a few things I would like to discuss."

Harry took a few sips of his tea and looked across at Edwards who was doing his best not to look all superior. He had never really forgiven Harry for "stealing" his girl back in their student-teacher days. As far as Harry was concerned she was never his property anyway.

"As you may well know," continued Cavendish, "some reports have come my way, reports of a rather disturbing nature. I have one or two statements I would like you to look at." Cavendish then ruffled through a dossier of paperwork and pulled out a couple of sheets. "It would be helpful if you could outline exactly what..."

Suddenly there was a furious knock at the door and in burst a year 11 student.

"Sir, sir there's an emergency! It's Scott Luckhurst. He's locked himself in the Maths store cupboard."

"Well just get the caretaker," said Cavendish impatiently.

"The caretaker's there already it's just that he sent me to get you because he's got Mrs Sheridan in there too."

"What! He's locked her inside with him?"

"Yes."

Cavendish stood up "Right, right." And then in one quick bound, he leaped through the door leaving Harry alone with a bemused Edwards.

"Shouldn't we help?" he spluttered.

"No," said Harry in a matter-of-fact fashion, "there'll be a number of people around. We'd just get in the way."

"Right," said Edwards. "Yes, you're right."

There then followed an awkward passage of time in which Edwards typed a few things onto his laptop and Harry hummed a tune. After a minute or two, Harry could see that it was irritating Edwards, so he did it slightly louder. Edwards parried his offensive with a deliberately disinterested look. Harry then took it upon himself to make a verbal thrust.

"You love this don't you?"

"What?" asked Edwards nonchalantly.

"This position of power that you are in, especially with me."

"I am not sure what you mean."

"Oh, come on. You've never liked me, have you?

"I am not sure what you are on about, but I can assure you I am simply doing my job, as are all of us."

"Simply doing your job? Hitler's cronies used to say the same thing when they put people in the gas chambers."

"I am not sure that you can equate what we are doing with Hitler's army," scoffed Edwards. "But I understand how people feel."

"Do you really?" said Harry indignantly. "If I had a penny for every time people like you used the phrase, 'I understand,' I'd be rich. Honestly, it's straight out of the management's handbook of how to elicit sympathy from the poor unfortunate victims you're shafting." Harry should have stopped there but he didn't. "I can see you lot standing over someone after you'd kicked them in the testicles acting all caring. 'Does that hurt? Oh, I'm terribly sorry I know how you feel. I understand.'" Harry repeated that last phrase slowly. "'I understand.' Do me a favour." He looked at Edwards who said nothing but simply frowned. "You do know that behind your judgements and condemnations there are people, real people in real communities. Do you know what people like you have done to these communities?"

"Yes, improved standards of education," said Edwards sharply.

"Really, is that what you call it?" Harry was pleased with himself. He got Edwards to bite back. For a millisecond the smarmy veneer slipped but then it returned with a more measured response

105

"Yes, we have all worked hard to improve standards. There is no doubt that results have improved, progress has been made, and teaching has become much more rigorous."

"And there we go again," replied Harry dismissively, "the same pronouncements dished up to anyone who questions your position. Massimo was absolutely right."

"Who?"

"Never mind but you, you think that if you spout off this rhetoric often enough or say it loud enough, it becomes true. Isn't that right?"

But Edwards gave no reply. Instead, he carried on typing behind his laptop. He wasn't going to be drawn into an unnecessary conversation and he certainly wasn't going to be wound up. Harry tried some more interfering tactics, a few scratchy coughs, some heavy sighs, and some incredibly annoying taps on the table, but Edwards didn't bite again. Harry was tempted to tell him that his former girlfriend was doing very well without him, but he thought better of it.

For the next few minutes his mind wondered. He imagined Cavendish coming back in, slipping a judge's wig on, and sentencing him.

"Harry Jones you are a habitual scoffer of new educational initiatives. Your irreverent swipes at authority and your increasing cynicism have become an educational blot on the landscape. Therefore, you have left me with no alternative but to sentence you to two years of sifting through data and target setting. Think yourself as fortunate. In some quarters this would be seen as a reward. And to ensure that you do not deviate from this path you shall serve out your sentence under the strict guidance of the guv'nor Mr Justice Nerd Prentiss."

Further imaginary scenarios came and went until finally, Cavendish walked in. He looked flustered. Beads of sweat could be seen trickling down his forehead.

"That proved a tad more difficult," he panted.

"Mrs Sheridan?" enquired Harry concerned about her welfare.

"She's okay thank you, she's an old stalwart."

"That's good that she's okay," said Harry "but a younger more inexperienced teacher…"

"Quite," said Cavendish He then stopped and looked at his watch. "Look, I think we'll have to leave this again. I'm terribly sorry."

"No problem," said Harry casually."

"I'll get Rachel to set another date."

Harry nodded in agreement. He then stood up and without any acknowledgement of Edwards promptly left the office. As he shut the door Edwards turned to Cavendish.

"He's got attitude that one."

16

GONE!

It was the sound of Harry's car leaving the campsite that woke up Massimo. Surprisingly, he felt quite good, despite having had a few too many glasses of wine. During the evening he'd made a very important decision. He was going to take the painting back to Naples. Perhaps it was the wine, the sense of place, or maybe last night's company that had prompted this decision. If he was lucky, very lucky, he could get the painting back before anybody knew that it had gone missing. He knew that "borrowing" the Caravaggio was a stupid and reckless thing to do, but at the time he couldn't seem to help himself, he was sure that Alfonso was going to destroy it. Maybe, when he got back, he could have another go at changing his boss's mind or even talk to the church authorities.

First things first. Massimo had to clean up! Five large empty wine bottles stood proudly on a small table whilst a smaller bottle that still contained a little grappa lay buried amongst some cutlery in the sink. He started by bagging all the bottles and then washing the cutlery and glasses. He smiled to himself as he cleaned some wine stains from the sink area and dusted down the table. He swept everywhere thoroughly and arranged the table and chair precisely in the centre of the floor space. He then folded his clothes neatly on the bed, but before he put them in the large suitcase, he decided to check one last time. He undid the zipper on the inside and fully expected the encased painting to peep out…but it didn't. His heart missed a beat. There must be a mistake. He unzipped all the way round. Empty! Massimo was stunned. His mind raced through some possibilities. He'd had quite a few to drink. Maybe he brought the painting out at some idiotic time in the night, perhaps to have one last look before he went to sleep. But he was sure that he would have put it away. Maybe he was drunker than he thought and had put it somewhere silly. He spent the next fifteen minutes searching through every nook and cranny of the caravan. Nothing. He sat down on the bed and went through recent events in his mind. The last time he saw it was a few hours before Harry came round and, in that time, he was sure that he never left the caravan unattended. Did Harry have something to do with it?

Massimo frowned. He'd been a big part of The Family for many years, nothing surprised him, not with people. He knew what greed could do. But Harry? How would he have done it? He'd drank copious amounts of wine and was completely inebriated…unless he was faking it. That was a possibility but if he was, he was a very good actor. Maybe he stole it without realizing thought Massimo. Could that be possible? As he searched for some answers he looked out of the window. A few people were starting to emerge for breakfast. He recognised an elderly couple sitting on fold-out chairs around their fold-out breakfast table. Without thinking, he walked over.

"Good morning," said Massimo. The old man and woman turned round and smiled simultaneously. "Sorry to disturb you but I wonder if you saw anything unusual last night. I've lost something you see…a small painting that is very dear to me. It was in a silver case. I can't find it. I think that someone may have taken it."

"Taken it?" said the man surprised. "What, you mean stolen it? Really?"

"Well, I'm hoping not. I had it last night and now it's gone."

"You've had a good look?

"Yes, of course."

"In the car?"

"Yes. Yes."

"Hmm, Is that yours, the black Audi?"

"Yes."

"You know you've got a smashed headlight."

"Yes."

"You need to get that fixed. It'll be no good for driving, the coppers 'll pull you up. I 'ad something similar and got stopped, didn't I Doris?"

Doris nodded.

"Yes, you are right," said Massimo curtly. "I am seeing a mechanic this morning."

"Who are you usin'?"

"Please, I am in a hurry, could we try and focus on last night? Did you see anything strange?"

Oblivious to the question Doris continued her husband's theme.

"Only Jack's always used Mike's up the road, haven't you Jack?

"Yep, never 'ad any trouble."

Massimo shook his head, on another day, at another time, he might have found this little enactment endearing.

"Please, I know you are being helpful but…"

"That your caravan?" interrupted Jack

"Yes but…"

That's usually Ted and Alice's." He turned to his wife. "They come here about this time. Don't they?" Doris nodded. "Was there a cancellation?"

"Yes," replied Massimo exasperated "but please can we..."

"Ever such a nice couple. Sometimes we've had a tea or a coffee together. They brought us the sausages last year. They were lovely, the best sausages you've ever tasted. I'm right, aren't I Doris?" Doris nodded.

"Yes, yes I am sure they were," said Massimo impatiently, "but did you see anything last night…somebody hanging around, somebody a bit suspicious, near the caravan?" But Jack and Doris were still thinking about the taste of those delicious sausages to give an instant answer. Eventually, it was Jack who broke the deadlock.

"Hmm. No, not really. You seen anything Doris?"

"No, No I can't say that I have."

"Are you sure?" said Massimo… "Anything?"

They both shook their head. "We're not saying that somebody wasn't there," said Doris, "it's just that we didn't see anything."

110

Massimo paused for a second or two and then watched as Jerry, their pet dog, suddenly sprang onto Doris's lap and gave her a lick around the mouth. Massimo recoiled as dog and woman revelled in a show of slobbering physical affection. Doris then gave the dog a bit of her breakfast.

"Good boy Jerry, good boy."

Massimo watched on in horror before gathering himself together. "Thank you, you've been most helpful," he said firmly. "Please, if you remember anything here is my number." The couple smiled as they took Massimo's note. Massimo couldn't wait to get away but as he marched up the path he stopped and looked back. He was touched by the look on Jack and Doris's faces. They seemed genuinely saddened by the fact that they could not help him. Even Jerry the dog frowned.

"Maybe at the reception," shouted Doris.

Massimo nodded but he was already on his way there. It was the most obvious port of call. As he circumvented a muddy patch, he asked God to let this be his lucky day. "Let it be there Lord please," he muttered out loud. He repeated it like some mantra as he approached some steps and opened a door.

The old man at the reception was sympathetic to Massimo's plight but just shook his head and shrugged his shoulders. "Well I'm buggered if anybody 'ere as stolen anything but you never know, there's nowt so queer as folk. We've 'ad some odd ones 'ere I can tell you." He then started to tell Massimo a story of a very odd couple that stayed in the caravan next to the two poplars just down the driveway. "They used to parade around in their caravan in each other's clothes, very strange they were…"

"Could they have done it?" interrupted Massimo.

"No, no they only stayed three times. Last time was a few years back. Peculiar, that's what they were, very peculiar. There was another time they…"

"Thank you," said Massimo bluntly but I really don't have time for your anecdotes." The old man looked puzzled so Massimo explained. "Stories…your stories. I do not have time for them."

"Right you are," came the crestfallen reply.

Massimo suddenly became aware of how irritable he sounded. "I am sorry," he said trying to be more civil, "but this

111

item is precious to me. Please, forgive my rudeness." The old man smiled sympathetically. "Do you think anybody here is capable of theft?" asked Massimo, trying to make his voice sound softer.

"Well, that's just what I mean," said the old man, "anybody is capable. Just because they don't look like thieves or criminals. I mean take me; people say I have a kindly face, but you never know. And you, you're well-mannered and you 'ave a kindly face, but for all I know you may be a right old tea leaf or part of a big criminal organisation. You never know. There's nowt so queer..."

"As folk," said Massimo finishing off the sentence. "Quite." There was a moment's pause before Massimo asked him in his most forthright manner if he knew anything, absolutely anything about his missing painting. When the old man eventually said that he hadn't, Massimo thanked him and sloped off.

He spent the next hour or so meandering about from caravan to caravan asking the same questions but there was no joy, nobody had seen anything suspicious or untoward. What's more, he couldn't see how any of these quaint English families could have committed any crime let alone steal a priceless piece of art, unless he was missing something. It was time to call Harry. He switched his phone on for the first time in three days and instantly it rang.

"I've been trying to reach you for days," came the familiar voice on the other end. "Where on earth are you?"

"Ah Maria."

"Yes Massimo, Maria."

"Is everything okay?"

"Yes, but more to the point, are you okay? I've been trying to get in touch but have been unable to contact you."

"Yes, no signal here. Sorry."

"Massimo, are you sure you are okay? You seem unsettled."

"No, I'm fine. Honestly."

"Do you know when you will be back?"

"Soon," said Massimo being deliberately vague.

"It's just that your boss has been trying to get in touch with you. He called round the other day."

"What, Alfonso? How was he?"

112

"Slightly agitated."

"Did he say anything?"

"No. Just that he needed to speak to you. What should I say if he contacts me again?

Massimo pondered his sister's words. "Nothing, not yet. Don't tell him that you have spoken to me."

"Massimo…"

"Look I have to go. I will explain everything later. Ciao." He didn't like being that abrupt, but time was of the essence. He quickly reached into his pocket and brought out a piece of scrunched-up paper that Harry had thrust into his hand during the night's festivities. He rang the phone number but there was no answer. He tried several times, still no answer. He looked at the note again. There was an address. He typed the details into the satnav, and in an instant the directions flashed up. Forty minutes away. There was nothing else for it but to drive there immediately and hope that in his drunken state, Harry had given him the correct address.

17

AN UNEXPECTED GUEST

Sometimes it was an effort to fit some of the remaining boxes of food into the tiny bit of space in the cupboard. It often required a shunt of a midriff to force anything in. Just as Mary was contemplating doing this, she heard a familiar voice.

"Here," said Tanya as she held out an inviting cup of tea. "Have this, you look as though you need it."

"Thank you very much. You're absolutely right and it is gratefully received," replied Mary.

"Is everything alright?" asked Tanya.

Mary smiled and sipped her cup of tea. "Yes, yes of course."

"You just seem a little preoccupied that's all."

"Well, I'm okay...mainly."

"What do you mean, mainly?"

Mary hesitated, but in the end couldn't help herself. "Well, it's Harry, he's having a bit of trouble at school. It's just the pressure of the job. I think it's getting to him."

"What's causing it?"

"All sorts, the kids, the management, and he's not getting any younger."

"That must be difficult for him and for you. How's he been this weekend?"

"I think he's ok. On Saturday I sent him off to the caravan to do some fishing and get away from everything. I think he had quite a nice time. He rang me last night to say that he wouldn't be home and that he was going straight to school from the caravan in the morning. But he sounded quite drunk."

"Really. I do hope he's not getting drunk on his own, that can be quite dangerous."

"No, no," interrupted Mary, "he met this Italian man. Well, they didn't so much meet as have an accident." Tanya looked shocked. "It's fine, absolutely fine, just a few scratches and dint on a car. But, and here's the odd thing, Harry discovered this chap was a fellow Caravaggio enthusiast. They ended up having an absolute ball together."

"Really! You don't think they are having an affair, do you?"

Mary chuckled. "Chance would be a fine thing. It might spice up our marriage."

They both laughed and in that moment Mary found herself becoming lighter.

"Someone's enjoying themselves," came a voice from across the hall. "Obviously not working hard enough." They both turned round to see a smiling Mrs Clitheroe walking towards them. "Sorry to disturb your happy moment." She looked at Tanya. "I think we've finished. Is there anything more we need to do?"

Tanya looked around the church hall. The boxes had been tucked away, the trestle tables had been folded up and stacked neatly and the floor had been swept. Any trace of there ever having been a food bank in the church hall had been removed with forensic-like precision. Tanya was, as always, genuinely grateful…

"Very impressive. Yes, yes thank you ever so much Janice I don't know what I would do without you and all the volunteers." The last bit was said loudly so that all could hear. It only added to the good feeling that swept through the ranks as they filed out. The food bank was providing much-needed support for the community. But it was Tanya's positive and affirming character that helped their sense of self-worth. "Well done all of you," she added.

Mary's chest swelled with pride; she was a part of a good team. And as she watched the last volunteer stride out, she suddenly remembered something.

"Oh, by the way, you've left something at the house, a yellow cardigan."

"Oh yes," smiled Tanya, "I wondered where that was."

"Come round and collect it now if you like," said Mary hopefully and then gave her a helpful nudge. "Remember I'm only just down the road."

"Yes, that's a good idea," replied Tanya enthusiastically.

As they gathered their belongings and left the church hall Mary looked out to the sky. It wasn't as sunny as the last time Tanya was round. In fact, it was quite dull. Some grey clouds had started to gather in the north sky. As they began to walk down the lane, Mary felt compelled to say something.

"I am sorry."

"I am not sure what you mean," said Tanya frowning. "What on earth have you got to be sorry for?"

"For Harry," said Mary quickly. "The other day, he was quite rude. He asked me to say sorry for his behaviour. He felt quite bad, he's usually friendlier."

Tanya looked at Mary's pained expression. "It's fine Mary, honestly."

"Are you sure?" said Mary a little unconvinced.

"No, really, it's absolutely fine, really. From what you said he's had a hard time with school and all. The last thing he wanted to see and hear when he came home was two silly women giggling away like stupid teenage girls, especially after a hard day at the office."

"Yes, I suppose," said Mary.

"It was fun though, wasn't it?" said Tanya quick to extinguish any hint of guilt.

"Yes, yes it was," said Mary wistfully. And as she opened the front door and walked inside the house, she became aware that the last remark of Tanya's had rekindled a little spark in her, a feeling of being more alive. She'd forgotten but it was there now. Mary suddenly felt nervous. She quickly walked over and picked up the cardigan.

"Here, here it is." It came out in a rushed kind of way. Tanya's mouth opened. She was about to speak when suddenly there was a loud knock at the door.

Mary jumped. "Who...what?" She looked at Tanya quizzically. "I am not expecting anybody. It can't be Harry, it's too early and he's got a door key. What would he be doing home now anyway?" The knock came again a little louder.

"I had best get that," said Mary. "You never know." They both smiled at each other. Mary then walked down the hallway. When she came to the door she stopped and took in one last deep breath of air and then exhaled slowly. That seemed to do it. The slight anxiety she felt before had now dissipated. She was now much more centred. She opened the door and was instantly taken aback. She didn't recognize the stranger.

"Yes, how can I help you?"

A balding well-dressed figure, early sixties with a neatly trimmed moustache answered.

"Hello. Mrs Jones? Harry Jones's wife?"

"Y...Yes."

"I'm so sorry to disturb you. My name's Massimo I am a friend of your husband."

Mary looked quizzically at the kindly face.

"We were at the same caravan site," exclaimed Massimo.

And then it clicked "Oh you're the fellow Caravaggio nut." Mary laughed.

"Quite," said Massimo sheepishly.

"Sorry I didn't mean to be rude," said Mary apologetically. "I think Harry had a great time. He rang me last night in the middle of your festivities. I've not heard him sound so jolly in absolutely ages."

"Yes, yes," said Massimo recollecting last night's events. There was a pause. "It is Harry I am after. Is he at work?"

"Yes, I am sorry he is."

"Do you know when he will be back?"

Mary thought for a second. "It's Monday," she said out loud. "There are no meetings, he's usually back early, so probably two hours." As Massimo paused and thought about his next words, Mary felt the urge to invite him inside. It was not like her, not with a stranger but right now it seemed necessary.

"Come in, come in," she said effusively. "Oh, this is Tanya,"

"Oh, I'm just going," said Tanya smiling.

"No, no please stay," said Mary frantically. "I don't know M.."

"Massimo."

"I don't know Massimo very well." She turned to him. "I don't know you well." She then turned back to Tanya. "And he

won't be staying for long." She then turned back to Massimo."
You won't, will you Massimo?"

"No, I suppose I won't."

Mary mouthed an exaggerated please to her friend and rolled
her eyes to the heavens. When Tanya agreed, she breathed a
huge sigh of relief. Mary turned back round to Massimo.

"Can I get you a cup of tea?" she said enthusiastically.

"Yes, that would be nice," smiled Massimo.

"I'll help," said Tanya who rushed into the kitchen a pace or
two behind her friend. As soon as they were both together, Mary
felt quite upset. She then hung her head.

"I'm sorry," she said tearfully.

"Don't be, it's fine," replied Tanya reassuringly. "You are
very thoughtful and kind to that man." Tanya reached over and
gave her friend a reassuring squeeze of her arm which seemed to
do the trick. "But I will be going as soon as Massimo is gone,"
Tanya added. Mary nodded meekly in agreement. She felt better
and then it occurred to her.

"I wonder what he wants."

"I have no idea, but I definitely think you should ask him,"
said Tanya. "It does seem strange that he is here."

Mary agreed. And then her husband suddenly popped into
her mind. "I hope Harry's alright. He has done some odd things
in his time. I think he got pretty drunk last night. People do
funny things when they've had a drink. He once stole a traffic
cone. It was on his fortieth. He had no idea. It was only when he
opened the closet door and it spilled out that he realised that
something wasn't right. You know the first thing he did was yell
my name."

Tanya laughed. "That's such a male thing."

They both continued to chuckle away as they walked into the
living room clutching a rather grand tea service. Massimo smiled
as he was offered some cake to go with his Assam tea.

"Thank you this is so.."

"English," chirped Tanya.

"Yes absolutely," said Massimo. He sipped his tea.

"Massimo. That name, is it Italian? But your accent it's quite
English.

Well, I was born and bred in these parts, but I've lived most of my time in Italy. Naples to be precise.

"So, what are you here for?" said Tanya in that forthright way of hers.

"Massimo paused and sipped more of his tea before answering. "I've lost something precious to me, a painting and I am hoping Harry might be able to help."

"Was he very drunk last night?"

Massimo nodded. "I am afraid so."

"Well Harry has done some strange things," confessed Mary, "you know – taken stuff when he has had a few." Mary then told Massimo about the traffic cone fiasco. He smiled meekly. There was a chance that something similar could have happened with the painting. As soon as Massimo had finished his tea, he insisted on waiting for Harry in his car. He didn't want to impose. He thanked them both profusely for their hospitality and bowed his head in deep gratitude. He then sauntered over to the black Audi. Once there he reclined in the front seat and pressed play on his phone. Mozart always helped him to relax. There was a glimmer of hope, but a lot depended on Harry.

18

WHO STOLE WHAT?

Just after lunch, Harry got a note from the office. "Get home quickly you have a visitor." It didn't say who it was, but he didn't need a second invitation to leave early and once the bell went, he was off. Chugging along gently in the school-run traffic, he reflected on the day. After that ridiculous meeting with Cavendish and Edwards, it was largely uneventful, apart from one or two minor episodes.

In the afternoon one year 11 student decided to do PE wearing a Mankini. Apparently, it was a full ten minutes before Hughesy noticed. By all reports, he was furious especially when the boy's genitals popped out. He was promptly sent home.

And then there was Emily Bradshaw who, according to Carruthers, had a fantastic art lesson. Harry was there when he burst into the staff room proud as punch and broadcast it to all who would listen. "Absolutely wonderful she was, a beacon of artistic skill and perseverance." Harry refused to be impressed by this privately educated southern softy and his flowery words. He said as much to Vicky who berated him for his ungenerous attitude towards somebody who was trying to make a difference.

Then there was a stint in the isolation room. There were a few tricky customers who had been sent out of their respective classes but nothing that he could not handle. Scott Luckhurst was there but he was fairly subdued. He could be like that, thought Harry, one minute doing something quite bizarre like locking a teacher in a cupboard or trying to stick a pencil up a student's arse, and then the next minute he'd be completely fine. He could, in fact, be quite a nice lad but he needed help, some proper counselling. Harry said as much to the school's counsellor, Kirsty Hart.

"I couldn't agree more," she said sympathetically, "but I haven't got the time. Have you seen the queues of students outside my door? I'm only on two days a week, I'm full – choc a block. I can sometimes give him the odd half an hour but it's not enough and besides, he needs more specialist help. Unfortunately, he'll be lucky if he's seen within the next eighteen months even though he's had umpteen referrals."

Overstretched and underfunded thought Harry. And the worst part was that this lad would probably flourish with the right help. Harry had a good old moan about this in the staff room and found quite a bit of support for his lament.

It was the last thing on his mind before he pulled up outside his front gate. For a moment he had forgotten about the note and the visitor He was quite looking forward to a nice night in, that is until he heard a voice. It called to him just as he stepped out of the car.

"Harry. Harry, it's me, Massimo."

Harry wheeled round. "Massimo? What on earth are you doing here?"

"I am so sorry," said Massimo apologetically. "I would not be here if it is not important."

"Yes, it must be important if you are here," said Harry considerately. "Do you want to come inside?"

"Yes," said Massimo gratefully, "but you do not need to introduce me to your lovely wife, Mary. I called round earlier."

Harry raised his eyebrows.

"I wasn't sure that it was the right address," explained Massimo, "and I wanted to be here as soon as you got home."

"Well come inside again," said Harry. "You seem a little concerned."

"Yes, yes I suppose I am," replied Massimo.

As they both stepped through the front door, Harry could sense that Massimo was watching him closely. He felt slightly uncomfortable and so turned his attention to Mary in the garden. She smiled and waved at both of them.

"I'll stay out here if you don't mind," she shouted. Harry gave her the thumbs up and then turned round.

"So, Massimo, what is it that is so important that you have driven down here to see me?"

Massimo considered his words carefully. "I have lost something, something very important."

"What do you mean, lost?"

"I had it safely tucked away in my suitcase and now it is not there."

"And you've looked all over, in and around the area?"

"Of course," interrupted Massimo forcefully. He paused. "And what is more, I know that just before we had our drink, it was there. I saw it just before I saw you."

"I am not sure…"

"Harry, if you have it please give it back."

Harry was taken aback by the authority in Massimo's voice. "I'm not sure…I'm not sure what it is that I might have," stuttered Harry. "I was pretty pissed. I don't remember but I know that I would never knowingly take anything that was not mine. Yes, I am positive."

Massimo said nothing but looked directly at Harry. It unnerved him. There was something unyielding about the Italian's grimace that seemed to fix him to the spot. And in that moment he knew that if he was lying, he would be found out. Harry was shaken. This was a completely different person. He was now sterner and possessed a stare that chilled him to the bone. It seemed to be an age before Massimo eventually relented.

"I'm sorry," he said slipping back into his more agreeable character. "I had to be sure."

But Harry was angry. "What? You had to be sure about me not lying ? Of course, I'm bloody well not lying!" He took a moment or two to recover. "I still don't get it," he stuttered. "You had to be sure. Do I look like a thief? Christ!"

Massimo smiled apologetically. "Mary told me about the traffic cone. Are you sure you didn't take it, not knowing. A slim silver case with a painting inside."

"No, I didn't. I am quite sure," said Harry sternly. And then it occurred to him. "Mary told you about the traffic cone? What else did she tell you about me?"

"I know that you are angry," said Massimo, "but please…"

"Look Massimo that was done for a laugh," spluttered Harry. "Once it fell out of the cupboard, I remembered what I had done, but I can assure you that I have not done anything like that with anything of yours. Why would I? It wouldn't be fun."

And then it went quiet. After a moment's reflection, Massimo spoke.

"It's a painting Harry, a very valuable painting, and it is very dear to me."

"I understand," said Harry calming down. "Look we can look in my car now."

"Do you mind?" said Massimo politely.

"Well, yes I do, but if it satisfies you then I am happy to oblige."

They marched over to Harry's car. Nothing was found but Massimo would not relent...

"Your caravan?"

"What? You want me to drive down now?"

"It's very important Harry."

Reluctantly Harry agreed.

After a forty-minute drive, a long search around every nook and cranny of his caravan and a final look in the car, Harry turned to Massimo, "See! Nothing there." But Massimo didn't look satisfied, he looked glum. "It must mean a lot to you," said Harry sympathetically.

Massimo nodded. "More than you think. His shoulders then dropped. Harry could see how upset he was and tried to lighten his mood.

"It's not a Caravaggio, is it?"

Massimo said nothing.

It was the seriousness etched all over the Italian's face that made Harry suddenly think the unthinkable. He repeated the question, "Massimo it's not a Caravaggio, please tell me it's not."

Silence.

"Oh, my Lord! It is! How on earth? Is it really a Caravaggio? Are you sure? How?"

"It does not matter how or why I have it, but I need to get it back. Do you understand Harry? I need to get it back." With Massimo's connections, Harry understood all too well. "Think Harry, think," urged Massimo. "Was there anything you noticed?" But Harry was still in a state of shock. All he could do was mumble.

"A Caravaggio, a bloody Caravaggio."

"Harry!" shouted Massimo.

"No, no I…I don't think so."

"Think again, a detail, something small?"

"No, I'm sorry." Harry then gathered his thoughts. "Have we any idea who was nearby?"

Massimo then explained all that he had done and the people he'd questioned.

"And Ray, what did he say?" Massimo looked bemused. "Ray, the old man at reception."

Massimo shook his head.

"Do you mind if I question him?" asked Harry. "I know him, he might be more forthcoming with me. He can be a bit meandering, and he doesn't care for foreigners, but he's got good eyes."

"Be my guest," sighed Massimo.

Harry led the way back down the path on the now dreadfully familiar walk to the reception.

Massimo's pace had slowed. He didn't look forward to revisiting the conversation with the old man.

"Ah Mr Jones," said Ray as the two walked in the door. (He ignored Massimo) "What can I do for you?" It was said in quite a bright and cheerful manner.

"He wasn't like this with me this morning," whispered Massimo.

"Old Ray can be quite warm and friendly," replied Harry, "you've just got to know the right buttons to press." He turned to Ray.

"Ah Raymondo my old friend," he effused, "what a fine establishment you run…quite ship-shape if you don't mind me saying."

"Well, I do pride myself…"

"Pride? Nonsense," said Harry. "A man like you from such humble origins, there is not a hint of arrogance. You are a fine and honourable man."

"Thank you," said Ray smiling.

"Now then," said Harry in a softer tone, "as you know my friend here has lost something valuable, maybe even had it taken. I...We were wondering if you may be able to shed some light on the matter."

Massimo could not help but be impressed by Harry's charm. He saw the effect it had on Ray who gave the matter much more serious consideration.

"Hmmm."

"Think Ray, think," urged Harry.

After a long silence, Ray spoke

"Well...erm, no I'm sorry. There was nothing that I can think of."

But Harry noted the hesitation. "There was something Ray, you were going to say something."

"Well yes, a couple of things went missing...not at all valuable so I can't think why anybody would take them. I thought I'd mislaid them but..."

"What things?" enquired Harry.

"Well, my remote control for the telly." Ray pointed to the screen just above Massimo's head. "Went missing a couple of days ago. Never could find it. I 'ad to go into the city centre, get myself a new 'un. Pain in the arse it was."

Something started to flicker in Harry's mind. "You said a couple of things, the other one, let me guess a pen, a key?"

"Yes, a pen. It was on my desk. I went inside the back to make a cuppa and when I came back it wasn't there. But nobody had been in. Strange."

"Could I have a look at your contact details of the people who have stayed this weekend?" said Harry forcefully.

"Do you know something?" said Massimo expectantly.

"Maybe," said Harry, "it is a long shot."

But Ray hesitated. He clutched a folder to his chest. "I am not sure I can give you this, Harry. Data protection and all that."

Massimo brought out his wallet, but Harry quickly pushed it away. "I understand completely. Ray, you are an honourable man but it's just the names I want to see not the contact details. I might recognise somebody." Hesitantly Ray handed over the folder. Harry looked through them and suddenly pulled one out.

"Ray, did you check any of these?

"Well, I look through them quickly but…"

Harry handed Ray a form… "Look at the names on this one."

"May and Lee King," said Ray.

"Yes, with daughters Fay and Jo," added Harry. Ray looked perplexed. "You still don't get it, do you?" Harry Then spelt it out. "Lee-king, may-king, jo-king and fay-king. Do you get it now?"

"Oh yes," said Ray, "very clever."

Harry turned to Massimo. "We can try the contact details, but I will bet you that they are fake.

"Nevertheless, we must try," said Massimo. He dialled the number quickly but soon found out that it didn't exist.

"Look at the email address," said Harry "jo-kingandfay-king@gmail.com. No, we will not be able to contact them, but tell me Ray, was it by any chance a girl who filled in the form, can you remember?"

"No, I never let youngsters fill in the forms," he said, hurt by the fact that Harry would even think such a thing. "No, it's got to be the parents or an adult."

Harry frowned but then Ray remembered something. "But she, a girl did hand it to me. Yes, but she was so sweet, very polite not at all like some of them."

"They can be like that," said Harry. "I'm always wary of a young teenager being too polite. It doesn't suit them. You say she handed it to you?"

"Yes, her mother had a bit of a migraine you see – filled the form out in the car or at least I thought she did."

"This girl… light brown mousy hair, quite thin probably got her hair tied back?"

"Yes, that sounds about right."

"And the mother?"

"I didn't see much of her; she was sitting in the car."

"Father?"

"No, I never saw him."

"Anybody else in the car?"

"I think there was another girl."

Harry wasn't expecting that, but suddenly it made sense.

"This other girl, glasses, blonde hair, about the same age?"

"Maybe. I couldn't tell, yes, I think so."

Harry thought for a second and then remembered something from last night that confirmed his suspicions. He looked at Massimo's eager face and then turned to Ray. "Thank you. You have been most helpful.

As he watched Mr Jones and his friend march off, Ray felt pleased with himself; so pleased in fact that he forgot to tell Massimo that someone had called round asking for him – a quite ordinary man in jeans and sweater, quite average really. "Oh well," said Ray out loud, "probably not that important."

19

A CUNNING PLAN

"Who is Emily Bradshaw?" said Massimo stepping into Harry's car.

"One of my students," said Harry shaking his head. "Those missing items, it is her modus operandi." He then turned to his friend. "A quite malevolent spirit, very cunning and opportunistic. Of course, it may not have been her who stole your painting, but I am quite certain that she was at the caravan site. It's not just the odd missing item, it's that joke name thing. She's used it before, usually to new staff when they ask who she is. She tells them it's Fay King, sometimes it's even been Vi King."

"But how did...?"

"If it was her, she probably bided her time. Once she recognised me, she lay in wait. She saw us drinking together...maybe even thought it was my caravan."

"But I never left without locking up...not even a trip to the toilet."

"She would have found a way believe me, slippery as an eel that one." Harry turned on the ignition. The Astra started up first time. "If it's her there's still a chance we can get it. She won't have done anything with it yet for sure. We call her the magpie. She steals things and then puts them in her 'nest'."

"And where is her 'nest'?"

"Well, it was her locker at school but I have no doubt she has one at home." Harry looked down at the details he'd obtained from the school office. "Hmmm it's the Dreadnought Estate

"Is that something we should be concerned about?" enquired Massimo.

"Could be," replied Harry. "It's quite a notorious neighbourhood."

"How long before we get there?"

"About thirty minutes."

Massimo suddenly had a thought. "What about the others in the car?"

"Ah yes, Mrs Beavis and her daughter. At least that's my guess. They sometimes take Emily out with them on trips. Mrs Beavis is a churchgoer. She thinks Emily can be saved; she would have no idea about what has been taken. Matilda might, she often stands there in admiration of her friend's exploits but there is no way that she would be directly involved. No, Emily works alone." Harry frowned. "I'm not sure what we are going to do when we get there. I don't have a plan, do you?"

Massimo shook his head. "Not at this precise moment, but thank you, Harry, thank you for doing this, thank you for driving me."

"No problem," said Harry, and indeed it wasn't. He felt rather excited. This was a little adventure involving the Mafia and a stolen Caravaggio. Episodes like this don't come along very often and Harry was going to try to make the most of it.

But when they arrived at the address, he felt nervous. Some heavy rain spitting on his windscreen added to his anxiety. The clouds that had gathered earlier were now spilling their contents over the red-bricked, non-descript houses of the Dreadnought Estate. Harry suddenly felt hemmed in. His breathing became shallower. What if somebody recognised him? He put his flat cap on, slid down in his seat and peered out of the car window, furtively.

"What are you doing?" said Massimo. "Please act normal."

"Yes of course," said Harry sheepishly. He quickly shifted to a more upright position.

"Much better, Harry. Now, we may have to stay here and watch the house for a while," Massimo looked at Harry. "We do not want to draw attention to ourselves, do we?"

"Absolutely not," said Harry effusively. "Absolutely not." Suddenly he was more than happy to let Massimo assume the reigns. Now that there was an element of subterfuge and cunning involved, he was happy to defer to a member of the Clan.

"This girl," said Massimo, "this Emily Bradshaw, how will she react if we question her?"

"From my experience, she will flatly deny anything." Harry shook his head. "The very fact that you question her on the matter will no doubt alert her to the fact that she will have stolen something important. She will be reluctant to simply hand it over or in any way admit that she even has it. Of course, she may not have it. We may be barking up the wrong tree."

"No, she has it," said Massimo assertively.

"What makes you so sure?" said Harry quizzically.

"I've just realized the belt from one of my pairs of trousers has gone. I may not have packed it but..."

As Massimo let the sentence trail off Harry grimaced. "It sounds like the sort of thing she'd do."

We have to be careful how we tread," said Massimo thoughtfully. "What about money? What if we offer her some cash?"

"Again, tricky," said Harry. "Emily has a very good sense of the value of things. Once you offer her money she will, again, be alerted to the fact that she has something valuable. So, whatever you offer, she will refuse – at first anyway. It depends how much time you have."

"I don't have any," replied Massimo.

"Well, it could take a few days, she'll barter for sure. By the sound of things that may not be an option."

"No, perhaps not," said Massimo pensively. He looked up. "But thank you, Harry, you have been and are being most helpful." He paused for a second. "I would not blame you if you wanted to drive back."

"No, absolutely not."

"Thank you again, Harry." There was a slight pause as if Massimo wanted to emphasise his gratitude. He then continued. "Would Emily have told her parents?"

"No. I would say not."

"Do you think it would be a good idea for us to talk to parents?"

"Not sure. They don't strike me as the most honourable. The school has a red flag against them. I know that social services are involved, perhaps even the police."

"Do we know what the problem is?"

"No, but rumour has it that they are involved in some of the more criminal aspects of the local community. So, if we are not careful, they may become involved. But I suppose with your background that would not worry you."

Massimo frowned. "Whilst it is true that I have had dealings with the more criminal aspects of Neapolitan society, I am never overconfident, Harry, particularly where people are concerned. Sometimes I am nervous. The secret is never to show that you are nervous. I do, however, think we must be careful and cunning."

"I think you're right," said Harry, "but do not underestimate her."

"She is just a girl, Harry."

Harry shook his head and said nothing. Massimo was going to have to find out the hard way, that is, if they managed to catch up with her. There followed a few minutes silence until Massimo eventually spoke again.

"We need to search their house. It will not need to be in all the rooms just her bedroom. Of course, we do not know which one is hers, but looking at their house the bedrooms are small; (and) it will not take long for us to search. There will only be a few places where the painting can be hidden, behind the wardrobe under the bed, in a drawer. I think five, maybe six minutes. It will be difficult, there appears to be somebody in the front room. We need to find some way of getting whoever is in there out and we also need to find a way of entering the house undetected."

"How do you propose we do that?"

"Have you anything that is combustible or can burn Harry, a newspaper, a book?" Harry looked around. There was nothing apart from Andrew Dixon's book on Caravaggio.

"I'm sorry, Harry, I know it is profane." Massimo then took the book from the back seat and began tearing up the pages and screwing them up."

"Is that necessary?" said Harry alarmed at what he was seeing.

"Absolutely."

"But it is a signed copy."

131

"Do not worry, Harry, I will replace it." Massimo then went quiet as he became engrossed in scrunching up the paper in a very deliberate manner. After a minute or two, he was happy with what he'd made. "There, it is finished," he declared. "It is crude, but I think it will do the trick." He turned to Harry. "When this goes off, we have to be ready."

"When what goes off?"

Massimo never answered. He was already out of the car. Harry saw him walk a few paces down the road, unscrew the petrol cap off what looked like an old Citroen and stuff a ball of sacred and profane paper just inside. He then lit it and ran back to their car. He stopped just outside the passenger door and gestured to Harry to wind down the window.

"It is a common misconception," he said putting his head through the window, "that when the petrol tank of a car is set alight there is an explosion, but that is not what happens. It just bursts into flames, but just in case, I will wait and see if any pedestrians are walking close by, and I will alert them of a possible danger. We don't want a nasty accident, do we?"

"Well, that's bloody good of you," said Harry, agitated.

"However, you may still want to put your fingers in your ear," said Massimo smiling. "You never know."

Harry slowly did as Massimo suggested. "I STILL DON'T UNDERSTAND," he shouted.

Massimo smiled as if to say it's alright don't worry. And then it happened. As Massimo predicted, it wasn't a big explosion, but it did go whoosh! A few seconds later and the car was alight.

"We needed a distraction," said Massimo, "that would bring all the neighbours out including Emily Bradshaw and her family."

"Yes, well, you haven't disappointed me on that one," said Harry. "There's nothing like a fire for getting everybody out."

"Precisely," said Massimo as the flames started to grow.

And then it occurred to Harry that his friend may have done something like this before. It all seemed very easy. Suddenly all and sundry poured out of their houses. There was no attempt by anyone to put out the fire, instead, they encircled the flaming, smoking car like a sea of ants swarming its prey. Harry watched on as youngsters threw anything they could find onto the burning heap. Parents chatted to each other and wrapped a protective arm around the very youngest. Occasionally stones were thrown in for absolutely no reason. It was quite a spectacle. Harry almost missed her but just out of the corner of his eye he spotted Emily.

"There, there she is but I'm not sure who she is with, maybe stepbrothers, I think that's stepdad. They look a bit odd, don't they?"

"No time to dwell on that," said Massimo cutting Harry short. "You stay here."

"Where?"

"Right here in the car. Be my lookout. Use the horn if you see them coming back in."

"Right," said Harry. "Right." He watched as Massimo stepped across the road up to the white front door and glided through the entrance as easily as a knife through butter.

"Sweet," said Harry out loud. For a second or two, he relished the subterfuge that he was involved in but then the doubts crept in. What on earth was he doing here? Why didn't he just bid Massimo adieu and wave him goodbye back at the house? A strange feeling of loyalty to his friend, and an allegiance to the painting had swept over him. To take part in the rescue of a Caravaggio, well that would be something to tell Mary.

But right now, his patience was being tested. Five minutes had elapsed, and Massimo was still not out. One or two of the residents were returning inside. With every second that ticked by, Harry could feel his anxiety increasing.

Suddenly there was a bang on his passenger door. It was a shock and made Harry jump. He quickly turned round. Two little urchins were squashing their faces up against the car window and deliberately making their noses go all flat. They were laughing as they did it, but Harry wasn't finding it funny.

"Oi, piss off," he said aggressively.

Suddenly one of them spat on his window and rubbed green/yellow phlegm all over the glass. The other put the middle finger up and shouted, "Fuckin' pervert!" Harry was incensed.

"Why you disgusting, little…"

And then they ran off. Bloody kids thought Harry. I know I was one once and I was no angel, but I never behaved like that. Suddenly he realised that his attention had been diverted. He wheeled round desperately hoping that he hadn't missed anything. The door was still ajar. Phew. But where was Emily Bradshaw? His eyes moved rapidly around the scene. He couldn't see her. Oh no! Panic. Harry tried to bib the horn, but no sound was coming out. He tried again, pumping away like a first aider doing CPR. Still nothing. "Shit!" He was pressing the wrong area. "Shit!" He pressed again this time it worked. He pressed several more times, six short blasts and then one long one. He expected Massimo to come running out possibly with a stolen painting in hand. He expected it to happen immediately. After twenty seconds he was still optimistic. But after a couple of minutes, he began to worry. After five, he realised that something had gone wrong.

20

A FINE MESS

At first, everything was fine. As Massimo entered the hallway he deliberately coughed. Nobody came out, the house was empty. Good. He coughed again and shouted hello just to be sure. No sound, nothing to hear but there was also nothing to see. The house was sparse. A loose hallway carpet partially covered old grey floorboards. A peep through the living room door showed little improvement. Basic furniture, big telly and no pictures on the wall. There was a smell of lighter fluid mixed with a hint of marijuana and lemony disinfectant. He'd seen and smelt this kind of place before in some of the back streets of Naples. No matter said Massimo to himself as he strode purposely up the stairs.

He opened the door to the first bedroom A king-sized waterbed dominated the space, clearly not Emily's. The second room was a grubby smelly affair that featured two single beds, a huge television, and young men's clothes strewn across the floor. Nothing much there. He stepped inside the third bedroom. The first thing that struck Massimo was the array of drawings blue tacked onto the bright pink walls. One, in particular, caught his eye – a chalk and charcoal late renaissance-style portrait with heavy use of chiaroscuro. He recognised it straight away. He was in the right place. He quickly knelt down and started searching feverishly underneath the bed. As he did so the door slammed behind him and a key turned the lock. He leapt up straight away and tried the handle but couldn't open the door. He was locked in.

Just then a car horn started tooting furiously. "Too late Harry," said Massimo softly, "too late. Merda," cursed Massimo.

"Murder? Steady on, no one's being murdered," came a girl's voice from the other side of the door.

"Forgive me," said Massimo politely. "Merda is shit in Italian."

There was a stifled giggle. "Well, you live and learn every day, don't you?"

"Yes, I suppose you do," replied Massimo meekly. He went to the window. There was no way he could climb down. He continued to search the room for anything, anything that would help. Underneath the bed, there was something, an old photograph in a small box. It wasn't what he was looking for nor did he expect to see it. He took it and put it in his pocket.

"Are you going to keep me here?" enquired Massimo.

"That depends," said Emily.

"On what?" enquired Massimo.

"On how cooperative you are."

He shook his head and smiled. Although he was annoyed at the predicament he was now in, there was a begrudging admiration for the ingenuity and brazenness of this young girl. But what was she going to do next? What did she mean by 'how cooperative you are'? What exactly did this Emily Bradshaw have in mind?

21

EMILY'S STORY

Emily walked over to the small sink in the corner of the caravan and turned the tap on. She had to wait a few seconds before the water came out. "It might not be that cold," she shouted.

"Not to worry," said Matilda trying her best to be as cheerful and as appreciative as possible. Emily shook her head. It wasn't enough that her friend was ill, now she was having to get her a glass of bloody water. "Here, take this," she declared. Matilda did as she was told and took the glass of water with both hands.

"Thank you," she said gratefully. She took three large gulps and inadvertently slammed the glass down. "That's better. Oh. I'm sorry for that slam. I didn't mean it and I'm sorry for being a bit sicky. It's not going to be much fun, is it? For you I mean?"

"No, it's not," said Emily caustically.

"I'm sorry," said Matilda tearfully. "I really am."

Emily smiled faintly. She hated Matilda's grovelling.

"I'm sorry I'm sick," repeated Matilda, "I know I'm whining…"

"Yes, you are, so shut the fuck up."

"Yes, yes I will," said Matilda submissively.

Emily shook her head. It was too easy. She could be as mean as she liked, and Matilda would still come back for more. She was so adept at making people feel small. Even older teenagers were wary of her.

"You know your mum asked me if I wanted to go to church with her this morning. Ha! Really? Do I look as though I would be remotely interested in spending this morning with a load of crusty old coffin dodgers?" She turned to Matilda. "You go sometimes, don't you?"

"Sometimes."

"Does it do any good?"

"Sometimes."

Emily thought for a minute and then watched as Matilda's eyelids grew heavy.

"It might do you some good," said Matilda as she lay her head down on the pillow.

"What do you mean?"

"All that stealin'," mumbled Matilda slowly sinking into the land of nod.

Emily bristled. "What do you mean?" But Matilda had gone. Her soft snoring only added to Emily's indignation. How irritating! It wasn't just that her friend had fallen asleep, Emily would have liked to reply. She would have told Matilda that going to church wouldn't help, because God didn't care and besides, she liked thieving too much.

It was the act of taking rather than any financial gain that gave her the rush. Things didn't have to be valuable. Sometimes they just had to be lying there, out in the open ready to be removed. If it inconvenienced people or just plain baffled them, then all the better. To see that look on their face or hear their befuddlement… "I'm sure I had that a minute or two ago, what on earth," or even "what the hell?" The teachers were the best. They were such easy targets, so naïve, leaving their classrooms unattended with bright shiny remote controls there waiting to be grabbed.

Emily looked around the caravan. There were a few things there to take but it wasn't worth it, no real challenge. She also found it difficult to steal from the Beavis's. She had taken a couple of things including an old photo, but she told herself that she was only borrowing them.

Just then the door opened and in walked Mrs Beavis in a prim white shirt and a bright yellow jacket. She smelled of church.

"Ah, Emily, how are you? Thank you for looking after Matilda. Is she…sleeping?"

Emily nodded. "I think she's fine, just tired."

"She's probably had what I had….it doesn't last long. Hopefully, she will be okay in the afternoon. Anyway, it will give me a chance to talk to you. How are you, really?"

It was Mrs. Beavis's earnest look that unnerved Emily. She hated people caring for her or sounding as though they meant well. She gave a short reply.

"Yeah alright."

"What do you mean alright?"

Here we go again, thought Emily. It wasn't that Mrs Beavis over did the God thing, it's just that after a good church service she seemed particularly caring. Okay, thought Emily to herself, let's give her a little bit of what she wants.

"Well, I know that I can be challenging but I am working hard to alter my patterns of behaviour."

"I'm not sure what you mean?" said Mrs Beavis smiling.

"The educational psychologist said that early childhood trauma can sometimes be responsible for the brain forming different neural pathways and wiring itself quite differently from the norm. That's the reason I can be so difficult and destructive. So, to combat this I am doing some meditation."

"Oh really," said Mrs Beavis disbelievingly.

"Yes absolutely. I find that doing something peaceful gives me some peace."

"Hmm. Well, how about doing a jigsaw puzzle with me, that's peaceful." Mrs Beavis then stretched over and brought out a 500-piece version of Van Gogh's sunflowers from the top shelf. Normally, Emily would turn her nose up at such an activity but, for whatever reason, she felt compelled to try it. As they started sorting out the edge pieces, Mrs Beavis opened a new avenue of questioning.

"Matilda tells me you are close to permanent exclusion, is this true?"

Emily shrugged her shoulders. "I suppose."

"I know you've had a difficult home life and things haven't been easy, but you know you owe it to yourself to try to get through." Emily listened. Mrs Beavis had a good heart, but the full truth of the matter was that she liked doing the things that she did. She once overheard a teacher referring to her as subversive and having looked up the meaning. She couldn't agree more, and what's more, she was proud of it.

"Emily are you still with me?"

"Yes, of course."

"And family, how are they treating you?"

"Fine, fine."

Emily could always put up a good front, but it wasn't fine. It was her dad, Jimmy, he was the worst. According to him, "If it ain't nailed down it deserves to be taken." Emily always used that mantra to justify her activities, but the family was never interested in what she had acquired. Terry, her stepbrother, poured scorn over the trinkets she brought home. "What a pile of crap. You must 'ave 'ad shit in your eyes." None of her stepbrothers were nice to her. From an early age, she knew it was something to do with her being a girl and having a different mother. She was the "little bastard runt." If only it would have been the "clever little bastard runt," that would have made her feel better – she knew she was smart.

The jigsaw only kept her interested for so long. In no time at all, Emily started to get bored. Matilda had recovered only slightly and conversations with her were brief and uninteresting. Mrs Beavis had done her best to keep her occupied, but Emily had to get away, and soon.

"I'm going for a walk," she suddenly pronounced. Mrs Beavis realised straight away that there was no point in trying to persuade her otherwise. She did, however, ask one question. It was rather nervously put.

"How long will… ?"

"About an hour," interrupted Emily as she waltzed out of the caravan door. As soon as she was out of sight she breathed a deep sigh of freedom. It was good to get away from the claustrophobia of a loving family. She spent the next hour wandering around aimlessly. She couldn't get a signal for her phone which increased her boredom. She was fast concluding that returning to the jig-saw was the only viable course of action when she came across a familiar figure, glugging away on a large glass of wine. Mr Jones! She watched transfixed as he and a strange bald-headed man continued to knock back the vino. She knew that if she stuck around then some opportunity would present itself. It wasn't long before her patience was rewarded.

As Mr Jones went to stand up, one of his legs suddenly buckled as though the weight of his upper body was too heavy a load to bear. Emily started to chuckle impishly as she watched him stumble around pissed as a fart. Suddenly this tiny boring world of caravans and their accessories seemed full of possibilities, and it got even better. Jones lost his balance and fell arse over elbow. And as the strange bald-headed guy tried to pick him up, he followed suit. For a second it appeared as though they were involved in some odd kind of strange homo-erotic wrestling match.

Emily saw her chance. She quickly nipped inside Massimo's caravan. Instinctively, she went straight under the bed to where the suitcase was and scurried through the contents. She found the thin silver case and without looking at what was inside, took it. The whole episode took no more than one minute. But as she stepped outside Jones clocked her. She wasn't worried, in fact she laughed as his rather shaky finger tried to point in her direction. She even laughed some more at the look of horror on his face. But she couldn't linger and enjoy the moment too much. The other guy was more with it, less pissed. If he saw her it may be difficult so, she quickly turned away and glided effortlessly into the dark recesses of the night.

As she approached her own caravan, she saw the curtains move and quickly threw the case underneath the caravan. The relieved face of Mrs Beavis appeared at the window none the wiser. As she stepped inside, she told herself that Jones was so pissed that he wouldn't remember anything but even if he did, she wasn't particularly bothered. She could just deny it. Nevertheless, Emily thought it prudent to be prepared, to have some story ready should Mr Jones remember and want to question her. It would be a completely ridiculous story. She would have great fun thinking it up.

The following day, memories of those events resurfaced as she saw Mr Jones parked across the road from her house. She had to do a double take. She wouldn't have noticed him if he hadn't looked so odd. Slinking halfway down his seat trying to make himself look invisible, what on earth was he thinking? Emily laughed out loud.

She watched through a gap in the curtains and saw a rather portly figure leave Mr Jones's car and trot over to a car nearby. She couldn't quite make out what he was doing but the next moment, whoosh – the car burst into flames. Emily rocked back in her chair. "I wasn't expecting that!"

As the whole neighbourhood stormed out of their houses, Emily followed suit, but kept half an eye on what was happening nearby. She noticed the bald guy make his move and in no time at all he was in her house. So, he's the thief! thought Emily, and good old Mr Jones is the lookout. Not bad, not bad. Then she had an idea. She quickly walked over to the two MacDougal brothers, who were busy throwing stones at the flaming car, and whispered in their ears.

"Don't look round but an old fat guy is sitting in a blue car opposite our house. He's a pervert, he's waiting for a chance to flash his todger. I dare you to go over there and do something, something that will piss him off and make him go away."

The two tiny terrors licked their lips in anticipation, wheeled round, and then ran towards the Astra with mischief in their eyes. Emily watched with glee as one of them spat out a ball of green and yellow phlegm on the window of the car. As soon as Harry's attention was diverted, Emily darted back towards the house. Once inside, she spied the stranger entering her room. Quick as a flash, she leapt upstairs, shut the door, and then turned the key.

"Merda," cried a voice from behind the door.

"Murder? Steady on, no one's being murdered."

"Forgive me, Merda is shit in Italian."

"Well, you live and learn every day, don't you?"

"Yes, I suppose you do. Are you going to keep me here?"

"That depends," said Emily.

"On what?"

"On how cooperative you are." A brief silence followed before Emily continued.

"So, what's a stranger doing in my house?"

"I'm so sorry I was a little dazed…the car, the explosion. Where am I?"

"You'll have to do better than that. I watched you leap up the stairs. Certainly didn't look dazed to me. Now I wonder what the police would do?"

"Please, I am not sure…"

"Mind you when my brothers and their mates come back in it could be worse."

"I was looking for something," said Massimo seriously.

"That's better. Now you are cooperating. And what was it that you were looking for?"

"Something personal that I had lost."

"And you thought that I had it underneath my bed?"

"No. Well, yes, possibly. Please there has been a mistake. If you could just let me out, I will not harm you."

"How do I know you won't?"

"I give you my word. I mistook you for somebody else. I think she took it."

"Took what?"

"I am not sure I can tell you."

"Well in a minute my brothers will be here so unless you start talking…"

"Okay, okay. I think that you took something of mine, a painting that is very dear to me."

"Why not just knock on the door and ask me for it back, talk to my parents, or better still why not ring the police?"

Massimo sighed, shook his head, and muttered quietly. "This girl Emily Bradshaw. She is as wily as a fox."

"What's that?" said Emily, "I can't quite hear you."

"Because if it is you that has stolen it, you may not be inclined to just hand it over and for various reasons, I do not wish for the police to be involved."

"And what reasons are they?"

Massimo stayed silent so Emily changed tack a little.

"How did you find me?"

"I am resourceful."

"I think Mr Jones told you."

"Mr who?"

"You know, your little accomplice, the one in the car, the one that tooted the horn a bit too late."

Emily chuckled. Massimo stayed silent.

Just then the front door opened and in walked the rest of the Bradshaws, lots of them.

"I'm going to let you out but don't run," whispered Emily through the door. Those voices they are my clan if you run, they'll 'ave you. Just do as I say and go along with me." She undid the lock and opened her bedroom door. Massimo stepped outside and felt Emily's arm push him to the bathroom; at the same time, she took her water bottle and sprayed Massimo's crotch.

"What...why?" sputtered a very confused Massimo. As her brothers looked up Emily patted Massimo on the back.

"Poor bastard 'e was right by the car when it went up in flames, 'es wet 'imself. I think 'es a bit ...you know. I said 'e could use our bathroom." Massimo was still pretty befuddled so he didn't need to act. He looked down at his damp crotch and muttered something in Italian

"Poor bastard doesn't know much English either." She turned to Massimo and spoke very slowly. "Are...you... okay?" Massimo was still quite confused but utterly transfixed with young Bradshaw's performance. Emily continued her affected pidgin English only this time a bit louder. "You... know... where... you... go?" She then did a thing with her fingers that simulated walking. Massimo nodded.

"Si, si senora. Grazie," said Massimo. She then practically pushed him down the stairs. He nodded politely as he shunted past a bemused group of gangly youths, their hoodies up, phones out and mouths agog.

22

ONWARDS AND UPWARDS

As soon as Harry saw Massimo step out of the front door unscathed, he breathed a great sigh of relief. But that feeling soon evaporated as there in the background smiling away and shouting, 'Arrivederci' was Bradshaw, Emily bloody Bradshaw. Just before she shut the door, she gave a little wave. Harry was sure it was aimed at him and not Massimo. "Damn," he said loudly. He half tried to hide his face with his hand but was painfully aware that it looked stupid, so he stopped.

"Yes, she knows you are here," affirmed Massimo stepping into the car.

"Never mind that," said Harry. "Are you okay? I don't understand. What was she doing there? Did you get caught?"

"Yes, Harry, I got caught," scowled Massimo.

"What was she doing just then?" asked Harry. "Why was she smiling and bidding you farewell in Italian?"

"Probably showing off," replied Massimo. "That Emily Bradshaw, she is a formidable opponent. I have underestimated her," he sighed. Harry felt like saying I told you so but thought better of it, "Unfortunately," continued Massimo, "I think that she is now fully aware that she has in her possession something valuable. I do not think that she is aware of quite how valuable, but it may not be long before she has an idea. Whatever we do we need to act quickly."

"We?" said Harry. "I am not sure I want to be associated with you. You have just made yourself known, along with me, to one of the more dangerous families of the Dreadnought Estate, you've just blown up a car, and one of the wiliest most cunning students that I have taught has something on me."

"My apologies," replied Massimo. "But in my defence, it is only a vehicle that has been hurt, and the car is most probably insured. If it helps, I have noted the number plate and hope that I can provide some reimbursement for the inconvenience but," said Massimo steadfastly, "I will do what it takes to get the painting back. If you want to take no further part in this, I am already grateful. You have done more than enough."

Harry saw the hard resolute look on Massimo's face and for a second wondered how much more than blowing up cars he had been involved in, but then Harry felt strangely compelled to see it through. "No, I'm in," he said firmly. "Just don't go setting any more cars alight."

"Absolutely not," said Massimo lying through his teeth.

"Where are we going?" said Harry as he drove past the last few houses of the Dreadnought Estate. "Shall I drive to my house?" Massimo was deep in thought and took the time to respond. Eventually, he spoke.

"Yes, I think so."

Harry was relieved. He didn't want to hang around the estate. He certainly didn't want to be around the Bradshaws.

"I think," said Massimo thoughtfully, "that the painting may be at school."

"Really. What makes you think that?" said Harry surprised.

"Because it wasn't in her room, and I am thinking that maybe she has had an art lesson today." Harry looked perplexed so Massimo explained. "I saw her drawings. I saw a copy of my painting of the Caravaggio on the wall."

Harry still looked puzzled. "I am not sure I follow."

"She took the painting in, probably in a portfolio," stated Massimo. "That way it wouldn't be noticed and then she drew from it in her art lesson in chalk and charcoal — materials from an art class." Massimo looked at Harry. "She does take art?"

"Yes," said Harry suddenly cottoning on.

"She took her drawing home and left the painting inside her portfolio at school. And why wouldn't she? It was probably more convenient to leave it there. At that time, she had no idea of its value."

"Right," said Harry. And then he saw through Emily's eyes the wicked irony of it all. Not only to have stolen the painting,

146

but to work from it in school underneath his nose. And she would have delighted in courting the outlandish praise of her art teacher. And then he remembered

"Carruthers. Oh God, he came in the staffroom at lunch positively wetting himself in ecstasy."

"I beg your pardon, Harry?"

"Oh, the art teacher," said Harry disdainfully. "He was ridiculously delighted in Emily Bradshaw working well for him. He practically had an orgasm." He looked at Massimo. "Was her drawing a good rendition?"

"Yes, surprisingly good."

Harry shook his head. "I am surprised he didn't bring Emily's work into the staffroom and show it off, make us all feel inadequate. He usually does. Any shitty kid that does anything, whoosh - straight in the staffroom, shows everybody. You know he's really saying how good *he* is."

"Maybe he's just enthusiastic."

"No, no he's 'sucky-uppy'. I've heard that he plays tennis with Cavendish. I can just hear him now. "Oh, good shot Michael, oh wonderful sir. Definitely one of the brown nosers. Probably got his nose halfway up Cavendish's back crack, snivelling away."

"Harry! Please!"

"Sorry. Yes, you are right I am just getting carried away."

"It is okay my friend. On another day I might chuckle at such remarks, but we need to keep a clear head. And Harry, right now we need to turn round and go to your school."

"Yes, of course."

Almost immediately there was a space in the road. Without hesitation, Harry executed a rather nifty U-turn. Emboldened by this manoeuvre, he gripped the steering wheel of the Astra tightly and thrust his chin out. "Onward and upward then."

Massimo smiled and winced at the same time. "Yes Harry, onward and upward."

23

THE BRADSHAW CLAN

On the other side of town, Emily had a big grin on her face. The look on Jones's face was priceless and the funny Italian guy was put well and truly in his place. Skipping up the stairs to her now unlocked room, she flopped on her bed and enjoyed the bounce of the spring mattress. She looked up at the few plastic luminous stars dotted around her ceiling and felt pleased with herself as well as excited. There was always a certain amount of adrenalin when she involved herself in such capers. The prospect that she might get caught out was part of the thrill. Emily had become extremely adept at extricating herself from what she described as her 'little scrapes'. The only thing was her family. She had to be careful there, very careful but that was part of the spice, and she was feeling good.

The day started off well, but not well in the way that Emily was used to. It did not have any sense of mischief, nor did it have any subterfuge. It was her art lesson. She liked the subject but found it frustrating and got angry when things didn't always go to plan. So, when she turned up in the first period and plonked her art folder onto the table it wasn't with any great sense of expectation. At first, she was reluctant to bring it out. She knew exactly what Carruthers reaction would be. And sure, enough he didn't disappoint. She took the silver case from inside her folio and unzipped it, and carefully took the Caravaggio out. Carruthers couldn't help himself. As soon as he saw it, he went straight over.

"Oh my," he said ecstatically.

"It's, okay sir, don't wet yourself, it's only a copy."

"Only a copy! Emily, you have brought something in. This is amazing. How utterly fantastic, how wonderful. You are a gem."

"Yeah well, there's lots of others that bring things in all the time."

"But Emily *you* have, this is wonderful."

"Can I just get on with drawing?" said Emily already growing impatient from her teacher's flowery language and over-the-top praise.

"Well of course. Yes, absolutely. I think some chalk and charcoal. Yes, that will enable you to create the chiaroscuro. Wonderful." In a world of rapture, Mr Carruthers then flew over to his stockroom and plucked out the materials from the red tray. "Here you are, have a go. Risk something. Play with the materials. Yes, play! Have no fear!" He then waved the chalks in the air drawing imaginary shapes with an artistic flourish. "Yes, have some fun." Everybody laughed at his mannerisms but there was a sense of fun with Carruthers. Emily didn't buy into it, but he wasn't bad. And that, for Emily, was an incredibly positive point of view on a teacher.

After his little flourish, Carruthers walked over and inspected the painting. "Is this…" He stopped for a second and looked even more closely. "The paint. It looks rather realistic." He then ran his fingertips over the surface. "Definitely not a print. This is paint. Can I ask where you got this?"

"No, you can't," said Emily sternly, "and if you don't stop asking questions, I'm gonna walk out and you won't have a chance to show Cavendish what I've done."

"Right, yes, yes, of course," said Carruthers meekly. Emily loved bossing her art teacher around. In between nicking chalk, charcoal pencils, rubbers, scissors, basically anything she could get her hands on, that was her favourite activity. She was, however, determined to concentrate on her drawing this time. The painting fascinated her, and she wanted desperately to catch a likeness.

Emily had never used charcoal before. She was hesitant. Carruthers was about to come over, but she gave him a look and he backed off straight away. She didn't want him buzzing around. The first few marks she put down on the grey sugar paper were interesting. She liked the looser, grainier effect. Suddenly she found herself smudging the chalk in. There was a surge of confidence as she realised that it was working.

Carruthers was always telling them to loosen up, "everybody's too tight." As she continued to push and manipulate the materials to achieve the dramatic light and dark, she began to understand what he meant. Before long, something recognizable appeared on the page. Time passed without her realising it. She surprised herself that she could have such involvement. This image had no graffiti that she loved to copy, nor did it have any Disney characters which she so loved to draw. There was no pop art or popular culture that she could relate to. And there was no screwing up of the paper in frustration, no melodrama, just a sustained effort. It was good. It was by far and away the best thing she'd drawn.

At the end of the lesson, Carruthers wanted her to leave her work with him so that he could display it and show off his teaching prowess. Much to his dismay she deliberately folded it up in front of his face and stuffed it in her bag. It was quite a violent act. She then looked at him with disdain and chewed on her chewing gum even more ferociously. Carruthers let out a cry of anguish that could be heard in next door's classroom.

"Yeah, so what!" said Emily provocatively. And as she eyeballed him, Carruthers backed away. Suddenly the bell went and she instantly strode off. As soon as she had left the room, she took out her drawing and with great care straightened out the creases and rolled it up neatly. She was proud of her efforts but she was never going to let that be seen, certainly not by a teacher.

Next up was a double drama, no writing just acting and being stupid. She always wanted to be the lead but a feisty Miss Smith usually made sure that didn't always happen. But this time it was definitely her turn. Miss Smith had no alternative but to grant Emily her wish and she didn't disappoint. Emily was at her maverick best, taking centre stage, bossing everybody about, and generally being as outrageous as she possibly could. Miss Smith said that her performance as a misunderstood and rebellious teenager with ADHD, dyspraxia, and Tourette's was, 'freakishly outstanding'.

And then there was RE with Biggsy. That was a blast. When they were discussing Islam and the Muslim religion Biggsy kept shouting out the suicide bombers' cry, "Allah Akbar." In the end,

Mrs Hall, the supply teacher, told him to get out. He laughed and called her vinegar tits. Mr Hughes had to come in and sort it out. Biggsy was excluded but it was a right laugh!

At the end of the school day, Cavendish asked her how her day had gone. "Good," she replied, "I've stayed in all my lessons!" They both laughed. As she walked home hand in hand with her friend Matilda; she was on a high.

But nothing topped the last half an hour. All that stuff with Mr Jones, the flaming car, and that fat Italian guy, absolutely priceless. Suddenly she sat up. "Priceless," she said out loud. It was like the ching of a till. Is that why they were trying to steal it back? Maybe it was already stolen. She never did buy the fat Italian's story. She quickly searched on her phone and soon identified the style. Carruthers was right, late Renaissance, most likely a Caravaggio. A Caravaggio! And if it was real, wow! She smacked her lips in anticipation. Even if it wasn't "real" she could tell it was a great copy. She read that even if it was done in the style of the artist at around that time it would still be worth something. She was going to get it right now from the art room. But she had to move quickly just in case Mr Jones and that funny man realized it was there. She would then store it at Matilda's house, but she had to go now. She hastily pulled her coat on, opened her bedroom door, hopped down the first stair, and then stopped dead. A posse of gangly youths headed by her stepdad stood intimidatingly at the foot of the stairs. They blocked the door. Terry, her stepbrother, eyeballed her.

"Where do you think you're going?" he asked menacingly.

"Nowhere," said Emily. They all laughed.

"Nowhere? How the fuck can you be goin' nowhere?" said Jimmy, her stepdad. He curled his top lip up and bit down on his bottom lip. Not a good sign. He walked up to her. "Now come on, where the fuck are you goin'?" Emily felt his nicotine-smelling breath explode on her face.

"My friend Matilda's," said Emily backing away.

"Why not just say that in the first fuckin' place?" scowled Jimmy.

"I don't know, I'm sorry," said Emily feeling the tension in the air. She needed to get out. She stepped towards the door, but they didn't move away.

Jimmy grabbed her arm firmly. "Not so quick." He turned to Terry. "Do you believe any of that shit?"

"Do I fuck!" said Terry. The narrow eyes that he'd inherited from his father squinted alarmingly. He looked and felt intimidating. It had been a while since either he or Jimmy had been physical. Suddenly Emily had a vision of hyenas circling their prey; nipping away at a weakness; waiting for their victim to stumble. The adrenalin that she normally felt in these situations was giving way to fear. It was Terry that she dreaded the most. With him, the violence bubbled away under the surface. When the smack or punch came it was a kind of relief. She often calmed herself down by telling herself that she deserved it, after all, she was a "lying little bastard".

It was the threat of what they could do that she found most difficult. It was there right now simmering away in the atmosphere. Emily tried to be calm. She'd faced their hostility before. The pitch of her voice had to be just right. "I'm just going to my friend's, honest."

"I'm not talking about that," growled Jimmy. "I'm talking about that funny fuckin' Italian guy and that totally fuckin' shit arse story you gave us."

"What shit story? It wasn't a shit story. He got all confused, he didn't know 'is arse from 'is elbow." Emily was desperately hoping that they would buy her act. But they didn't.

"What's she up to?" said a voice from underneath a hoody.

"I don't know," said Jimmy, "but I wanna know what that fat fuckin' Italian guy was really doing 'ere."

"Do you fink she knows 'im?" said another voice from underneath the hoody.

"Maybe," said Jimmy. "Maybe if we ask 'er nicely."

"Emily come here please." Emily complied. "Emily dear, who was that man?"

"What man?"

"What man? Very fuckin funny. Don't play fuckin dumb."

At this point, Emily had to be careful. Jimmy and Terry were getting wound up. She had to be convincing.

"Now let's try this again," said Jimmy. "Please answer the question."

"I don't know 'im honest. I don't know," pleaded Emily.

THUMP! Right in the ribs. Emily gasped for air. She was half expecting it, but it still took her by surprise.

"Now then, who is he?"

Emily barely heard the question through the sound of ringing in her ears. She just managed to gather her senses together enough to splutter out something coherent. "I'm tellin' you (gasp) I've never seen 'im before." (gasp) But despite her efforts, she could sense another blow coming. "WAIT! I'm tellin' the truth. (wheeze) I don't know him, but he was after something."

"That you'd stolen?"

"Yes."

What 'ave you stolen?

"A necklace. He said it's his mother's an' I stole it. It was at the caravan site."

"Go on."

"Well, I saw an opportunity. The door was open, and it was there lyin' on the table. I was gonna tell you." Jimmy ignored those comments for the moment.

"How did 'e find you?"

"I don't know." Jimmy grabbed her hair hard and twisted it. Emily yelped. "'E was the one who torched the car."

"Go on."

"It was a tactic to get us all outside. I think the necklace is already stolen. That's why he didn't tell the police. He came to steal it back."

"And where is it now, this necklace?"

Emily fought back the tears of anger and pain. "I 'ad to give it 'im back."

"Really?"

"Yeah really." Emily wiped the snot off her dripping nose with her sleeve. "I was gettin' in too much trouble."

The others laughed that horrible sneering laugh again. "Do you believe 'er?" said Jimmy.

"Not a chance," said Terry, smiling.

"Well, it could be true." Jimmy looked round laughing and smiling with the others and then suddenly WHACK!! Another thump right in the side of her ribs again. "But then I don't think so."

It caught Emily off guard, and she keeled over. Cue sadistic smiles from Jimmy and Terry. It wasn't just that they enjoyed it, they were careful. No head shots nothing on the arms or thighs nothing that could be seen by others. They looked on as Emily wheezed and gasped for air.

"Get 'er phone," said Jimmy. There was no resistance as Terry took it from her back pocket.

"Password," said Terry coldly.

Emily shook her head in defiance.

Terry raised his fist to her face. "PASSWORD."

Emily remained tight-lipped.

Whack! This time right across the side of her face. Jimmy tutted. Terry had let his anger get the better of him, there would be a bruise and swelling that would need explaining. It took a minute or two for Emily to come round. When she did, she was broken. Through her swollen lip, she whispered the password. "141179."

When Jimmy heard the numbers, he realised the significance. "Ah your dead mother's birthday, sweet."

At that point, the clan simply ignored Emily and gathered around Terry as he scrolled down her recent searches and texts. They quickly worked out that it was a painting that she had stolen and by the sound of it, it could be worth a lot of money. Jimmy turned to Emily.

"Where were you really off to?"

"School," said Emily groggily.

"Because you have left it there?"

Emily nodded.

"Right then," said Jimmy full of gusto, "let's go." He pointed at Emily. "You! Get some fuckin' makeup on, cover up that fuckin' bruising."

Emily got up gingerly from the floor. It was a struggle. Her left side was in agony. Deep down she always knew that life was not a game and the exciting world of illicitness that she had created wasn't real, but she just wanted one thing of her own that her family wouldn't take from her. It didn't matter that it was ill-gotten. That painting was precious. And as she wiped the snot from her nose, she realized that it wasn't precious simply because of its monetary value. It was precious because it had reached out to her and touched her in a way that she could never have imagined.

24

A GHOST STORY

The traffic jam was making Massimo impatient. He wanted to get to St Peter's quickly. "Probably some dodgy lights not changing when they should," said Harry sensing his friend's unease. "It's happened before. Don't worry it won't be too long." Massimo smiled and closed his eyes. As he did so an odd feeling of calm descended. Apart from the slow hum of the engine, all went quiet. It seemed at odds with what had gone on in the last few hours. This silence didn't sit comfortably with Harry. He needed to say something, maybe start a conversation.

"You're not married are you, Massimo?"

"No Harry. I am afraid not."

"You didn't find the right girl?"

"I think I did, but that was a long time ago." His voice tapered off but then picked up. "We met at university, and I suppose we fell in love." Massimo sighed. "I told her my background Harry, and my connections. Was that a mistake? Maybe, but I had to be honest. But it proved an obstacle that could not be overcome. She didn't see herself being a part of The Family. I could understand that."

"Were you not tempted to leave it all behind? For her I mean," said Harry inquisitively.

"Yes, I was very tempted, but I couldn't. I was ambitious. I could see a position for myself, a very valuable position in The Family so I made a choice to be in Naples, and besides, I didn't want to be like my father."

"What do you mean?"

"He probably had a similar choice and for a time chose to be with my mother. I think he loved her but then he left and went back to Naples. He left me behind too. There was a terrible sadness at that time. I was very young, but I still remembered my mother crying a lot.

"I understand," said Harry. "You did not want history to repeat itself."

Massimo smiled in acknowledgement. It went quiet again before Harry changed the subject.

"So why Caravaggio? Was this love affair with the great master a slow burner or was there a special moment?"

"It is not a love affair," said Massimo dismissively, "that implies something fleeting. It is more deep-felt than that. But if you must know I believe that there was a moment, a moment when a great connection was made. It is something that I will never forget." Massimo paused, gathered himself, and then continued. "I had just turned 12 years old, and my mother had just died. I loved her very much. It was a terrible shock to me and then out of the blue, my father came over from Italy to collect me. I had never previously seen much of him. After the funeral, I had to go with him to his home in Naples. I did not want to leave England. I did not want to leave my friends, but I had no choice. I was a very sad and lonely young boy in a strange and foreign land. One day, shortly after I arrived, my father took me to the church, The Pio Monte della? Misericordia. Perhaps he thought it might help. And indeed, it did because it was there that I came across my first Caravaggio, The Seven Acts of mercy. I beheld its beauty and suddenly I started to cry."

"You must have still been grieving," said Harry. "Perhaps it acted as a trigger, all that emotion poured out."

"Yes, Harry, I think you are right, but it was more than that. I cannot explain or put it into words but maybe something akin to a spiritual connection. And then Harry, I felt a hand on my shoulder comforting me. I thought it was my father but as I looked up, I saw my father standing there talking to my uncle Marco. I turned round to see whose hand had been on my shoulder and through my teary eyes, I saw the face of a man I did not recognize. But I was not worried. I found his touch strangely comforting. I said nothing but turned back around and looked again at Caravaggio's masterpiece. My father saw that I had been crying and came over to me. I never felt the stranger leave me but when I turned round again, he'd gone. I asked my father who the stranger was. "What stranger?" he said. "I have not seen anyone else. There has not been anyone in this room apart from me, you and my brother Marco."

"A ghost?" said Harry smiling.

Massimo said nothing.

"Really?-You believe that?" said Harry.

"It may not be as incredible as it sounds," replied Massimo. "After returning from the church, I went to the library and looked up all I could about Caravaggio and it was there that I recognized him."

"Who?" said Harry fascinated.

"The stranger of course. He was in the paintings. His face appeared many times. It was him, Harry. It was Caravaggio himself."

"No!" said Harry shocked.

Massimo smiled. "Of course, Harry this may be the result of a traumatised boy undergoing huge changes and the loss of a loved one. The mind can create odd illusions to provide comfort. I know this and I have to admit that my story may appear outlandish, but I have never been able to shake off that feeling that it was real, and that his spirit is still with me. I have only ever told my sister of this, but you understand don't you Harry?"

"Yes, of course," he replied. "I am not sure that I believe in ghosts but you know…whether or not I or anyone else believes your story, for you it was real, and that is all that counts."

"Precisely, Harry, precisely." There was a short pause before Massimo asked Harry about his passion for Caravaggio.

"I am afraid that it is nothing so dramatic," stated Harry. I did the life and times of Caravaggio as a module in my degree. I loved it, and that passion for his life and work never really left me. I have seen a number of paintings in many places but for whatever reason, I have never been to Naples." Harry frowned. "And I cannot think why."

"You must come, Harry. I will make it my personal mission to show you around and I promise not to set anything on fire." They both smiled.

"Do you think, Harry, that we would have become friends, I can call you a friend?"

"Yes, of course, absolutely."

"Do you think that we would have become friends if it were not for…"

Suddenly the toot of a horn sounded. It was Mary who'd pulled up in the next lane beside Harry. They both wound down their windows.

"What? Where are you going?" said Harry.

"Your school, remember? I said I'd help Sally with the drama production, you know the make-up and all that."

"Yes of course," said Harry who'd completely forgotten.

"And what about you? Surely you're not going back to school?" inquired Mary surprised at the possibility that Harry might be so conscientious.

"Back to school? Yes, I just need to pick up something."

"Really? Well, is Massimo staying for tea?"

Harry looked at Massimo who shrugged his shoulders.

"Yes, I think he is."

"Is he vegetarian?"

Harry looked again at Massimo who shook his head vigorously.

"No," said Harry, "definitely not."

Suddenly the lights changed.

"Right," said Mary, "might see you at school then."

"Right," said Harry. He turned to Massimo. "Is that okay?"

"Yes," said Massimo, "you are very kind."

Harry then put his foot down on the accelerator and just made it past the lights before they turned to red. As he did so, he found himself reflecting on that last piece of conversation with Mary and how strange it was to talk about what to have for tea in the middle of what felt like some action movie. And then he realized that he didn't need to let his imagination run away with him and visualise some odd flight of fancy. This was real and what's more, it wasn't over. He had a feeling that there was more to come.

25

POSSESSION

As Harry arrived at the school entrance with Massimo in tow, he was greeted by a fraught Sally Smith, the drama teacher. "Thank God you're here," she spluttered. But Harry didn't want to know. He and Massimo had more pressing matters to deal with.

"I'm sorry, I've got no time," he said abruptly, but Sally was insistent.

"It's Steven Biggs. He's set Shami Iqbal's head on fire."

"What!?" Harry looked over to see a forlorn figure sitting disconsolately on a chair in the corner.

"Can you look after him?" implored Sally, "just till parents arrive? Pleeease."

"He seems alright to me. His head looks fine."

"Yes, it is, mostly, apart from a few singe marks," agreed Sally.

"But I thought you said that his head had been set on fire," argued Harry.

"No, sorry, well yes. Biggs made Shami wear one of the wigs he'd nicked from the drama studio. I think he sprayed some stuff on it from the science department and then put a match to it."

Harry turned to Shami. "While you were still wearing it?"

"Yes," said a rather pathetic voice.

"What a plonker. Why on earth did you let him?"

"I'm sorry Harry," said Sally, "but I've got a drama production to run, can you just take care of him?" Before Harry could protest Sally had rushed off.

"Bloody drama teachers," he said, exasperated, "everything's a bloody drama." He looked at Shami. "Right then you'll have to come with me." He then turned to Massimo. "I can't leave him here unattended he does look a bit peaky, if he faints and I'm not here…"

"It is fine Harry," replied Massimo, "let us just get to the art room."

"Yes of course." He turned to Shami. "Oi, you plonker let's go."

The young Indian lad gingerly got to his feet and meekly followed them up the stairs. Suddenly he spoke. "The flaming heads sir," he said out of the blue.

"I beg your pardon!" said Harry somewhat perplexed.

"That's the name of our band," said Shami enthusiastically. "Biggsy was going to take a photo. It was going to be used for marketing purposes."

"Then why didn't *he* do it? Why didn't Biggsy take the risk and put the wig on?" said an annoyed Harry as he entered the art room.

"He said the flames would look better against my dark skin." Harry shook his head.

"Just sit there."

By the time Harry had finished talking with Shami, Massimo had already made a start on searching through the racks of portfolios. Suddenly the door opened.

"Ah there you are, Harry," said Mary. "One of the kids told me you were heading in this direction. What on earth are you doing here? What's Massimo doing?" Before Harry could answer Massimo shouted.

"Here! Harry, I think I have it. He unfastened a black portfolio and pulled out a thin silver case. He unclipped that and pulled out a small canvas ever so slowly. He felt like a person going through a winning lottery ticket not quite believing he'd obtained the prize. But it was there, thank God.

"It is here! Yes, definitely here." He went to pull the painting right out when Harry looked over slightly alarmed.

"I can hear voices." A quick peep through the window of the door confirmed his worst fears.

"It's the Bradshaw clan," said Harry. "They're coming up the stairs. There's quite a few of them."

"Merde," spluttered Massimo as he quickly zipped and buckled everything back up.

"I don't think we'll be able to over-power them," said Harry. "Too many, and besides we have Mary and Shami with us." Massimo frowned.

"Harry what the hell is going on?" said Mary pensively.

Harry ignored her. Instead, he grabbed the folio from a startled Massimo, chucked it in the stockroom, and turned the key that had been left in the door.

"Harry!!"

"Not yet, Mary. Will explain later." He quickly turned to Massimo. "Make it look as though you are still looking. Maybe it will work." Massimo duly obliged. Suddenly the doors burst open.

"What have we here then?" said Jimmy menacingly.

"I'm not sure what you mean," said Harry.

"You!" said Jimmy pointing to Massimo "Haven't I seen you somewhere before?" Massimo smiled as disarming a smile as he could muster. Jimmy scowled. "You aren't lookin' for something are you?"

"As a matter of fact, I am," said Massimo, "it is my niece's favourite piece of artwork. It is a beautiful piece." He then went into a lavish description of the painting. Jimmy was having none of it.

"I think I've had enough of this fuckin' rubbish." Without turning round, he issued a command. "Emily, get the fuckin' painting." He looked at the others and smiled. "You fuckin' lot stay right where you are." He looked at Shami. "Apart from you. You can fuck off." The young boy complied instantly.

As Shami left, Emily stepped out. Harry was shocked. He hadn't noticed her until this point. She didn't want to be seen and Harry could see why. She was an awful sight shuffling along like some old woman with arthritis. "Christ what's happened to you?" he muttered. But Emily seemed oblivious. Harry then caught sight of her face. The thickly applied make-up couldn't hide the swelling on her cheek and jawline and there were some fresh spots of blood coming from the corner of her loose-lipped mouth. The cocky, malevolent spirit had been broken and beaten.

"You bastards," spluttered Harry. "What the hell have you done to her?" He went over to help her and was immediately repulsed by a couple of strong arms.

"Stay right where you are, Mr Jones," said Jimmy forcefully.

"She can manage," added Terry disdainfully.

"Harry, what's happening? That poor girl," cried Mary.

Massimo put his hand on her arm. "It's okay we will sort this out." The soft tones of his voice calmed Mary down to a point. Harry wanted to fight but thought better of it. He needed more time to think. He stood back and watched as Emily searched valiantly in the spot where she last put her folio. Mary looked across at Harry and then the stock room door. He knew from the look in her eyes that she wanted to say something. She needed to say something. Harry understood, of course, but he wasn't going to give up that easily. He was bloody angry over the sight of Emily. He looked at Mary, shook his head, and mouthed "no," through clenched teeth. His wife looked frightened but said nothing. They didn't have long, maybe a few minutes before they realised that the folder wasn't there. And then what?

Harry looked across at Massimo. He could see his eyes searching around the room for a possible opportunity. Given his background, he'd probably been in this situation before. Harry was hoping that he would come up with something, anything. Time was nearly up and there was no car to set alight for a distraction.

Harry then weighed up the opposition. If there was a fight, who would he tackle first? Maybe Jimmy. Knock the leader down and the others will fall. But there was something uncompromising about Jimmy, something hard. He wouldn't stop. Long after you were down, he would carry on punching and kicking to teach you a lesson. Harry had doubts. Maybe Terry first. Harry looked at him closely. He was the one who yanked his chain and wound him up. It was the sneer, that sadistic sense of enjoyment over the infliction of pain. It was written all over his face. Harry wanted to punch his lights out but unfortunately, Terry's fighting prowess was well known in the area. He was also more violent than Jimmy. He could do some real damage, particularly to a face. What's more, Harry thought he could see a knife handle peeping out through his belt strap. Maybe not. A step behind Terry was Robbie the youngest and then Cousin Joey. They never spoke but just obeyed orders. Harry could have a go at one of them, but they were no pushovers and what would be the point? Whilst he was involved with either one of them Terry and Jimmy would sort him out.

It was easy to see that the "Bradshaw Boys" were related. They all possessed similar characteristics, furrowed brows, deep-set eyes, high cheekbones, and a wiry well- muscled physique. It was Tom Bailey who said that they could all be Jack Palance's offspring. And then the first few notes of a spaghetti western started to sound in his head. Thankfully he was able to kill it. Now was not the time.

Emily turned to the rest of her clan. "It's not here," she said glumly.

"Are you sure?"

"Yes positive."

Jimmy turned to Harry and Massimo. "Where is it?"

Massimo smiled. "I don't know what you mean by 'it'."

"Don't play silly buggers with me old man. It is somewhere in this room otherwise you would 'ave left by now." Jimmy looked at Mary intently. Under his scrutiny, she couldn't resist a furtive look at the door. Jimmy clocked it and walked over to the stock room. He tried the handle...

"Locked! Okay who has the key?"

Think, Harry, think. You need to do something now. He looked out of the window. People were coming for the drama show. Maybe if he could alert them. Suddenly he picked up a stool and threw it at the window, only for it to hit the frame and bounce right back. It ricocheted off a desk and hit Mary flush on the side of her head and knocked her out.

All of the Bradshaws laughed.

"You couldn't fuckin' dream this one up. This is definitely value-added," said Terry chuckling away. Harry and Massimo rushed over to where Mary had collapsed.

"I think you've killed 'er," said Jimmy laughing. Harry was distraught.

"She is not dead," said Massimo reassuringly.

Harry shook his wife gently. "Mary it's me, Harry. Mary, wake up! Please."

Mary stirred. Thankfully, she was coming round. Harry sat her up and comforted her. He then turned to Jimmy. "You know if anything would have happened..."

"You'd do what?" sneered Jimmy. "Now give us the key, Mr Jones, there's a good boy." Harry felt an adrenalin rush in his arms and fists. It was all he could do to restrain himself.

Massimo put his hand on Harry's arm. "It's okay Harry. Let me deal with this. Give me the key." Harry didn't take his eyes off Mary, nor did he protest. He simply reached inside his pocket and slipped the key into his friend's hand. Massimo grasped it and then stood up. He puffed out his chest and looked his foes in the eye.

"Now then gentlemen," he said, "this key which I am about to give you will unlock the door to the treasure. We all know what is behind that door. It is a valuable painting. But what you do not know is that it is not my painting. I have merely been looking after it. It really belongs to one of the most fearsome clans in Naples. They are Camorra and they are ruthless. Do you understand? I need to make it clear to you that if you take it, they will come for you and they will find you. They will not hesitate…"

"Stop!" said Jimmy. "You're cracking me up." He turned to Terry. "He thinks he's on some set of the fuckin' Godfather.." Jimmy shook his head. "Just give us the key."

"You have been warned," said Massimo sternly as he handed it over. Jimmy ignored him sauntered over to the door, opened it, and picked up the folio. He brought the painting out of its case and laid it out on the table. He looked at it closely.

"Hmm really quite interesting," said Jimmy mimicking some art expert. He then spat on his sleeve and used the saliva to wipe a bit of imaginary dirt off. "You don't mind, do you Mr Godfather?" said Jimmy laughing. Massimo's moustache twitched. He was absolutely enraged but trying desperately hard not to show it. Harry left Mary for a second and put his hand on Massimo's shoulder. This time it was his turn to be the calming influence.

"Thank you, Harry," said Massimo acknowledging the gesture "This is not your fight, but you have been drawn in. I am sorry. There will be another chance for me, Harry. I am not finished. This is not over. And more importantly, we need to get your wife to the hospital. She has taken a nasty blow to the head."

"Mary, yes of course." But as Harry turned round, Mary was already standing up. She wasn't at all wobbly. She was firm and solid,

"Mary, are you alright?"

But Harry's words tapered off as he saw his wife stride over to the Bradshaw's. Her gait was different. The stride was purposeful, less feminine more macho. She caught Terry's eye immediately. He nudged Jimmy who was in the process of zipping up the folio. He stopped what he was doing and looked up at Mary. They both laughed but Harry was very alarmed.

"Mary! what on earth..."

Without turning round, she put her arm out. "Stay back old man." It was something in her voice that was commanding. Harry found himself doing as he was told.

"This could be fun," said Terry smirking.

"The Caravaggio," said Mary firmly, "hand it back now or you will get hurt."

"Really?"

"Yes, really, you ugly piece of shit."

Jimmy looked at her for a good few seconds. "Terry put her back in her box," he said smiling. "Or better still put her with those two fat bastards and lock them in the stock room."

Terry went to carry out his father's instructions and sauntered over to where Mary was. He shook his head and laughed again. Perhaps it was the blow to the head, but Mary seemed ultra-confident. She was going to do something. Harry wasn't sure what it was, but something told him to wait. He was nervous. What happened next shocked him to the core.

As Terry went to grab Mary's arm, she reached into her pocket, pulled out a small screwdriver, which she'd picked up from the teacher's desk, and drove it hard into Terry's thigh. Chunk! It plunged right up to the hilt, right into the muscle.

Terry howled in pain. "Fuck, fuck!!" He looked at Mary in disbelief. For a few seconds, everybody stood rooted to the spot and time seemed to freeze. It started back up again when the main art room door swung open. Such was the normality of the man that walked in, Harry thought he was a parent.He wore a grey sweater and light blue denim jeans. He was of medium build with an affable if slightly chubby face. Nothing really stood out. He looked directly at Massimo.

"Ah, Mr De Rosa. I'm not interrupting anything, am I? I've been trying to find you for some time. Is everything okay?

"Who the fuck are you?" said Jimmy aggressively.

The stranger ignored Jimmy. Instead, he talked to Massimo and said something in Italian.

"I said, who the fuck are you?" repeated Jimmy, who was now even more furious that he was being ignored in such a fashion. The stranger ignored that statement too and simply carried on his conversation with Massimo as if Jimmy wasn't even there. Harry watched with bated breath as Jimmy marched over in a rage-filled stride. At the last second, the stranger stopped his conversation with Massimo and punched Jimmy hard in the throat. It was done with such disdain and yet had such a debilitating effect. Jimmy staggered back unable to catch his breath. He collapsed to the floor trying desperately to gulp for air - completely incapacitated. Far more effective than a punch to the face thought Harry in a surprisingly detached manner. Terry then lurched forward as best he could, but Mary's stabbing had left him short of any real agility. It was an easy dodge out of the way for the stranger who then gave Terry a hard punch into his left kidney. Harry noted that it had the same effect. And as Terry collapsed to the floor the stranger set his eyes on the other two members of the Bradshaw Clan....

"Boys, you're not going to do anything are you?"

Robbie and Cousin Joey looked blank and for a second the question didn't register. Their minds seemed in a place that was far away and neither of them could muster up a reply. "Are you?" repeated the stranger firmly. And then it was as though everything about them suddenly switched on. Their eyes became focussed and they shook their heads vigorously.

"No, no honest. Absolutely definitely fuckin' not," they spluttered.

"Then get you and your fucking trash out of this building."

Like some scene from a battlefield, Robbie and cousin Joey helped the wounded and shell-shocked to their feet and began the evacuation of the classroom. Harry took the silver folder, there was no resistance. But it wasn't quite over, there was still the issue of Emily.

"Wait!" cried Harry. "She's staying." Jimmy and Terry stopped and turned round snarling something or other.

Harry didn't wait for their protests. "I said she's staying. She's not going home with you." He clenched his fists. He wasn't going to back down. The Bradshaws could see that, and they were in no fit state to fight back.

"Fuckin' 'ave 'er," growled Jimmy, "she's a useless twat anyway."

But Emily was hesitant. Harry could see that the pull of being with her family was strong. Abuse can be addictive. "Come here, love," said Harry warmly. "You're safe with me." But Emily was frightened. It wasn't easy to make that step. She tried desperately to find a small ray of hope – something to hold on to. She found it in the chunky palms and thick fingers of Harry's outstretched hands. She reached out. Harry quickly clasped her thin bony fingers and gently pulled her towards him. He gave her a great big hug and Emily burst into tears. She wrapped her hands around his large stomach and wouldn't let go. They were there for an age. Neither of them could speak.

"When you're ready, Harry," came the more familiar voice of Mary.

Harry wheeled round. He didn't quite know what to say to her. What she had just done, was hard to put into words. He couldn't explain it. But as he looked at his wife, there was something different from the screwdriver-wielding Amazonian of a minute ago. She seemed more like herself.

"Mary, what on earth, are you all right?"

"Yes, of course, why wouldn't I be?" said Mary chomping on an apple.

"But the Bradshaws, the screwdriver, you fighting…"

"Are you sure you're alright Harry?"

Harry looked at Massimo who shrugged his shoulders. "She is back with us," was all he said.

"What was the last thing you remember?" asked Harry.

"What a strange question," said Mary, "but now that you ask me, I am not quite sure. I remember setting off to see you. Were there more people here? But I can't quite remember how I came to be here, not exactly." She suddenly looked at the apple, "Or where I got this from. Was it from my pocket?" Harry smiled. Mary suddenly felt the side of her head. "It hurts here. Did I have a bump or something?" Harry nodded and stroked the side of her head. Mary touched Harry's hand affectionately. "But other than that, I feel fine. No, more than fine. I feel very, very good."

26

THE AFTERMATH

In the aftermath of the battle, the wounded figures of clan
Bradshaw shuffled out of the art room and just about clambered
down the steps. As they limped into one of the side corridors
Cavendish clocked them. He immediately left the parents that he
was with and marched up to the dishevelled bunch.

"Just fuck off," said Jimmy in a low growl.

"Yes, of course," said Cavendish, who quickly backed away.
There was no way he was going to argue, but despite feeling
intimidated, he plucked up the courage to enquire.

"Do you mind telling me what's been hap..."

"You heard the man," groaned Terry. "Fuck off."

A bewildered Cavendish shut up instantly. He didn't quite
know what to do, so he did nothing but simply watched as Clan
Bradshaw hobbled past him through the side entrance and out
through the double doors. Considering their ailments, they made
a relatively quick getaway in a large white builder's van.
Cavendish breathed a huge sigh of relief, he then turned to the
open-mouthed parents and explained that it was probably part of
the drama production.

"They are getting into character," he said confidently, "part
of the method acting I do believe. You didn't hear what was said
did you?"

"No, we didn't hear..."

"Ah that's good, very good, they can get a bit carried away.
I'm sorry, do you mind showing yourself out? I just have a few
phone calls to make." He said goodbye and virtually pushed
them out of the door. "So sorry, again, but I have a brutish
timetable this evening, operational matters you understand." As
soon as Mr and Mrs Samuels were out of sight, Cavendish was

on his walkie-talkie to the caretaker. He then followed some
spots of blood up the steps to the art room. He stepped inside and
surveyed the scene. On the surface, everything looked okay but
there was clear evidence that a mess of sorts had been cleaned
up. Clearly, the Bradshaws were involved but there had to have
been others, but who? "No matter," he said out loud, "we'll see
what we've got on CCTV."

Harry was pleased that they'd managed to exit the school
without further mishap. He'd just managed to evade Cavendish.
It was stupid really, hiding in the stockroom but it worked. They
weren't seen. He looked in his car mirror. Emily and Mary were
fast asleep in the back seat. He turned to Massimo.

"Who the hell was that back there? He had the moves of
Jackie bloody Chan? Wait, don't answer. It was a member of
The Family. Is that right?" Massimo nodded sheepishly. "How
the hell did he find you?"

"I'm not quite sure," replied Massimo with a shrug of his
shoulders. "Maybe they went to my apartment, saw something,
hacked my computer, who knows?"

"Anyway, I'm glad he did find you," said Harry, relieved.
"God knows what would have happened if he hadn't come in at
that moment."

"Quite," replied Massimo concisely.

"I didn't understand a bloody word you two were saying. I
take it whathisname..."

"Kurt."

"I take it Kung Fu Kurt is a friend of your boss. Good God,
he looked so...normal.

"They don't all come in dark suits and spats, said Massimo."

"But he did mention the name Alfonso. Are you in trouble?
Is the game up?"

"I'm not sure," said Massimo with a frown. "Alfonso wants
me back urgently, but for some kind of financial crisis.
According to Kurt, he needs my 'business acumen' and my
'mediating skills'."

"No mention of the Caravaggio?"

"No," said Massimo, pensively.

"Maybe he doesn't know...

"I'm not sure."

"Well Kurt would have taken it or at least asked about it wouldn't he?" said Harry patting the silver case.

"Yes, I suppose he would," said Massimo, still looking perplexed.

"All this macho posturing," said Harry, "the fights, threats, battles, stolen goods. Is it like this for you back in Naples?"

Massimo smiled. "It is possible that it is like this for some people, but not so much for me, although I must confess, I have seen some interesting things. Once I was there when a man got shot in his backside, but that is a different story. Mostly, I have business meetings and phone calls. Sometimes I am asked to smooth over some things.

"I have never seen anything like it," said Harry shaking his head. "Was that really my wife? Tell me, Massimo, tell me that I wasn't imagining what she did."

"It was really your wife, Harry, and you didn't imagine anything," said Massimo sombrely.

"Mary's never done anything like that," exclaimed Harry. He shook his head. "What on earth was she thinking? She remembers nothing but she, my wife of thirty years, was completely different. If I was a religious man, I would say that she was possessed. Do you think we need a priest?" joked Harry. Massimo smiled. "No, I am serious," said Harry fearfully. "I don't want to wake up one morning with a sharp object at my throat."

"I am sure that this will not happen, although I would not rule out the supernatural."

"I beg your pardon!" said Harry. "What on earth makes you think that?"

"Because I have felt this presence once before," said Massimo earnestly, "in the church."

"I'm not sure I follow."

"The Pio Monte della Misericordia. The hand on my shoulder, the ghost, you remember the story?"

"Ah yes, Caravaggio's ghost. But surely, you're not saying that my wife's actions were the result of his possession? Massimo, she bumped her head and for a few minutes became a different character – perfectly understandable and scientifically explainable. In her confused state, she may have thought she was part of a film or a character in a book that she'd recently read."

"Perhaps," replied Massimo." There followed an awkward silence. During this time Harry spent time reflecting on a number of concerns. Although they had been triumphant, the issue of the Bradshaws would not simply go away. They were not the type to lie down and accept defeat. Harry knew that there would be repercussions, they were a nasty bunch. He was already bracing himself for what might happen. Would it be a machete hacking him and Mary down in some dark alleyway or maybe a kneecapping in some old, abandoned warehouse?

And what about Emily? She was staying at his house tonight. They couldn't take her to the hospital, there would be too many questions. The Bradshaws would be contacted, and the police would almost certainly be involved. That wouldn't be good for Massimo, and Mary would have to explain her assault…no it was too much of a risk for everybody. But a vulnerable child staying at his house? It was going against all procedures and protocols. Cavendish was bound to find out and that would be the end of his teaching career, an ignominious exit.

Harry suddenly thought more deeply about Emily and what a terrible position she was in. Who would want to have a family like that? What future did she have? And Massimo. He'd stolen from the Mafia. What was going to happen if they found out? And Mary, she had absolutely no idea what she'd done. How would she feel about knowing that she'd stabbed somebody?

That night Harry had some terrible and disturbing dreams. Emily Bradshaw took a selfie of herself in his bedroom with him in the background fast asleep with his semi-naked big fat stomach bulging out just about hiding his genitals. And in this grotesque vision, the photo was soon shown all-round the community and then on the front page of the tabloids. He was up for child molestation and shamed before the school. And Cavendish presided over everything with one of those judge's wigs on, laughing away as though it were some big joke. As that vision melted away it was replaced with a more hideous one of Mary in spectral form hovering over him knife in hand. Only it wasn't quite Mary's face, superimposed was Caravaggio's all distorted and demon-like. And then it spun round and laughed hideously. That face then gradually metamorphosed into Terry Bradshaw's complete with terrible scarring on his right cheek. He hovered over Harry, knife in hand, stroking his cheek and laughing monstrously at the same time. In the background the Mafia – all dark and unseen, a presence that seeped through every apparition. He woke up in a cold sweat. Oh Lord, he said to himself what is to become of me?

The following morning Harry got up early, put on his dressing gown, and walked bleary-eyed down the stairs. He had an awful night's sleep. He yawned and stumbled into the kitchen only to see Massimo buttering a piece of toast. He seemed quite perky.

"Would you like some, Harry? Is this bread homemade? It smells delicious." Harry stood there speechless and motionless. "Are you alright, Harry?" continued Massimo. "What about a cup of tea? I know the English like tea, especially first thing in the morning."

"Yes, I think so, yes," stuttered Harry. "Massimo are you okay you don't seem at all worried?"

"That is because I am not. I have made up my mind. I am going to tell Alfonso everything."

"But why? You would still have a chance to get the painting back without him knowing."

"The chances are that he already does know, Harry. He is no fool and besides putting it back won't be easy. At least this way I have a chance to appear honest and remorseful. There is the possibility that he will look upon me favourably. As you well know this was not a crime of deceit. There was no money to be made. It was for the love of art; it was for the passion."

"Are you sure that he will look upon you favourably?"

"No, I am not but there is another reason. I know that when Alfonso hears what has happened and what you have done for me at such a cost to you and your family, he will give you some protection."

"What kind of protection?"

"He will sort it. Trust me, we do not need to go into detail but the Clan's influence stretches wide and far. I would not worry too much about the Bradshaws." Massimo paused before continuing quietly. "But I would ask one more favour, Harry. I know that you have to inform the authorities about Emily, but please could you not do so until perhaps late morning. By that time I should be well on my way to the continent. Could you do that Harry?"

"Yes, of course."

Massimo patted Harry on his shoulder gulped a last cup of tea and took his jacket from off the chair. "Then I must bid you arrivederci. I will be in touch. If you need any help, anything please don't hesitate to contact me."

"Sure," said Harry and before he knew it, Massimo was off and the house was quiet.

Three hours later, Mary and Emily came down, pretty much together. In some ways, that was fortunate. For his own protection, he knew that there was no way he should be with the girl on his own. It was only as Emily gingerly stepped inside the kitchen, that Harry could see the full scale of her assault. She looked a mess. As she shuffled along, Emily caught sight of her reflection in the mirror and in particular the bruise on the side of her cheek.

"That's a bloody corker!" she blurted out. "Cor, they've given me a right smack."

"That's because they're a lot of fucking bastards," said Mary.

Harry was quite shocked and looked at his wife with surprise.

"Well they are," said Mary ignoring Harry's frown. She then walked over to Emily and gave her a big hug. "We're going to make sure you are alright. Don't you worry."

"How often has this happened?" asked a very distressed Harry.

Emily just shrugged her shoulders. "Sometimes they have hit me, not so much lately, never quite as bad as this, but I've done some bad things…"

"Stop right there!" said Harry sternly. "You do not deserve it no matter what you have done. Mary's right, they are bastards for treating you this way."

Emily smiled meekly, and suddenly Harry felt guilty. He knew that she had problems, but he couldn't get past her appalling behaviour. He knew she was a victim but he couldn't

175

see it. Was it the years in the institution that had hardened him? He looked at Emily.

"I'm sorry I didn't see it. I should have, we should have…"

"And you can stop right there, Mr Jones," said Emily. "It's not your fault."

This time it was Harry's turn to smile meekly. And then he changed the subject.

"Mary, I'm wondering if there was anything you could lend her. She has some spots of blood on her shirt."

"Yes, that's a good idea, Harry – back in a tick."

As soon as Mary had left the room, Harry turned to Emily.

"What do you remember about last evening back at the school?"

"Not much, I was too busy feeling pain."

"Do you remember Mary, and what she did?"

And suddenly Emily's mood changed She became quite animated. "Are you talkin' about the woman who did the stabbin'? That's your wife aint it? Wicked! I mean she kicked ass." Emily then made a gesture that simulated one of Mary's battle manoeuvres. "Heyyaaaah!" she cried.

"Quite," said Harry. "Well, here's the thing, how can I put it? I would appreciate it if you didn't say anything."

"You want me not to say anything?"

"About Mary," said Harry quietly, "and you know …the fighting."

"What, you want me to lie for you, sir? Is that right?"

"No, just leave that bit out."

"It will cost you."

Harry's face dropped.

"Only kidding," laughed Emily. "I'll just say I blacked out, couldn't remember nothin' about anythin.'"

"Really?" asked Harry enthusiastically.

"Yes, it's easy. I lie all the time."

"How do I know that you are not lying now?"

"Because I'm not," said Emily sternly.

There was a moment's silence before Emily made a suggestion that surprised Harry.

"Sir, Mr Jones, it might be best for you if you took me round to Matilda Beavis's mum. She's always been good to me. She'll put me up. The social services and the police can see me there. That might be better for you."

"Yes," said Harry appreciatively.

Just then Mary walked in with a nice shirt and blouse.

"Here, come upstairs and try these on. They're almost as good as new, from Barnardos."

"I'm not wearing dead women's clothes" blurted Emily.

"But..."

"Just give her some of yours," said Harry submissively.

Mary complied, and after a good breakfast and a few phone calls, Harry took Emily round to Matilda's mum's house. She was more than happy to have her. Harry watched as the young waif of a girl stepped inside the hallway. He always knew that she was resilient and resourceful but living in those circumstances. That was incredibly difficult and in the midst of last night's episode when she reached out for him, he saw a vulnerability in her that affected this gnarly old teacher. As he drove off, he pondered whether or not this might be a turning point for Emily. He had seen another side to her, maybe he'd helped. It was only after Harry put on his jacket and reached into his pocket that he realised that there was a ten-pound note missing.

27

THE DATA DRAGON

Harry did eventually make it to school just after lunch. He only had one lesson. He could have taken the whole day off but in his view, nothing was wrong with him apart from having a world full of worries on his mind. He just didn't want to spoil his attendance record or be seen as some kind of shirker. He went up to the art room to see if everything was okay. Carruthers looked perplexed at his enquiries and wondered why he was in the art room at all, seeing as though he never usually ventured up there.

"Everything is fine," he said, "why wouldn't it be?" Harry looked around and agreed.

Afterwards, Shami Iqbal came to see him to show off his new skinhead haircut. "I preferred the burnt look," said Harry, "and that smell of singed hair was sure to have been a real hit with the girls."

Shami laughed and stroked his head. "Cheers sir." He said 'Cheers' at nearly every comment that came his way. He was always a good kid (for a teacher to use). It didn't matter if an attempt at humour was ridiculously poor, Shami would always say 'Cheers' and say it with a smile. Definitely a good 'un to have in your class, thought Harry – does wonders for the old self-confidence. He turned to the kid.

"So, what did your mum say?"

"She didn't mind."

"You didn't tell her, did you?"

"No, sir."

"Has she seen it?"

"No, sir, I put a baseball cap on this morning."

"Are you scared?"

"Yes, sir, my mother is a beast."

"You could always use some shoe polish; you know, make it look like close-cropped hair."

"Cheers, sir."

"Listen Shami did you see anything last night."

"You mean the Bradshaws?"

Harry nodded.

"I didn't see what happened, but they looked pretty beaten up when they came down the stairs."

Harry winced. "Do me a favour, please, don't mention it."

Shami's face squirmed.

"You've already told somebody haven't you?"

"I am afraid so sir, Mr Jones."

"You told Biggsy didn't you?"

Shami nodded.

"You know you might as well have broadcast it over a loudspeaker."

Shami smiled his lovely infectious smile. "Cheers, sir."

"Shami it's not a joke. And you can't go on saying cheers after every comment that comes your way."

"Yes, sir, thank you, sir, cheers."

Harry just shook his head.

"Just go Shami."

"Cheers, sir."

As he went Harry smiled. He needed something light to cheer him up. He was dreading seeing Cavendish but that never happened. He was out on a course. The rest of the school day went by in a blur. When he got home Mary was out. She'd left a note saying that she was round at Tanya's and that there was some food in the freezer. He sat down with a glass of beer and waited for some probable phone calls from the police, but they never came. By the time Mary came in, he was in bed, whacked, fast asleep.

When Harry arrived at school the following morning his worst fears were confirmed. Rumours of his conflict with the Bradshaws had spread. Biggsy and Ali came up to him and started talking in this ridiculous gangland style.

"Respect man, a mean da big respect."

"Are you taking the mickey?" asked Harry, indignantly.

179

"No, mon," said Biggsy, who then extended the forefinger and little finger of each hand in a very odd rapping style gesture. Others waded in.

"Aaaiiiii, mon."

"Give it rice, Mr Jones."

"Da Bradshaws, man you wrecked dem heathen."

"Yo da man."

The comments were usually followed by some kind of salute and then a ridiculous attempt at a high-five. Biggsy was most prominent, puffing out his chest, ultra-strutting style. Harry smiled faintly, wishing that the ground would swallow him up. It all helped lighten his mood until he sat down at his desk. Then he felt nervous. He still had this feeling that the police were going to call round. Nevertheless, he turned on his laptop and opened his emails. Usually, he couldn't be bothered, but this time they provided a much-needed distraction.

There were, of course, the usual daily reminders to use the computer operating system to fill in all target grades for the students. That was to be expected, but there were also reminders to fill in the actual grades, currently working at grades, homework grades, attitude grades, and effort grades. Then there were the additional emails that attempted to clarify what this meant. There was also the command to log all behaviour incidents, as well as any parental contact made, as well as a brief report about any conversations that took place. There were emails about learning walks; emails about observations; emails about incorporating reflective time in lessons; emails about lining up the children correctly incorporating the 'one foot in and one foot out' mantra; emails about assembly time; emails about seating plans; emails about being careful not to shout. You name it, there was an email about it. All this was topped off by a letter from the CEO thanking everybody for their hard work. "Bollocks," said Harry out loud, and just deleted the whole lot...and then he had to go to get Vicky's help to get into his deleted folder, to get an important email. There it was in big bold letters...**Urgent meeting 2.30 Mr Cavendish.**

One day, thought Harry, I am going to slay the form-filling, target-driven monster that lies in waiting in every academy. And suddenly he had a vision of himself as a kind of heroic St George type figure manfully defending himself and the school against the fire-breathing algorithms of the data dragon. To the left the number crunching dwarves ready to crush any semblance of unorthodoxy, to the right the stat-analyses goblins ready to trample all over any mutinous off-piste pedagogy. The only weapons Harry had at his disposal were his mighty maverick lance and the sharp-bladed sword of truth. Despite repeated thrusts with both of these impressive weapons, Harry could not pierce the armour-plated scales of infallibility that protected the dragon's heart of data. This did not deter him as he fought on. It was certain death but still, he wrestled valiantly against overwhelming odds…

"Are you okay, Harry?" said Vicky, who'd just popped her head round the door.

"Yes, of course," said Harry snapping out of his daydream.

"The office told me you had a bit of Deli-belly yesterday morning."

"Ah, yes," said Harry rubbing his stomach.

"You still don't look right Are you sure you should be in?"

"I've got my meeting with Cavendish today."

"Have you still not had it?"

"No, not yet, but this one's typed in bold black."

"Ooh, that sounds serious, but surely he's not got that much on you, apart from a few stupid phone recordings."

"He may have much more, but to be honest I don't care."

Vicky seemed surprised at Harry's defeatist tone. She didn't know what to say except, 'Good Luck' and that he could always 'come and talk'. Harry was touched by her kindness, and it cheered him up. It certainly helped him get through the first lesson and into break time.

28

THE GOOD LISTENER

Harry always had the idea that he might go out like something
from 'Goodbye, Mr Chips'. The congratulations of his students
and his peers would be ringing around his ears. Ghost-like
figures from his past saying, "Goodbye, Mr Jones," and, "Well
done, old man" or simply, "Thank you!" Each one would pat
their hand on his back as they floated by. There might also be a
grand, 'Hurrah' from some of the old boys. They would be there,
the characters of yesteryear. Mr Hayward, the science teacher,
who used to have a bed and television in the stockroom so that
he could watch test match cricket when the class was doing a
test, Frank Stubbs, the old caretaker, who used to swear at
students and teachers alike, just for the fun of it and good old
Goody Goodwin, who regularly gave good tips for the horses
and was your best pal on the rugby trips…all long since retired
but now back to give Harry a good old send off. They'd be
plenty of guffaws as old tales and comic episodes would be
recounted. Harry would be the good-natured butt of the jokes.
Then, as is the customary fashion, he would be clapped out of
the hall amidst firecrackers and wild yelps of delight. "Well
done, Mr Jones, Well-done, sir, Good show," echoing round the
old hall. His friends Tom and Vicky would give him a hearty
handshake. 'Well done, Harry, Well done, Thank you for all that
you have done.

But as he knocked on the door of Cavendish's office he knew
that this may be his last hurrah. It was never going to be
'Goodbye, Mr Chips'. Unfortunately, he may have left
Cavendish with no choice. He'd realized that there were cameras

around the school. How much they'd captured he didn't know, and he was past caring.

Fortunately, there was no CCTV in the art room, but there was a camera near the art room doorway which showed quite clearly the odd comings and goings of a number of people, including Harry and his friends. When presented with this Harry chose to say nothing. When asked to explain the injuries to the Bradshaws he said that he couldn't. And when asked what he was doing there, he said that he wasn't sure. The one positive for Harry was that neither Emily nor her family was prepared to offer statements. Harry spent most of the interview looking out of the window at the bright blue sky and the fluffy white clouds that gently rolled by. He'd had enough. He didn't listen to Cavendish's summing up. He knew that there were too many unanswered questions and too many improper procedures. Harry was being suspended. He was just about to say that it was time for him to go, to leave for good when the principal handed him a card. Harry looked at it. The heading, "The Good Listener" appeared in soft blue typeface at the top. In the centre was a light pink and grey dove. At the bottom was a phone number again in soft blue.

"It is a counselling service," said Cavendish with his most sympathetic face on. "The Academy bought into this last year, it's really rather good. It's there if you need any help."

For a second Harry said nothing but just looked vacantly at the card and then he scratched his head in an irritated sort of way.

"Well, I suppose this covers you," said Harry, flippantly.

"I am not sure what you mean."

"You, the academy can say that you have offered me support. The box has been ticked."

Cavendish smiled a crumpled kind of smile. It peeved Harry more than ever. He wanted to say something, but he could see that Cavendish was well prepared and well trained to absorb any emotional outburst. He'd been on all the courses. Harry didn't want to give him the satisfaction of losing it but that card, the blue and fluffy good listener pissed him off. He couldn't stop himself.

"Is this what it's come to? A bloody card? You know there was a time when education had a soul and people cared for each other, I mean genuinely cared. You lot say all the right things, you even sound good but..." He looked at the card again and shook his head. "How much does this cost you?" Cavendish sat there tight-lipped. "I bet it's one of your chums that runs this service, making an absolute fortune! Cavendish still said nothing. "Well, if it's not your mate then somebody from the academy hierarchy. They've all got their snouts in the trough...making money out of our fucking misery!"

"Would you like a glass of water, Harry?" said Cavendish passively.

"No thanks," said Harry politely, "and if that's all, I'll be off."

As Harry left the room, he felt disappointed with himself. He'd lost it and it was the one thing he wanted to avoid. Suddenly a familiar voice shouted out.

"Yo de man."

Harry wheeled round and there was Biggsy, doing his usual, walking round the corridors, along with several other students, who didn't fancy their lessons. Several of the senior management were in tow, tracking their movements and relaying information on their walkie-talkies. Prentiss was right behind Biggsy, walking in his slipstream, talking to him, trying to get him back in lessons. Biggsy simply ignored what he saw as ineffective mutterings, but then he suddenly stopped and turned round to look at Prentiss. He pointed to Harry. "He de maaan." Harry smiled and looked at Prentiss.

"I see we've got this nicely under control."

But before Prentiss could reply, Biggsy walked right up to Harry.

"Yo de man."

Harry thought for a second and then replied. "I was de man," he said softly, "I was *dee* man." And with that, Harry thanked Biggsy and left the building.

A few days later he got the formal letter "Temporarily suspended pending further investigations." Strangely, it didn't particularly phase him. There was that one moment in Cavendish's office that upset him, but other than that he was quite happy tending to his gardening and catching up on some of his favourite authors.

A few days later a parcel came from Massimo. Much to Harry's delight and amusement, it was a replacement copy of Dixon's biography of Caravaggio and a little note inside which simply said, "A passionate man." Well, it's certainly not me, no passion here, thought Harry as he scratched an itch on the back of his leg with the frayed edge of his brown and grey slipper. But something happened that changed that opinion of himself. It was all to do with Mary.

He was out in the garden one day gently pulling some dead leaves away from his prize petunias when Mary came out and offered him a glass of Chianti. As he sipped it, she put her arms around him and gently brushed the side of his cheeks with her lips. Before Harry knew it, they were in bed, having sex in the afternoon! He thought that those days had gone but maybe he was wrong. Mary seemed different. A few days later pretty much the same thing happened. She instigated it and Harry was more than happy to go along for the ride, especially as she was on top!

He was feeling quite chipper when he got a phone call from Massimo. He too sounded in a good mood, almost as good as his.

"Ciao amico!"

"You sound happy," replied Harry.

"Yes, life is good. All is fine with me and Alonso! I will tell you about this later but first to you Harry. How are you? And the Bradshaws, I trust that you have had no dealings with them. And what of school and Emily? Please tell me everything."

Harry then explained what he knew and that he was on gardening leave. He stressed that he was quite enjoying the break and seeing more of Mary. He didn't go into any detail.

"They will not sack you?" said a concerned Massimo.

"I don't know," said Harry.

"But you did nothing wrong."

"No, but there were signs of blood all over the art room floor and stairs, even though we did our best to clean up. CCTV cameras caught us lot going in the art room along with the Bradshaws. Clearly, there was an incident – they came out looking like they'd been in world war three. I came out with

Emily and a strange bald-headed guy – you. I wouldn't give any
answers to Cavendish."

"But they can't prove anything, especially if nobody is
saying anything."

"That is true, but there have been other recent episodes of a
dubious nature. Each one on its own may not be enough to
condemn me, but put together it makes for grim reading.

"But you will fight, won't you?"

"I'm not so sure."

"Harry! You can't let them sack you. You are a good man.
You were protecting people. I am happy to help. How can I
help?"

"Massimo, it's fine honestly, I feel good. Me and Mary,
we're getting on. And there has been nothing from the
Bradshaws, thank God. And Mrs Beavis says that Emily is
recovering well."

"Good, good," said Massimo.

"But what about you and Alfonso?" asked Harry.

"Ah yes," said Massimo. "Well Harry, I think I am going to
be okay. In fact, it's worked out better than expected."

"Phew! I'm glad, but how?"

"So, after I left you, I rang him and turned up with the
painting. I then told him about the whole episode. He just
laughed. I couldn't understand his reaction, Harry. I thought he'd
be mad and at the very least I would be excommunicated. Why
are you laughing I asked him. He replied that very shortly the
painting would be deemed worthless. As you would expect I was
speechless. He then explained that he had hired some experts and
paid them a lot of money to discredit the idea that it was a
Caravaggio. Can you believe it, Harry? "I will be damned if I let
those pious bastards get the better of me. If it's not a Caravaggio
they've got no claim and can go and fuck themselves." Those
were his exact words. He thought that all the lengths I'd gone
through to get it back, all the angst I'd suffered over something
that would prove to be worthless, was hilarious. He started to
laugh again and continued laughing for a good few minutes. He
patted me on the shoulder and then told me to look after it."

"Look after it?"

"Yes, Harry. It is in my apartment on my wall. I am staring at it right now in the most beautiful frame. It is my pride and joy, the centrepiece on the main wall. You must come and see it." And then Massimo spent the next few minutes describing the splendour of his apartment that overlooked the bay. He was in full flow when Harry noticed a letter on the breakfast table propped up against a teacup. It was addressed to him; it was Mary's handwriting. And as Massimo continued to wax lyrical about his good fortune, Harry opened the letter and read it.

Dearest Harry,

We have had such a wonderful time over the past few days. You are so dear to me, but I need to go away. I am sorry but I am not sure for how long. I cannot fully explain but if I stay here, I will die. I don't know how or why but I have changed. I can see colour in the world where once I saw grey and I have to go out and explore that new world and I have to do this on my own. Dearest, Harry, I cannot assure you of anything. I cannot say anything about what or who I might find. I do not expect you to wait for me. You have your life to lead. Please do not put it on hold. Please, please, please do not contact me. I will try to contact you, but I cannot guarantee that I will. I know that you will not understand but I hope that you can forgive me, my dearest Harry.
    Love Mary x

"Harry are you still there, Harry?"
    But Harry couldn't speak. He gently put the phone down and stumbled backwards onto the kitchen chair in shock. He read the letter again, and then some more. He tried to see something, a redeemable feature or some ray of hope but he couldn't. However many times he read the letter, the plain and simple truth was that his wife had left him.

29

EIGHTEEN MONTHS LATER

Harry was in a rush. He hated the possibility of being late. He gulped down his cappuccino and thanked Bruno, the waiter, in his best Italian. "Grazie, Bruno, era delizioso." The waiter smiled. "Prego, Signor Jones." Harry was quite pleased with himself. His Italian was coming on, but he had no time for too many self- congratulations. He needed to be at the church in 10 minutes. In his haste, he nearly forgot his hat, which he'd purchased some months ago from a rather posh shop in the town centre of Naples. It was an expensive cream-coloured Panama. He never usually indulged himself in such frivolous items but as soon as he tried it on, he knew he had to have it. But it didn't just look good or offer some shade it made him instantly recognizable, an essential part of his job.

The church wasn't too far away. He tried to walk quickly through Spaccanapoli but as always found it difficult. The narrow streets were wildly chaotic. Even in the morning, there was a hustle and bustle; a toot of scooters; shouts of small stall holders; and a cry of a shopkeeper, yelling at someone who'd trampled some dirt onto his freshly mopped floor. There were all manner of balconies cascading with beautiful flora; early morning laundry flapping gently on the warm breeze; numerous artisans plying their trade; graffiti on the walls; old women carrying loaves of freshly baked bread up steep hills; and stray dogs pissing against yellow-stained walls – there was always something to see. It was a far cry from Preston and Appleton Drive.

As he turned the corner Harry saw his tour party congregated by the steps of Pio Monte della Misericordia. He'd got to know a few of them quite well over the past few days. One of them, an elderly Chinese woman, going by the name of Rita, greeted him enthusiastically.

"Hello, Mr Jones. How are you? Oh! I am so looking forward to what you have to tell us today. We have learnt so much already." Suddenly all of them were giving him a wave.

"Well, it's so nice to see you all here," said Harry warmly. "Today you are in for a treat." Rita clapped her hands. "Thank you, Rita but I haven't told you what it is yet."

"No, you haven't. I am very sorry, Mr Jones," said Rita giggling. Harry looked at her over his glasses and waited for her to stop, which she duly did. He then winked at her, and she giggled some more.

"Firstly, a little bit about the church," said Harry in his newly formed tourist guide voice. "Pio Monte della Misericordia, meaning pious mount of mercy, was founded in August 1601 by seven young nobles, who met every Friday at the Hospital for Incurables. In 1602 they established an institution and commissioned a small church built by Gian Giacomo di Conforto and the church was consecrated in September 1606." Harry then dropped his formal guide voice for the next part. "There were, of course, additions and annexes and I could tell you who did, what but if I am completely honest, I don't think you will remember and if you are that interested you will read about it. The real treasure is inside. This is my passion and I hope it will be yours too. Now, if you will follow me," said Harry brusquely.

He led his cohort through the entrance and into the main space of the hall and then stopped to address them. "Usually, I leave the best till last," he said, "but this time I am going to start with the best, and it is by far the star of the show." He turned around and gestured to the large panel that was behind him. "The Seven Mercies," by the artist Michaelangelo Merisi da Caravaggio, simply known as Caravaggio. Now before we go into detail about this masterpiece, I think we should hear a little bit about this interesting character. I have talked about him already so can anybody remember anything about him, maybe one or two of you have read up on him. Please, just call out."

"He was born in 1571."

"Good, good," said Harry encouragingly.

189

"He lost both his parents to the plague when he was a child."

"He died in 1610."

"Yes, yes all very good but is there anything more interesting?"

"He did some bad things and went to court at least 11 times."

"Now we are talking."

"He suggested that one of his contemporaries wipe his backside with his own painting."

"Yes," laughed Harry, "that was an insult that Caravaggio gave to Signor Baglioni. Our great artist was quite contemptuous of other artists, particularly that one. Unfortunately for Signor Caravaggio, he really couldn't keep his mouth shut or his temper under control. He once smashed a plate of artichokes into a waiter's mouth and slashed a man across the cheek for insulting him. He even tried to castrate a man over an argument about a woman and ended up killing him instead."

"Oh my!" gasped Rita. "What happened?"

"The pope gave him a death sentence," replied Harry. "But that's not all. He had his own face disfigured in a brawl. He was also very promiscuous having had many relationships with both men and women. He was, in today's parlance, 'a love cheat'. But amidst all of this, his art was pure genius." Harry paused and then with great reverence delivered the next few lines. "Caravaggio brought humanity, warts and all, into the divine. In many of his great works, we bear witness to how the profane can become part of the sacred, of how perfect God joins with imperfect man. When we place ourselves in his theatre, we too reach out... and God touches us. But it is not just drama, Caravaggio gives us the emotion and feeling of this tumultuous event. That is because he is a passionate man "un uomo appassionato."

Harry looked at the transfixed faces and like a good actor let a moment's silence speak volumes before continuing. "And so, we stand before one of his greatest works, 'Sette opere di Misericordia', 'The Seven Acts of Mercy.'" Originally conceived as several different panels, it was commissioned by the church here in Naples and was completed in 1607. It was his first masterpiece after killing a man, no doubt trying to earn some leniency from the pope." He broke off for a second. "Rita, have you any idea what the seven acts of mercy are?"

As Rita started to answer Harry saw a balding, portly figure with a small neatly trimmed moustache enter the chamber and stand by one of the pillars. Harry acknowledged him and then refocused on his audience, "Well done, Rita, you have identified three of them. What are the others? Look at the painting. You can all help her." Harry waited whilst his audience inspected the panel. Eventually, with a little help from him, they identified three more: feeding the hungry, giving shelter to the traveller, and clothing the naked.

"That is six," said Harry. There is one more, look to the side of the painting in the corner."

"Is that the feet of a corpse?" cried a voice from the audience.

"Yes, well done," said Harry. "So, what is happening? What are they doing with the body?"

"Burying the dead," blurted Rita, excited that she may have got the answer right.

"Of course," affirmed Harry appreciatively. "Now it is interesting that this one was harder to pick out than the rest because it wasn't originally part of the acts of mercy as described by Matthew in the gospel. Why do you think that was?" There was a brief silence before a voice piped up.

"I am Jewish," said Angela a rather plump sixty-something with a kind face. "I know that we have a long tradition of how we bury the dead. Even now it would be considered by some to be unclean to touch or handle a dead body. In some orthodox branches of our religion, they would still go through the purification process, sometimes fasting or not even handling food for days. It would be considered the highest grade of uncleanliness to be defiled by a dead body. So perhaps it would not be seen as an act of mercy for a stranger to help bury the dead."

"Interesting," said Harry. "Thank you so much for your insight."

"They may also be carrying disease," came a voice from the crowd.

"Absolutely. I think you both may be right, so either Matthew decided not to mention it or the Jewish scholars of the day decided not to include it. But Christian theologians decided to add this act of mercy later, after all, how can offering a pauper help to bury their dead, not be a true mercy?" Slowly and surely, Harry was drawing them in. Even Massimo who'd heard it all before listened intently.

Harry's skilful use of questioning got them all to notice things they wouldn't have otherwise noted. Jens, a silver-haired accountant from Salzburg who fancied himself as an academic, observed that Mary, the infant Jesus, and the angels, were all lit by the same light. "They cast real shadows – they are no different from the earthly figures below. They have no halos or heavenly glow. The divine and the earthly, the celestial and the terrestrial, are all depicted in the same way."

"Yes, absolutely!" said Harry excitedly. So, what is Caravaggio saying about our relationship with God?"

"That God is not so remote; he is there with us in our suffering."

The audience wheeled round. It was the voice of a rather shy Anne Maria Derain from the outskirts of Paris. She never said much, but when she did, it was often quite profound. There were nods of affirmation and another clap from Rita. Suddenly more questions were asked by different people.

"Is that man singing? Why is he singing?"

"What's that figure doing on the right?"

"Why is Mary draped in so much fabric?"

Jenny, a very buxom ex matron, leaned forward and looked more closely. "Why is that woman letting the old man suckle on her breast? That's rather shocking, isn't it? Is that one of Caravaggio's little fetishes?"

"No, no," said Harry. "This alludes to a story in classical Rome where a daughter visits her imprisoned father. He is starving so she feeds him with her breast."

"Oh! Come on Mr Jones, you are having a laugh, and so is Caravaggio," said Jenny indignantly. "From what you have told us about him it's probably one of his things, feeding on women's breast milk. I know of men, particularly those who have lost their mother early, who have need of this kind of nurture for sexual purposes."

Harry laughed. "I am not going to argue with that!" He was enjoying the interaction. They were getting confident enough to voice opinions and discuss them with each other. Harry had done his job well but needed to bring things together. He called for their attention. Once all eyes were on him, he spoke.

"But here's the thing," he said, "when you look at this painting, we may see God's mercy in a different way or we may appreciate a brilliant use of chiaroscuro but it isn't just a piece of dramatic theatre or a clever interpretation of the gospel, this is Naples, Naples as it was, under Spanish rule: an overcrowded city with massive poverty, where people died on the streets and prisons were terrifying. But Caravaggio, in line with his patrons' wishes, shows a different Naples. It is one where mercy holds sway, and where good deeds shine in the light of darkness."

Rita clapped her hands again.

Harry smiled. "Any more questions?"

"Mr Jones," said Jens, "you say that Caravaggio never did any preliminary sketches but wasn't there supposed to be a painting to accompany this, a small study of one of the acts of mercy?"

Harry looked over at Massimo and then back at the questioner. "I think you are right and for a long time it was believed to be authentic, certainly the family that had it in their possession thought it was."

"Is it not authentic?"

"Well, originally all the evidence gathered by the family suggested that it was. The only problem was that if it was real then the church here in Naples had a justifiable claim on its ownership, after all, it was part of their commission. It caused much conflict between the church and one of the main families here in Naples."

"Was it ever resolved?"

"Yes and no. To be absolutely sure, the painting was put under the most severe scrutiny with all kinds of tests carried out and art experts called in. The conclusion was that there were some serious doubts as to its authenticity. The church backed down and relinquished its claim, the family kept the painting and all the fuss died down."

"That's convenient."

"Yes."

"And the family still has it?"

"Yes, I believe so."

"But it may be worthless."

Harry looked at Massimo. "Not to some."

"What do you mean?"

"Value cannot always be measured in monetary terms. A painting or any artefact for that matter does not necessarily need to have a judgement of authenticity or a prized signature to be beautiful or treasured. Whether or not the painting in question is a true Caravaggio may be open to debate but, because of its part in such a dispute, and being the centre of controversy, it has a history and because of that, it has a spirit. It is also beautifully painted."

There were nods of approval from the gathered, including Massimo. Eventually, after some more questions, the session finished and in typical fashion, Rita was effusive in her appreciation. "Thank you, Mr Jones, thank you, thank you, thank you." But it wasn't just Rita, all of them applauded. As they slowly filed out, a familiar voice greeted him.

"Well done, Harry, as good as ever," said Massimo applauding his friend.

"I hope you didn't mind, about the painting?"

"No, absolutely not," said Massimo smiling. "But I'm surprised you didn't tell the ghost story, you know the one about the sad little boy who'd just lost his mother and was comforted here in this church by the ghost of Caravaggio."

"I didn't want to scare Rita."

"Understandable," said Massimo, "she did seem a little skittish. Anyway, let's get a coffee and pastry at Gambrinus. I know it's a bit of a walk, but I feel like a treat. I've got some news I want to share with you. I'll see you down there. I've just got a phone call to make."

"Sure," said Harry. He popped on his Panama and sauntered out of the church. As he walked past the small piazza, now filling up with tourists, he found himself in a reflective mood and afforded himself a wry smile. If only the tour party knew that he had lunch with the family at the centre of that dispute only a few weeks ago. Alfonso de Rosa was happy to confess that it cost him a lot of money to bribe the experts into formulating an opinion that was agreeable to him and his family. It made Harry feel rather smug that he knew the truth and that he could see that truth staring back at him from the main wall in Massimo's apartment each time he visited. Of course, talk of that painting brought to the surface memories of a traumatic period in his life. And suddenly he remembered that note from Mary. It was such a low point, but it wasn't quite the lowest.

30

A REUNION

As Harry took a seat at Gambrinus, he allowed the strong heady aroma of java to gently waft its way up his nostrils, down his throat, and through to the back of his chest. It felt good, the sun was shining and underneath the large parasol the temperature was very pleasant. In fact, everything was pleasant. Any lingering memories of a painful time were soon suppressed as he pictured a large piece of lemon cheesecake sitting on a small delicately patterned plate complete with a nice shiny silver teaspoon. That would be just right thought Harry. Something beautiful to eat whilst I watch the world go by. There was an elegance and tradition to this place that Harry loved. Overpriced? Absolutely, thought Harry but worth it in so many ways. Then, out of the corner of his eye, he saw a portly figure striding towards him, slightly red-faced and out of breath.

"So sorry to keep you waiting," puffed Massimo as he joined Harry at the small round table for two. "Have you ordered?"

"No, but I am about to." He called the waiter over. "Duo espresso e Crostata alla crema di limone," said Harry in his finest Italian.

"You have tempted me with cake," said Massimo. He patted his waistline "That is not good…but the Italian, that is good. Now about that news. We, you and I, will be having some guests round tonight at my apartment, that is if you are free." Harry nodded "One person, in particular, is very interested in seeing you, Emily, Emily Bradshaw."

"Emily, really?" Harry was quite thrilled.

"Yes, with her foster carer, Mrs Beavis and her daughter, Matilda."

196

"That is great, are they here on holiday?"

"Yes and no," said Massimo but more of that later. I have spoken to Emily, and she is very excited as are all of them, but particularly Emily. Harry, I think that she is so grateful for the help you gave her. I believe she achieved some good results in her examinations."

"I didn't do that much," said Harry, "just a few pointers here and there and a little bit of online tutoring."

"You gave her something precious, you made her believe in herself."

Harry tried to brush it aside but then it suddenly dawned on him. "I am confused. Have you been in contact with her much? I didn't think that you would be talking to her."

"I have spoken to her a little," said Massimo, "but it is really Matilda's mother that I have spoken to."

Harry was intrigued. "I am not sure I follow."

"I think I will surprise you," said Massimo. "All will be revealed, just be there tonight at 7.30."

"Okay," said Harry smiling. "I can't wait."

Later on, that evening Harry arrived on time wearing his nice new floral patterned shirt that he recently purchased from the high street in Via Toledo.

"Your wardrobe has definitely blossomed," said Massimo chuckling to himself. "Where has all that English conservatism gone? And that Panama, do you ever take it off.?"

"I'll have a wine," said Harry trying to change the subject. "Some of your nice pigeon-footed, red shitty piedorosso if you don't mind."

"But it suits you," said Massimo ignoring Harry's scornful remark, "you should keep up this homage to early seventies culture."

"Thank you, Massimo, though I am not sure whether or not to take you seriously, especially coming from someone who often looks and dresses like a private investigator."

"That is a fair comment," said Massimo submissively. Harry took the glass of wine that was offered to him, took a sip, and then stood back to admire the painting on the main wall of the apartment.

"I will never tire of looking at this," said Harry.

"Nor will I," said Massimo appreciatively. And then the doorbell rang.

"Right," said Massimo, "brace yourself for the whirlwind that is Emily Bradshaw."

And sure, enough she strode in first, bold as brass. She walked over to Harry and gave him a hug that took him aback. "Mr Jones," laughed Emily, "you've lost some weight. I can get my arms around you!"

"Only a bit," said Harry slightly embarrassed. "Now there is not as much of me to go around. But you look different too," he said, suddenly noticing her. "You look better, healthier." There was something else thought Harry. It wasn't just that she was taller and fuller, it was her face. It seemed more symmetrical and better aligned, the features more striking. The small, damaged flower had blossomed.

"She is a lot better," interjected Mrs Beavis, "but there are still some issues to resolve, but yes (she looked at Emily) you are a lot better." Emily smiled.

"I'm sorry," said Harry realising that he hadn't greeted anyone else. "Hello, Mrs Beavis.

"Please, call me Pauline."

"Pauline, so nice to see you in the flesh so to speak." Harry reached over and gave her a warm embrace. "Matilda, nice to see you." He shook her hand generously. Matilda smiled but appeared embarrassed. But Harry's generous greeting was nothing compared to that of Massimo and Pauline. They embraced each other like long-lost lovers. A bit over the top thought Harry.

"Are you two okay?" he asked quizzically.

"I'm sorry, Harry," said Massimo, "this is my cousin, Pauline."

"I beg your pardon. What, how? I don't know what to say," said Harry incredulously.

"I do," said Emily. "What about a drink my mouth is like the inside of a budgerigar's cage."

"Yes, yes, of course," said Massimo. He poured some drinks and looked at Harry. "You are thinking how on earth this possible. Yes?"

Harry nodded still slightly befuddled.

"Well, first of all, my mother was born in Preston, I grew up in Preston and I went to school in Preston," laughed Massimo, "so it is not much of a coincidence that I have relatives in Preston. But I would not have made my discovery if it were not for Emily." Harry frowned and Emily smiled.

"Yes, Harry, Emily," continued Massimo. "It was in her little nest underneath her bed. That day when she locked me in her room whilst I was searching for the Caravaggio. You remember Harry?"

"How could I forget?" said Harry drolly.

"Well, I found it in a little cardboard box alongside some trinkets and jewellery, an old black and white photograph of two women. One of them was my mother. I recognised her instantly. I thought that the other was her sister, my aunt Edith but I wasn't sure, and I wasn't sure how it came into Emily's possession. It took me a while to get to the bottom of it all, but eventually, Emily told me that she "acquired" it from Matilda's house."

"That was one of my most treasured photographs," said Pauline. "At the time I wondered where that had gone."

"Sorry," said Emily.

"No matter," replied Massimo. "But once I got in touch with Pauline, she confirmed that it was her mother, my aunt Edith. Sadly, however, she died a few years back."

"It would have been lovely if she would have been here," said Pauline. You would have had so much to talk about."

Massimo nodded in agreement.

"So good things can come from bad deeds," piped up Emily.

"I beg your pardon," said Harry.

"Well, I did a bad thing," said Emily. "I stole the photo and something good came of it. You say that in your history lessons. I remember the lesson on slavery."

"You remember one of my lessons?"

"Well, I try not to. Anyway, you said that however terrible slavery was, some good came of it. You said that things like transport, road systems trade routes were all improved. So, in a way, it doesn't matter what I do or if I do bad things because it is most likely that somewhere along the line some good will come of it."

"Emily you can't use that argument to justify your criminal activities. And you can't quote me out of context. When you stole the photo, you didn't do it believing that something good was going to happen. You stole it..."

Suddenly Emily was laughing. "I can still wind you up, sir."

Harry smiled. "Yes, and you do it so easily." He shook his head and tutted. "So why did you steal it? It seems an odd thing to steal."

Emily shrugged her shoulders. "Dunno really, it looked like a nice family photo, one that I hadn't got." And then suddenly she grabbed Matilda by the arm. "Can we have a look round?"

"Well, I am not sure," said Harry feeling rather awkward that he'd asked that question.

"I'm not gonna nick anything if that's what you're worried about."

"Massimo looked over at Pauline. She gave a hesitant thumbs up and a slight nod of approval. "Okay," said Massimo. Matilda and Emily then went skipping off down the hallway.

"Can we trust them?" said Harry.

"Yes, I think you can," Pauline replied. "Matilda will keep an eye out but stealing's not really the issue anymore. There are other things. She just doesn't trust anyone and who can blame her? The moment she gets too close to anyone she pushes them away, me included. It will take time. Regular counselling has helped.

"I'm surprised you got any kind of help given the state that the children's services are in," said Harry.

"Well, that's right, but we made sure that Emily was a top priority and I have to say the support has been good. You know Harry, you are one of the very few that she really trusts. I think that you have inspired her."

"Why do you say that?"

It is all those online tutorials that you have given her. She's done very well and now she has her heart set on doing a history and art degree. And let us not forget she saw you take a stand against her family, and you put your job on the line. For her, you are the real deal. There have not been many people in her life like that. If I may say so, it's such a shame that your job ended the way that it did. I never believed in the rumours about you and the drugs."

"I keep telling you Pauline that it's true," said Emily who'd just skipped back into the room. "Mr Jones bought some weed from Biggsy's older brother Buggsy. Tell her, sir. It's true, isn't it?"

Harry suddenly had a flashback of the time just after Mary had left him. He was feeling low and had just gone out for a fair old drinking session with Tom Bailey. As he staggered out of the pub he saw a hooded figure selling something illegal. It prompted a real urge in Harry to smoke some weed. He had toked a few joints in his college years, and it seemed so tempting to obtain some for "home relaxation." He walked up to the young lad and bought the stuff really easily. Little did he know this young lad was the older brother of Biggsy who was there with his phone and recorded the lot. The next day at school the proverbial shit hit the fan and he was gone.

Harry didn't want to talk about the subject. He was quite ashamed, but he knew that Emily was telling the truth. She was right there looking at him now, he couldn't lie.

"I am afraid it is true," said Harry sheepishly. "I have never taken drugs before and will not do so again but I was at a low point. I was already suspended and my wife, Mary…" Harry stopped himself, he saw no need to explain himself any further. "Let's just say that it was a difficult time for me, one of the lowest points of my life."

Pauline looked a little crestfallen but put an understanding face on. Emily was completely the opposite. She got quite excited as a kind of street-style speech took over.

"Mr Jones is legend Pauline. I mean beatin' up on me old man and bro, smoking dope bein' a rebel. And that wife o' yours, she is wicked." Harry suddenly waved a hand and mouthed no. "Don't worry sir, I aint gonna say no more about her, but she is wicked, and you are a legend. They done a rap about you. Biggsy says that you is a utube boi."

"Yeah," said Matilda who suddenly appeared very animated, "a wicked Utube boi." The two girls laughed.

"Did you understand any of that, Massimo?" said Harry.

Massimo shook his head. "No, not a word."

"I get the gist of it," said Harry. "Apparently I've got some kind of cult status." He turned to Emily "Is this true?" Emily nodded. "They've done a song about me and I'm on utube, correct?" Emily and Matilda both nodded. "Well, I'll take that. At least I've left some kind of legacy behind."

"It looks like you still tokin' the weed Mr J," said Emily.

"What do you mean?" spluttered Harry.

"That shirt!" Emily then made this exaggerated gesture with both palms out like somebody advertising some great product on the shopping Channel. "Only a geezer on the whacky baccy would buy that."

Suddenly everybody started laughing which set the evening up beautifully. It was noticeable how relaxed Harry was, how at ease he was with the youngsters and how sociable he was with Mrs Beavis. They had lots of catching up to do. Emily was a real storyteller. Her recounting of that night on the caravan site – the night she stole the painting was pure gold. It was the description of Harry's drunken stupor that was so beautifully evocative, and when she imitated his wobble, stumble and fall, they were all in stitches. Best of all was Massimo's ridiculous break-in where she locked him in her bedroom. Much to Harry's amusement she made Massimo sound like some country bumpkin. But it was the water on the crotch incident – Emily did an impression of Massimo just after she'd splashed him. She called it "Rabbit Poirot Caught in headlights." Her face was a picture. Everybody creased up with laughter.

Every so often, in the middle of all the merriment, Harry caught the young woman looking up at the painting, her thoughtful stare revealing a different side to the brash extrovert that had bustled through the door.

They stayed longer than they originally planned, and it was quite late when the taxi arrived. As Pauline urged her two charges to gather their belongings together, Harry turned to Emily. "What about Jimmy and Terry? Do you see anything of them?"

"No, they got busted. Somebody grassed them up. The police raided the house and found a stash full of drugs. The funny thing was that they never usually had much at the house, maybe a kilo of weed but they found quite a bit more, and some other stuff.

Jimmy swears that it was planted. Harry looked over at Massimo who simply smiled. "Anyway, they went down, I don't see them at all."

"Good," said Harry firmly.

A sharp toot of a horn sounded from the taxi, so they quickly sorted themselves out, said their fond farewells and in the blink of an eye Matilda, Emily and Pauline were gone. Suddenly all was quiet. Harry took in a deep breath...

"What a night!"

Massimo agreed but appeared deep in thought. It took him a few seconds to respond.

"You know Emily has a point...good things can come from bad actions. It wasn't just that I found my cousin through Emily's theft of the photograph, I broke into their house, I set fire to a car. I wouldn't have found the photo if it wasn't for my so-called criminal actions. And Mary, if she hadn't stabbed the Bradshaws, if she hadn't used violence then most likely young Emily would still be trapped in an intolerable and abusive situation.

"That was more foolhardiness or according to you, demonic possession.

"Yes, that may be true but her use of violence was excessive." Harry was about to disagree but remembered the aggression in Mary's thrust of the screwdriver. Massimo continued his line of thought. "If my friends had not planted the drugs, the Bradshaws would still be at large terrorising a great many people including you, and let's not forget I stole the painting in the first place."

"Surely you cannot be attempting to justify bad actions. Emily was joking, wasn't she? And I'm not sure where I fit in with your hypothesis - my wife left me, and I lost my job buying drugs."

"No Harry, you misunderstand me. I am saying it more as a matter of irony. I don't really believe it. But even your ridiculous attempt to buy drugs and then getting caught reaped some benefits. If you hadn't embarked on that transaction with that young man, at that time, then you might not have been sacked. You probably would have died a slow death, fighting to stay in an institution that you no longer believed in. You have said it

yourself; you are much happier now. Look at you. The years
have melted away, the frown has gone. I know that the thing
with you and Mary is complicated but the change has worked for
you and possibly for Mary. You are in a job that you like, living
in a place that you adore. Everything is new and fresh, and you
are learning a foreign language."

"Yes, I suppose you are right."

"And it has worked for me, Harry. I have a new, odd kind of
respect from Alfonso and the family members. I stole their
painting, yet they seem to love me even more. They see me now.
I am not just the fat man with a small moustache crunching
numbers. I am just glad I gave it back."

"That wasn't a bad thing you did," said Harry.

"But it could have had disastrous circumstances."

"You did it for a love of art and a passion that overrode
everything. By the sound of things, you couldn't stop yourself.
You had to steal it."

"And if I had stopped myself, what then Harry?"

"What are you trying to say, Massimo?"

That we shouldn't always stop ourselves. Sometimes we
should give in to desire; be reckless. I was when I stole the
painting. And yes, looking back I have no regrets. I am glad I did
it. It is not a crime to let your passion run over. It is not, and
should, not be the domain of the young. It might be what's
needed particularly, at our age, we're just so afraid of risk or
change."

"Yes, I think you have a point," agreed Harry.

"If we could just say once in a while to hell with the
consequences," continued Massimo now on a roll.

"Maybe when the mortgage has been paid."

"Harry!"

"I was joking, Massimo – no, to a large degree I think you
are right we shouldn't just accept shit. Change things, follow our
hearts - if that's what's needed. Yes, leave things behind and
whilst you're at it, leave people behind, loved ones - if that's
what is needed – despite the pain." Harry's voice slowly tapered
off and then he went quiet.

"I am sorry, my friend," said Massimo, "I can see that this conversation has caused you to think of her. When is she next coming to see you?"

"Three days' time."

"I hope all goes well."

"So do I," said Harry, "...so do I."

31

DANGEROUS LIAISONS

Harry hadn't seen Mary in quite a time. He never knew when she was coming until a week before. She insisted on their liaisons being conducted in this way. She never liked to have plans too far in advance. She didn't expect Harry to drop everything. If he couldn't make it then they would simply arrange something for the following week, and if that was not possible then some other time. If he didn't want to see her that was understandable, but Harry always made sure that he had that time available.

The first time she returned to see Harry was about three months after she left him. He was still living in Appleton Drive. The pain of his dismissal had subsided, but the pain of her leaving was still quite raw. He hadn't come to terms with any of it. Mary's departure had left a great hole. Her final letter only added to his confusion. Every time he read it, he felt hurt and muddled. The words were caring but the underlying message appeared so abrupt. It was a shock. Since she had gone, all he had been able to do was potter around the garden, read the newspaper, and watch some TV. He'd tried to motivate himself to do other things, but he found that difficult. He needed to move on and start something new. Deep down he knew that, but it all seemed too much effort.

Massimo tried to help. He was the one who suggested that he take up some offers of private tutoring in Naples. He said that he had connections, and the job would be very well paid and if he fancied it, he could make up any shortfall in hours as a tour guide. It was an interesting proposition and one that he was beginning to entertain until he got news from Mary that she was coming to see him.

That drive up to the train station – that first meeting, prompted a mass of conflicting emotions. The thought of seeing her again caused a nauseous feeling to unfurl in the pit of his stomach. He was still angry and hurt. But he was also excited – a nervous excitement like a first date. He had questions, so many questions. What was she going to say? He was anxious. He hadn't seen or spoken to her in such a while. As per Mary's instructions they had had little contact – a curt one-line email every month from her to say she was fine and one from him to say pretty much the same thing and that was about it. That was what she wanted.

As he walked through the gates onto the platform, Harry felt unsure of everything but at least he was nicely on time. That was important. Then, as her train pulled in, Harry could feel his pulse quicken. He watched nervously as the passengers disembarked. His eyes never left the scene as he studiously scanned each woman that walked by. He didn't want to miss her. But as the last passenger got off and the train started to pull away, he realised that she wasn't there! He started to panic. There was a very attractive youthful woman right at the end of the platform, the last one off –maybe he could ask her if she'd seen a person of Mary's description. He frantically marched towards her. Why was she smiling? Was his walk funny? Had he dropped something? It was only after she called out his name that he recognized her. She ran over and gave him a big hug and kiss.

"I've missed you," said Mary.

Harry didn't know what to say. He expected something a little more reserved, maybe even colder but this was wholehearted and a very pleasant surprise. Mary had missed him! He held her firmly in his arms and then looked at her properly.

"I didn't recognise you. You look different."

"I feel different," said Mary.

Harry immediately noticed the vibrancy in her voice. But it wasn't just the voice.

"Your hair?"

"Oh! I've just let it grow," said Mary casually, "I don't think about it."

"It's a lot lighter."

"It's the sun. I think it's bleached it."

Harry was thrilled. "It looks fantastic, and your face, it's brown!"

His words were short and breathless. He stepped back to get a good look at her.

"The clothes!?" he exclaimed.

"Oh yes, the bell-bottom jeans. I love them!" said Mary laughing. "Do you like them, Harry? I hope you do. I love the whole get up, everything."

Harry agreed, but it was the white, loose-fitting blouse that hung gently over her breasts that he was particularly fond of. The beads and sandals were fine, just not as sexy. Then Harry noticed her hands. They were quite rough and coarse.

"Oh yes, the hands," said Mary. "I've been picking some fruit down in Italy."

"Italy, goodness me," said Harry, "you must tell me all about it." And she did. Harry was enthralled. He in turn told her more about the unfortunate episode with the drugs and that he had now permanently left teaching.

"Oh Harry, I am so sorry, nobody deserves to go like that." She was genuinely upset. Harry thought he could see a tear in her eye. He then told her about the move that he was thinking of making to Naples, and about Massimo's offer of some private tutoring along with the possibility of some tourism work. Mary's face lit up.

"You must take it," she said, "absolutely." She said it in a very confident way like she knew that it would be good for him. That sadness she felt over Harry's dismissal from St Peter's quickly dissolved. It was as though she didn't want to expend too much energy remaining in that place. She was now bright, breezy and self-assured. Harry found it very attractive. She had an energy about her, and it was catching. He very nearly asked her there and then if she wanted to be with him. Instead, he resisted the urge to say something. The big questions could wait. Instead, he asked her more questions about her experience and she was more than happy to oblige.

In no time at all, they pulled up outside Number 4 Appleton Drive. Harry took Mary's luggage, walked up the steps, and opened the large red front door. Mary hesitated. There was something that made her anxious. Harry felt the need to say something quickly.

"I've got your favourite on. Vegan nut roast with baked beetroot, parmesan crisps and creamy mashed potato," spluttered Harry.

"Oh, Harry you are so thoughtful. You didn't need to do this, but yes, thank you, I am hungry." As Mary stepped over the threshold, she could see that Harry was relieved. "That meal, it must have taken you hours," she added.

"No, no it was quite easy really." They both knew that it was a lie.

"Cuppa?" said Harry cheerily.

"Yes, but could I have some mint tea?"

"I don't know if I have any, it's not your usual."

"Of course, yes, I am sorry. Any tea will do."

As Harry started to faff around the kitchen, Mary couldn't resist getting up and peering round the corner into the garden. Would it be as beautiful as she remembered? Of course, it was. She took in the scents with a deep, sumptuous intake of breath. This was the place she missed most.

Meanwhile, back in the kitchen, Harry was plucking up the courage to ask Mary if she wanted to move back in, maybe even come with him to Naples. It wasn't his original intention but after seeing his wife, and feeling her throwing her arms around him, he suddenly felt as though there were possibilities for their future together. Yes, they'd have to work things out and Mary would need to explain things and she'd have to be genuinely sorry, but he was a forgiving sort of bloke.

"There you are, Mary," said Harry cheerfully, "a nice cup of mint tea with the stringy bit dangling on the side so you can easily pull the tea bag out when it's brewed."

Mary smiled and thanked Harry adding that the living room looked "very clean and tidy."

Harry's chest puffed out. He was pleased that she'd noticed. He'd spent the whole morning tidying up. "I saw you looking at the garden," he said smiling. "I've planted some new roses that have just started to bloom. Do you want to have a closer look? Honestly, Mary, I think this year has been particularly good –

209

"Harry, I need to tell you a few things," said Mary interrupting Harry's flow. There was something in her voice that made Harry stop talking instantly.

"I am with someone," said Mary quietly.

"Someone? What do you mean with someone?"

"It's not emotional. It's just…physical."

"Oh well, that makes it fine then."

"It won't stop us from being together tonight or this week," pleaded Mary.

"Well with that information playing around my head it might."

"I am determined to be honest, Harry. I don't want to hide anything from you."

"Why not? You can hide that if you wish."

"He is just a lover, Harry, I'm not in love with him and I won't ever be."

"Well, that helps, that really bloody helps. It makes me feel a stack better. Couldn't you have waited…maybe an hour or two instead of jumping right in with this information?"

"What do you mean?" asked Mary quizzically.

"Couldn't we have just enjoyed a little more before you started saying all this? What the hell has happened here? You're different. Weird different. When I first saw you at the station, I thought wow! But now I think you've just gone doolally. You know Massimo was convinced you were possessed by the dead spirit of Caravaggio. I scoffed at the idea but now I'm not so sure. He, Caravaggio, was into all that taking a lover crap."

"That's ridiculous," said Mary.

"No, no it isn't," said Harry firmly. "Mary, that time in the school with me and Massimo you stabbed a man with a screwdriver, and I mean really stabbed him. You called him an ugly piece of shit and you told him to fuck off. And we're not talking about any old person we're talking about the Bradshaws!"

"Well, I can't remember a thing, so I feel nothing," said Mary firmly. "I have no guilt because they were bad people and deserved it."

But Harry persisted. "It was the bump on the head. That's when it all started. You were different from that point."

"Do you really think I was, or I am possessed, Harry?"

"I am not sure."

"Harry I am still me, but yes, I will admit that after that accident I felt different, I am different. I know this." Mary paused for a second. "That bump on the head, it was as though a blockage had been cleared. The best way of describing it is that when I got up off the floor, I felt for the first time in my life that I flowed. I could feel it in my heart and the pulse of my blood. I clearly don't remember anything of the fight, but I remember feeling good, self-aware – confident even. And that surprised me because I have never really felt that confident before. I am not too bothered about whether or not this can be attributed to some dead artist's spirit. I am happy. I feel alive."

There was a pause whilst Harry took it in. He didn't know what to say.

"Harry, I still love you, I always will," stated Mary. But it didn't offer Harry any reassurance. There was something in what she said and the way she said it that instantly made him realise that what he had to offer here in Appleton Drive was never going to satisfy her...

"You're not staying, are you?"

"No."

"How long?"

"I was anticipating a week, maybe a little more, maybe a little less."

"And what then? You can't go fruit picking, the seasons done."

"I have some work lined up."

"What kind of work?"

"Modelling."

"Modelling?"

"Life modelling, actually."

"What, naked modelling?"

"Yes."

"At your age?"

"Yes, I have met a group of artists."

"I suppose you've bedded them."

"Harry, you are being ridiculous."

"Am I, am I? I don't think so," said Harry answering his own question. "Look at you, all very quaint but the flower power era has long since gone. You are a woman out of time pursuing a stupid dream. Mary, you're fifty-seven for God's sake. Anyway, it's just plain selfish and self-centred."

"I can understand how you feel," said Mary calmly.

"Can you? Can you really?"

"Yes, Harry, I can."

"Tell me something," said Harry accusingly, "if the opportunity arose would you sleep with one of them? I mean if he were attracted to you, and you were attracted to him…physically."

Mary said nothing.

"Well, your silence says it all," said Harry bitterly.

"We have a limited time Harry, so please let us make the most of it," implored Mary.

"I am not sure how I can," said Harry as he stormed off into the kitchen. He then brought the vegan nut roast out, complete with baked beetroot, parmesan crisps and creamy mashed potato. It was supposed to be his pride and joy. He'd spent hours over it, but he placed it on the table in a joyless kind of way. Mary smiled faintly. After a few mouthfuls, she complimented him on his cooking and his effort. He acknowledged this begrudgingly. He wanted to ask more questions but he wasn't sure he wanted to hear the answers, so he ensured that any conversation was confined to the mundane – until Mary added quite an odd comment.

"Oh, by the way, please don't call me Mary. It doesn't feel right. I never did like it. I go by my middle name now."

"What, Pollyanna?"

"Polly, for short."

Harry tried to say something, but couldn't, as a parmesan crisp became lodged in his throat. Eventually, after coughing a few times, he got his breath back.

"Look Harry," said Mary sympathetically, "I realise that this is a lot to take in, so I have made provision for myself just in case."

"What do you mean?"

"I will be staying somewhere else tonight."

212

"Where? Who?"

"I will be at Tanya's."

"Oh, good Lord," said Harry. "I am not going to ask so please don't tell me."

After Mary left, Harry sat down and poured himself a brandy. He was utterly bemused but one thing was for sure, he was never going to call his wife Polly. It was and always would be Mary. Maybe others would call her Polly but not him. And for the following few days that curmudgeonly mood hung over him like a dark cloud. He was unable to function properly not knowing whether to call his wife or stay silent. He opted for the latter in the hope that silence would somehow punish her.

Suddenly out of the blue Mary called him.

"I've booked Lorenzo's restaurant!"

"What for," said Harry sarcastically.

"Please, Harry, it would be so awful if I just left. I can't change what I've done and what I've said. I don't want to anyway, but I am leaving tomorrow. I thought that if it were possible, we could see each other. We always used to like to eat out."

Harry thought long and hard. Every part of him wanted to just put the phone down but in the end, he agreed.

Mary was so pleased, it seemed to set the tone for the meal. Harry was surprised they got on as well as they did. They had a good laugh about some of the best memories of the past and it was great, but Harry just didn't want to talk about certain things. Mary understood and didn't drop any more bombshells. It was as they were leaving the restaurant Mary turned round and kissed Harry slowly and gently on the lips. They went back to the house and without realizing how it started they made love. The next day Mary left. She said something about absence making the heart grow fonder and short times of greater intimacy and intensity were better than longer times of mundaneness and conformity. He felt helpless as he watched her board the train for a new adventure in Paris.

That night Harry had one of his dreams, no doubt influenced by recent events. It started rather nicely. He was having sex with a colleague from school, and he was enjoying it. Members of

213

staff were standing around the bed applauding him. He'd had this dream before and was settling down to enjoy it when all of a sudden, the faces changed and the characters became quite different. They looked more like hippies from a love-in commune and instead of applauding they frowned and started to comment about his performance.

"Can't you do any better?"

"Is that it?"

"Is that all you've got?"

"Polly said that we were much better lovers."

And then Tanya stepped up and looked him in the eye.

"You do know that we satisfied her in a way that you couldn't."

That last comment was particularly disturbing and caused Harry to wake up in a cold sweat. At that point, he knew for sure that it was time for him to make the change and move to Naples.

32

A FRESH START

Leaving Appleton Drive, the house that he and Mary shared for twenty years, wasn't as difficult as he thought it might be, nor was leaving friends and colleagues behind. Once in Naples, he found a place to live relatively easily. That was largely owing to Massimo. He set up Harry with a nice one-bedroomed apartment overlooking the bay. He also helped set up his little business of private tutoring and within weeks he had a few very decent clients, who paid well. He also managed to obtain a couple of days a week as a private tour guide. He'd always fancied himself as some knowledgeable Andrew Graham Dixon-type figure talking enthusiastically about the secrets of great art.

He met several people through work and often found himself invited for meals. On days off he would go walking. Sometimes he would go with Massimo but often he would explore on his own. It surprised Harry how well he'd taken to his new life. There were times when he woke up feeling anxious, but he told himself that that was to be expected. There were other times when he could not shake off a kind of bewildered depression about Mary. They kept in touch still and were able to say a little more. Mary insisted that communication was no more than two paragraphs, and that contact would be every four weeks. Reluctantly Harry kept to his side of the bargain. He found it difficult; he had much more to say and even more questions to ask.

Three months after Mary's first visit she contacted him again. It was a simple text telling him all the details of the flight and times. She also told him how much she was looking forward to seeing him. Harry could once again feel the butterflies dance in his stomach. Lately, he'd been managing quite well without her but that short message reignited something he'd forgotten was there.

When he saw her again, she looked just as beguiling as ever, if not more so. It made him quite breathless. Just like before she walked over and gave him a great big hug. This time it was Mary's turn to step back and tell him that he seemed different. Harry smiled and asked if it was a good different.

"I think so," said Mary. "I hope so. Oh! I'm sorry, Harry. I didn't mean to offend you by hoping that you are different, it's just that you were…"

"Not in a great place," said Harry completing her sentence. "I can see that now, although I did enjoy that last night together."

"So did I," said Mary warmly. That was almost enough for Harry. He didn't want to ask her about who she'd been with or how long she'd be staying. That could come later, right now he was just happy to be with her and he'd made up his mind that he was going to show her a good time. He was going to show her the sights and sounds of Naples.

He started off in the old town and went to his and Massimo's favourite place, Pio Monte della Misericordia. There he showed Mary, Caravaggio's great work of art and delighted in telling her all about the painting and its history. She, in turn, seemed enthralled, more than before, more than she ever seemed to be. She asked lots of questions and Harry took great pride in answering them, but he got more from Mary's genuine adoration of the great painting. There was a passion there that he had never seen before.

He took her to some of the back street cafes, the ones that only he and the locals knew about. They drank Vecchia Romagna and traditional Italian coffee and tucked into sfogliatella. They shared the most beautiful strolls around the Santieri degli Dei and the Punta Campanella. They walked hand in hand along the bougainvillea-strewn hills. But he could only avoid the elephant in the room for so long.

They were sitting on the balcony of his apartment when Harry asked the question he'd been dreading. "How long are you staying?"

"I'm sorry, Harry, I really am. It is the day after tomorrow. No, I will stay a little longer maybe a week. Oh Harry, I never expected to…"

"To what?" said Harry impatiently.

"Find it so difficult."

"Then stay."

"I can't."

"Why not?"

"I have to be true to myself."

"And staying with me wouldn't be?"

Mary said nothing but Harry wouldn't let it rest.

"What is there out there that you cannot find with me here in Naples? Have we not had the most gorgeous time together?"

"I can't explain."

"Try me," said Harry annoyed.

"We're not ready."

"What?"

Mary was starting to get upset. "Harry, it's painful for me too."

"What? Painful for you too? "Painful for you too?" he repeated. And then his ire came out in three rage-filled words. "YOU LEFT ME!"

"Harry p…please, please don't get angry."

But it was too late Harry let rip about how hurt he'd been, how selfish she was, how she didn't understand…

"I'm sorry, Harry," said Mary weeping, "perhaps I'd best go."

"Yes, maybe you had," said Harry gruffly. As he watched Mary gather up her stuff, he could see the tears rolling copiously down her cheeks. He wanted to say and do nothing as a kind of penance –to show her that he didn't care, but the problem was that he did.

"No, don't," said Harry calming down. "I can't understand it, but I don't want to part like this."

"No, neither do I."

"But, Mary, I know you want to be honest and all that, but can't you just lie to yourself, just a little bit? Just for me?"

Mary smiled and sniffed. "I wish I could." She reached over and stroked Harry's cheek and suddenly a small tear formed in his eye. She kissed the slow watery trickle. Before he knew it, they were undressed and, on the bed, caressing each other in a way that Harry had not experienced before. A few days later Mary left again. This time it seemed worse than before. He and Mary were quite distraught, but still, she went. He'd never really cried before, even when Mary left him the first time, he just felt sorry for himself and tended to his roses, but now alone in his apartment he could feel real pain and one small tear soon became a torrent.

After that last visit, Mary and Harry agreed that there should be a change in the way that they communicated, and it made a big difference. Neither of them could keep to the curt one-liners anymore. They had too much to say but it was Mary who suggested that they corresponded through letters, and Harry loved Mary's letters. They were great descriptions of the sights and sounds of where she was staying. He loved her insights and wry observations about the people that inhabited her world. She even included some poetry. Harry loved that too.

He tried to craft some tender responses, but his letter writing didn't have quite the same flow as Mary's. She did, however, remark that, "...at least it came from the heart." He suggested that Mary write a book based on her collections and experiences. She suggested that he take a lover. And much to his surprise, he did! Although even he had to admit that having sex with a member of his tour group, for a couple of days, wasn't exactly taking a lover. She was attractive and was probably on a similar journey to Mary. He enjoyed it and he thought that she did, but he couldn't get past the feeling that he'd cheated on his wife. The strange thing was that just recently, despite all of Mary's "infidelity," he never really felt that she cheated on him. That's not to say that he accepted it, he still found it difficult to come to terms with. How long he or they could sustain this relationship he didn't know. As much as he became thrilled with her visits and the anticipation of her arrival it all ended in such pain and misery. Harry couldn't take it anymore. Perhaps the next visit would be the last. Like pulling a tooth out without anaesthetic: one big yank, lots of pain, and then free...to a degree.

33

SOCKS

"I hope all goes well." Those hopeful words from Massimo were still on his mind as he approached the station. When Mary stepped off the train, she again looked adorable. Harry loved her light brown hair all over again. It was the first thing he always noticed. Each new time that he saw her, it had grown a little more. It was now down to below her shoulders. Her face was still tanned and her eyes, already bright and expectant, lit up even more when she saw him. They embraced fondly and walked hand in hand to the taxi.

"You know I've tried calling you Polly, but I can't," remarked Harry.

"It's okay, Harry, you are the only one. You have a special pass."

They smiled at each other knowingly. A few intimate words were shared but they didn't say much on the journey. As soon as they got to Harry's place they went straight to the bedroom, undressed, and embraced each other on the cool white linen. Mary fell asleep in Harry's arms. When she woke up, Harry had made her a basil, tomato, and Mozzarella salad. He handed it to her on a slim white tray along with some crisp white wine.

"I thought you might be hungry," said Harry.

Mary smiled appreciatively. "Let's have this on the balcony." She slipped on a light dressing gown that Harry had put by her bedside, walked out, and took a good deep breath of the warm coastal air. Harry watched as Mary took in the view. A late afternoon sun lit up the side of her face bathing her soft cheeks in a warm golden glow.

"It is quite something out here, isn't it?" commented Harry.

"Gorgeous," replied Mary," who arched back and closed her eyes so that all her other senses could take in the scene. She breathed in again, this time even more deeply. She then let out a thoughtful kind of sigh. "Harry, can I ask you something?"

"Of course."

"Were you happy at Appleton Drive?"

Harry thought for a second or two. "I don't know. I thought I was but now I'm not so sure. I'm not sure about anything. It's all an accident really."

"What do you mean?"

"If it wasn't for that car accident with Massimo, I would still be at Appleton Drive tending to my roses, moaning about all sorts. I wouldn't have done anything. And now I have done something, but I feel uncertain. I had things mapped out for when I retired, not in any great detail, just things I wanted to do, with you, of course, but now I don't even know whether I will be here in Naples in a year's time. Sometimes I wish I was back there feeling safe. I am not sure about this future. But if I am honest, I wake up each morning feeling…"

"Expectant?" said Mary finishing off his sentence enthusiastically.

"Yes," said Harry as though it was some kind of revelation. "Yes, you're right. It just hurts that you're not…" He stopped himself. Not yet, don't talk about it, just a few more hours. No ultimatums, no heartache, not yet. "I'll just get some more wine," said Harry.

Mary smiled sympathetically. On a small shelf close by she noticed a few books. On the top was 'A History of Mr Polly' by H G Wells. She picked it up.

"You know we did this at school."

"What's that?" said Harry carrying in the wine and another plate of salad. Mary waved the book in the air. "Mid-life crisis of man."

"Ah yes, good old Mr Polly," said Harry smiling at Mary's comment. "We have a bit of fun with him at the end of my English lessons. His "Pollyisms" can be quite a laugh."

"You know Mrs Polly got a rough deal," said Mary. "Ever since I read it, there was always something in me that resented

Mr Polly being painted as something of a hero. It made me quite angry.

"I'm not sure I follow," said Harry quizzically.

"What about Mrs Polly? She was the poor unfortunate woman that married him. He was an absolute buffoon who couldn't communicate properly, bungled his own suicide, and then left her so that he could find a better life, which he did. Meanwhile, poor dull unimaginative Mrs Polly stays where she is and remains exactly the same. Her limitations make her incapable of change. It would have been braver if the author would have depicted the hero as Mrs Polly and developed a storyline whereby, she leaves him - she is the one that changes, whilst he remains the same. Of course, back then it would have been much more difficult to have published such a shocking story. People might not have accepted it."

"I'd never looked at it that way," said Harry. "Is that how you see yourself in our story, as the hero for leaving me? And am I the dull unimaginative dotard that you left behind?"

"No, of course not, and simply walking out is often such a cowardly thing. Harry, this sounds terrible, but I could not help myself. It was as though I had no choice, but I never really left you." For a second Mary's voice wavered and then she continued. "But I kept coming back hoping that something between us would change. I never gave up hope, but we had to want each other and miss each other. But you were never dull, Harry, *we* were dull. It has been painful for both of us, particularly for you, my dearest, Harry. But in our story, you are nothing like Mrs Polly and look at what you have done, you've moved on and despite what you think, you have changed things. It wasn't just an accident. And, Harry, I am certainly no hero."

"But it was brave, what you did."

Maybe. Maybe it is something to do with the spirit of Caravaggio and maybe it's always been there, this desire to be free. I mean, why do we refer to marriage as wedlock? It sounds like imprisonment. That's how I saw our relationship, Harry, in the same way you felt chained to an institution, I felt locked into a role I no longer cared for.

"Don't lock me in wedlock I want a marriage encounter," said Harry out of the blue. It surprised Mary.

"Yes, Harry. Yes! That's right! But how…"

"Denise Levertov," said Harry, "you recommended her to me."

"Did I?" Oh! Harry you remembered. But I let it happen. Yes, I let it happen. I knew it for years, but I said nothing."

"No, said Harry, it was both of us, but at least I can plead ignorance. I never even saw what you saw."

"Ignorance is no defence against malpractice," laughed Mary.

"Yes, I suppose you're right," said Harry, and he too started to laugh. Their conversation became heady and light. They laughed at themselves and each other. But as the night drew on Harry had to ask that question, the question he was dreading to ask, the one that would pierce their idyllic bubble. It was as if Mary could sense that it was coming and before he could say anything, she spoke first.

"I was worried, Harry, that if we got back too soon it would just go back to what it was or something similar."

"I can see that," said Harry. "I couldn't before, but I can now."

"I tried to explain before but couldn't."

"I know," said Harry," growing impatient. The signs were looking good, but he wanted an answer.

"You know I'd never had lovers before. I never considered taking one, but the French and the Italians consider it a remedy for some of life's ailments." Mary laughed. "It seems so absurd, but their way is far too clandestine for my liking, as though they were doing something wrong but I never considered what I did was wrong. It was never betrayal you must believe me." Harry gave a faint smile of understanding. "But you've never asked me about them. I can understand why, and I've never told you about them but if you would have asked I would have told you. If it were possible to have met them in another life, you may have even liked them. I am sorry that you have found that part of my journey difficult, but I have no regrets." Mary paused. "Harry, I'm not sure how to say this." Her voice trailed off and Harry's heart sank.

"Socks," said Mary out of the blue.

"I beg your pardon," said Harry surprised.

"Maru Mori brought me a pair of socks which she knitted herself with her sheepherder's hands, two socks as soft as rabbits."

"I recognise the poem," said Harry. "'Neruda's Ode to My Socks', but I don't understand."

Mary smiled. "There are lots of things you don't know or understand about me which you will find out over the next few months. But the poem, Harry, I love that poem. It's so tender and loving. That gift was so ordinary and yet so precious. You remember the socks that you once tried to knit for me?"

"Yes, they were bloody awful."

They both laughed.

"There was something tender in those times, Harry. Yes, the socks looked terrible but nobody, but you could have made me something so horrible and yet so beautiful. I have begun to feel a strange yearning for those socks."

"Really?" said Harry expectantly. "I can always knit you some more."

Mary thought for a second.

"Yes Harry you could, but they need to be different. Why don't we pull two chairs together, you and I. And with the softest, most precious wool, sit by the fire and knit something new."

The end

Brian Smith

ABOUT THE AUTHOR

Brian was brought up in Cheetham Hill, Manchester. Although he now lives in Dorset, he still considers himself a Mancunian. He has forged a successful career as an art teacher whilst continuing to produce his own paintings and drawings. Art has always been important to him and will continue to be so. He is married to Deb and they have two children, Jess and Luke. Brian didn't start writing seriously until his mid- fifties so there is hope for us all.